This book is a work of fiction. Names, characters, places and incidents are the product of the author's imagination or are used fictitiously. Any resemblance to actual events, locales, or persons, living or dead, is coincidental.

Published by Baldhir Singh

Book cover design: Emily's World of Design

ISBN: 978-1-7386704-1-3

B. SINGH

This book is dedicated to my amazing readers.

Fasten your seat belts for a roller coaster ride.

Siba - The Eternal Quest

- Chapter 1 -

The Grass Thief

"Watch your left!" shouted the leader of the golden eagles. Before the angel could maneuver to his right, blinding lightning struck across the dark clouds, just missing his left wing. The very next moment, deafening thunder numbed everything. The angel and the accompanying eagles held their nerves and pushed through the expanding wall of clouds. The leader of the eagles anticipated growing dangers and feared they would get lost. He yelled, "I can't help you if I can't see where we are going. The storm is escalating into a tornado. We won't be able to withstand these powerful winds for long. Everyone, move up above the thunderstorm. We'll resume our journey from there."

The angel and the eagles listened to the leader's call and flew up above the clouds. Looking down on the thundering clouds, the leader took a deep sigh of relief. He quickly turned his head toward the others to check their condition. "What happened to your wings?" the shocked leader screamed at the angel.

The angel looked instinctively on his sides. There were no wings but flapping arms. A sudden gush of panic infused in him as he realized he was just a boy and not an angel. Right away, the horrified boy fell into the dark mushrooming clouds, screaming from the bottom of his gut. His arms and legs kept flailing in despair until he disappeared into the dark swirling storm.

A fully drenched priest, braving the stormy winds, chased the young boy caught up in the tornado through the muddy paddy fields. The boy, along with several chickens and broken branches, was swirling high inside the twister. Passing through the water-logged paddy fields, the giant funnel was sucking water and feeding the dark clouds above it. The powerful gusts were making it hard for the priest to keep his eyes focused on the boy trapped inside the whirlpool of destruction. But he still kept chasing the tornado valiantly without getting intimidated by the roaring winds or the rain drops that were hitting him hard like bullets. Even the constant lightning strikes and the thundering sky couldn't dampen his spirit to save the boy.

Suddenly, the massive rotating wall of dark clouds picked up speed and zoomed toward the village, wreaking havoc along its path. It uprooted trees and bushes that came in its way and hurled them away like a nasty brat. Upon seeing nature's brute force in full swing, the priest's hope dwindled. He fell upon his knees and prayed to the Lord for the safety of the boy and his village. Suddenly, a bolt of lightning struck right in front of him, blinding him momentarily with the divine light, as if the heavens heard his prayers. He rose again with a renewed vigor and began pursuing the dark swirling monster with full strength, dodging the flying debris.

The tornado headed straight toward a bamboo grove at the periphery of the fields, as if it wanted to rip them from their roots and engulf them whole. But the flexible bamboo wall held its ground firmly and acted as a windbreak, weakening the arrogance and intensity of the funnel-shaped giant. The weakened vortex of dark clouds flung the boy onto a grassy field and changed its direction. It spared the village and headed toward the woods.

Struggling to see in the torrential downpour, the priest placed his hand above his eyes to get a clear view of the boy who was not moving. The priest panicked and rushed toward him. The boy's lean body, partially covered with mud, was lying lifeless in the field. The priest lifted the head of the unconscious boy and screamed, "Siba! Get up, son. Open your eyes. Please talk to me. Siba! Please open your eyes."

Siba groaned and slowly opened his big brown eyes.

The priest looked at the dark sky and said, "Thank you, Lord! Thank you for showering your grace and saving your innocent child."

"What happened? Where am I?" the boy asked the priest, touching his forehead with pain.

The priest, wiping the mud from the partially visible bruises on the boy's forehead, replied, "Don't you remember, you were swept up by the tornado? It touched down next to you and picked you up. I shouted 'watch your left', but the winds were too loud. You must not have heard me."

"No, I don't remember anything. I felt like I was an angel, flying with a group of eagles in a thunderstorm," Siba answered.

"They were not eagles. It must be chickens. The tornado picked them up from the field, just after it swept you up."

"It felt so real. I can still feel the presence of the eagles."

"You are in trauma." The priest helped Siba to sit up. "You are lucky that you survived. You should have listened to your friends and taken shelter inside the temple along with them, instead of running to your home. When they told me about you, I became really worried and at once, moved out of the temple to look for you. But before I could rescue you, the tornado swirled down from the sky and picked you up. What was so urgent that you had to rush to your home?"

Siba looked down nervously.

The priest resumed, "To err is human. Don't worry. Next time, when the winds are this strong and it's raining cats and dogs, take shelter and wait until the storm dies out. Anyway, I am glad that you are fine except for this minor bruise on your forehead. Something must have struck you inside the twister and knocked you unconscious. The tornado moved toward the forest, away from our villages. Thank God, it didn't cause any serious damage of life and property."

"Yeah! Please don't tell anyone about this incident. Else, everyone will become worried about me. You know nothing happened to me. I'm alright." Siba touched the bruises over his forehead. "Just my forehead is hurting a little bit. It should be fine within a few days."

"Don't worry. I won't tell anyone about this. But if you don't feel ok, see a doctor. The winds have slowed down now and the rain too. The twister tossed you in village fields. Your home is not that far from here. Let me take you home."

"No, thank you! I can walk home." Siba stood up and looked at the dark cloudy sky with his arms spread out. "This drizzle is nothing for me. You know I like dancing in the rain."

"Well alright then! You should go home and take some rest. I will tell your friends that you reached home safely."

"Ok!" Siba smiled. He ran swiftly over a puddled road toward his village. He stopped in front of an old, dilapidated house. A broken fence was guarding the house. Its walls were fully covered with vines. Discolored and torn curtains were swaying through the broken windows as if ghosts were waving at the outsiders. From the first look, this haunted house looked completely abandoned that could crumble at any moment. But Siba carefully sneaked inside it through the broken side of the main door.

"Baaa!" A sheep's bleat broke the melody of the rain.

Siba looked at the stable situated on the right side of the porch and rushed toward it. He lifted the old, patched curtain hanging on its door and entered swiftly inside it. Nine sheep were sleeping there peacefully. But a big sheep with thick white fur and a peculiar black spot in the middle of her head stared at him. It seemed as if she was waiting for him to arrive so she could ask for more grass.

Siba stared at her with a smile and walked toward her on the straw-bedded stable floor. "Celine! Sorry for getting home late today. Do you know? Today, I was picked up by a tornado. That's why I am late. Can you forgive me?" He ran his fingers through her thick fur, patting her. "How can you forgive me? You don't even understand what I said." He pressed his lips. "Anyway, let me grab some grass for you before Uncle comes home."

Siba carefully lifted one side of the old, patched curtain hanging on the door and poked his head out. He prayed in his heart, "It's almost evening. I hope Uncle is not home yet." Then he carefully tiptoed toward a small pile of fresh-cut grass lying on the other side of the porch. He hurriedly picked some grass for Celine. But as he turned back toward the stable, his foot hit a beer bottle lying next to the pile, and it rolled across the floor.

"Thief! Thief!" squawked a scarlet macaw, on hearing the sound of the rolling bottle.

"Hush, Rouble! It's me, Siba. Go back to sleep," he whispered to the large parrot perched on a nearby slacking clothesline.

"Who's there? Who's stealing my beer?" a crooked old man yelled coming out of a dark room with a cane in his hand. "You little scum! So it's you, who's stealing my grass."

Siba didn't say anything. He lowered his head, maybe in shame for getting caught stealing or helplessness of not being able to help his favorite sheep.

The old man shouted, "In a few months, you'll be a teenager. Grow up now, and stop stealing for that gobbler. I don't buy grass only for her. You and this incessant rain will starve my flock to death. I should have just sold her to the butcher on that day. At least her bleatings in the middle of the night won't disturb my sleep. I don't care if she's hungry or not, but if she disturbs my sleep one more time, I won't yield to your tears. Is that clear?" He gave a nasty look at Siba and asked, "And what happened to you? Look at yourself. You look like a pig, all covered in mud. How did you get these bruises? Did you fall again climbing the mango tree?"

Siba just kept staring at the floor and didn't utter a single word.

Pointing his cane toward the bottle, the bald and scrawny old man shouted, "Get me that bottle. I better finish it before you break it." Siba didn't move. He was frozen at the spot like a Greek marble statue. "Throw this grass back and get me that bottle," the old man yelled, whacking the boy with his cane.

Siba tossed the grass back grumpily. Holding back tears, he picked up the beer bottle, handed it to the old man, and dashed to the stable. In one corner of the stable, there was an old bed. He jumped onto that bed, dug his face into a pillow, and burst out crying. Still weeping, he sprang from his bed and hugged the sheep.

Siba sniffled, "Sorry, Celine! I couldn't get grass for you. Uncle doesn't care that you eat more than the other sheep. Because of the last five days of continuous rain, you couldn't even go out in the forest meadow to graze. Uncle spent his entire money on his beer and didn't buy enough food for all of us. Tomorrow, I'll go by myself into the woods and bring grass for you. I promise I won't let him sell you to the butcher." He wiped his tears and said to her, "The sun will shine again, maybe not today, but definitely someday." Siba collapsed to the floor, exhausted. He wrapped his arms around Celine's neck and, in no time at all, fell asleep.

Ω

"Wake up, Siba! Robby and Masai are here. Wake up, Siba! Robby and Masai are here," Rouble squawked, fluttering his wings on the boy's face. The young boy woke up rubbing his eyes and straightening the tangle of his long, messy hair.

"Siba, are you ready for school? Don't make us late again," a stout boy, lowering his umbrella, shouted from the porch.

"I'm up, Robby. Hold on. I'm coming," Siba shouted from inside the stable.

In the meantime, Robby asked his skinny friend, "Masai, did you bring food for Siba? Today, it's your turn."

"Yes, of course. I brought two sandwiches; one for me and one for Siba. Nubina informed me yesterday that next week, she and Yasmine will take care of Siba's lunch," Masai told Robby, placing his umbrella on the porch.

"Why Nubina always tells only you? What's the reason behind this special treatment?" Robby teased Masai.

"You were sitting next to Siba, and I was sitting next to her. That's why." Masai blushed.

"Yeah! I'm noticing that from the last few days, you're always sitting next to her." Robby gave a mischievous grin.

"There's nothing like that." Masai, lowering his gaze, tried to hide his smile.

Just then, Siba came out on the porch with a pale look on his face. He was coughing and shaking and pretending to be sick.

Staring at Siba's miserable condition, Robby inquired worriedly, "Hey champ! What happened to you?"

Siba sneezed and spoke in a shaky voice, "Dancing in the rain. That's what happened to me. Now, I'm sick. I don't think in this wet weather I can walk to the next village to attend our school. Please tell our teacher; I'll come tomorrow."

"Oh, Siba! That's not good. I understand our village is the last settlement before the forest but does that mean, we shouldn't have a doctor? Now what should we do in a situation like this? Every time we have to run to the city for medical help. That's not fair," Robby complained. "Do you have medicines or should I bring some from my home?"

"No need. I have medicines with me. Don't worry. I will be better by tomorrow." Siba smiled. "Thank you, Masai for bringing my school bag. I'm sorry for this trouble. Yesterday, when the stormy winds ripped my umbrella, I should have listened to you. Instead of handing my bag to you and running home, I should have taken cover in the temple along with you."

"No worries. Your bag is not that heavy," Masai said to Siba, handing over his school bag. "Alright, take care of yourself. Next time, listen to me. Look, we both are fine and your books are not even wet."

"Yes! They are completely dry." Siba looked inside the bag. "Thank you, Masai! Next time, I will listen to you for sure."

Staring at Siba's forehead, Robby asked, "Priest told us that he dropped you home safely. Then, how did you get these bruises? Did you get injured from the tornado?"

Siba replied nervously, "Oh no! I just slipped on the porch. Don't worry. They'll heal in a few days."

Masai grabbed both sandwiches from his bag and offered them to Siba, "Take these. I had a heavy breakfast before leaving home and the four of us can share lunch. You're sick. You need to eat more to recover quicker."

"No! One should be enough." Siba plucked one sandwich from Masai's hand.

"You must take both. I insist." Robby took the other sandwich and placed it in Siba's hand.

Siba wrapped his arms around Robby and Masai and squeezed them tight. "You both are my best friends."

"Goodbye, Siba!" Robby and Masai raised their umbrellas, waved, and left for school.

Siba watched them for a while, and when they disappeared around the corner, he rushed inside the stable. He grinned at Celine and patted. "Don't worry, Celine. I won't let you starve, and I won't let anyone take you away from me. I am going to the forest to bring grass for you and your sisters. Uncle doesn't know. He will think I went to school. I'll try to be back on time. You stay inside and don't get wet in the rain. Do you get it?"

"Baaa," Celine bleated. Siba smiled and hugged her tightly. "Baaa," she bleated again.

Siba secretly went into the storage room. The room was littered with empty beer bottles. Without disturbing them, he grabbed a sickle from a broken closet. He quickly hid it under his shirt and dashed back to the stable. Rouble was sitting on Siba's bed, bobbing his head.

Siba shooed the bird, "Move! Move away!"

Rouble fluttered and sat on one of the sheep. Siba folded his blanket, hiding the sickle in it.

"What are you doing?" Rouble asked Siba.

"Nothing!" Siba said sharply. He picked up the blanket and both sandwiches and hurriedly moved out to the porch.

"Nothing? It sounds weird. Where are you going?" Rouble asked, fluttering behind him.

"Shhh! I'm going to the forest meadow to get grass for Celine," Siba whispered.

"Did you tell your uncle?" Rouble whispered.

"He doesn't know. I'll be back soon."

"I'll go with you."

"No. It's raining outside. You can't fly. It's better for you to stay inside."

"Forest is no place for kids. You can't go alone. I'll go with you. If you don't take me with you, I'll tell your uncle."

"Really? A parrot is blackmailing me? Fine! Sit on my shoulder," Siba whispered.

Siba chopped a leaf from a banana tree planted in his backyard and covered his head with it. He looked around and ran out swiftly toward a grass trail, leading to the woods. The trail was flanked by thick trees. He kept running in the drizzle without caring whether he was stepping in puddles or on the slippery grass. He was determined to save his most beloved sheep.

When they reached the end of the settlement, suddenly, a big black dog leaped out from a tree hollow and barked at Siba, blocking his way. At first, Siba became scared, but soon, he realized that the dog was hurt and hungry. He moved a few steps back. When the dog calmed down, he threw a small piece of sandwich toward him.

The dog limped forward, sniffed the piece, and ate it. The hungry dog gave a puppy-eyed look, asking for more food. Siba threw the rest of the sandwich toward him. The dog sat down on the wet grass and started eating it happily. Siba moved closer and patted his back hesitantly. The dog was engrossed in eating the sandwich and paid no attention to the affectionate patting. Siba noticed that a big thorn was stuck in the dog's front paw. He carefully lifted the dog's injured leg and pulled the thorn out. The dog howled in pain. Siba panicked and at once, dropped the injured leg. The dog snarled and grabbed Siba's arm between his jaws.

"Grrr!" Rouble, sitting on Siba's shoulder, growled at the dog. He released Siba's arm at once and moved away. Siba was surprised to see that and asked Rouble, "What did you do?"

"I told him to leave you and back off," Rouble replied casually.

Rouble's answer perplexed Siba. He asked curiously, "Do you know how to bark?"

The scarlet macaw boasted, "I know many languages. Don't I speak your language?"

"Yeah!" Siba paused. "How do you know all these languages?"

"It's the emotions," Rouble told him. "Emotions are the basis of all languages. Language is a tool to express emotions. I correlate emotions expressed by the animals with the voices they make. It's as simple as that. I'll explain the rest to you on the way. Now pick up that leaf, or else you'll get sick for real."

While picking the banana leaf, Siba requested, "Please don't forget to teach me later."

As they proceeded further toward the forest, they realized that the dog was following them. After noticing him following them for a while, Siba asked Rouble, "What does he want now?"

Rouble inquired from the dog and told Siba, "You gave him food and helped him with his leg. So he wants you to become his master."

"Alright, but tell him only if he won't bite me again," Siba told Rouble in a stern voice.

"Bow-wow!" Rouble instructed the dog.

"I'll call you Limpoo," Siba said smilingly, patting the dog.

Limpoo wagged his tail with excitement, and they began marching together toward the forest meadow under the drizzling rain.

After crossing the woods, an overflowing river halted their journey. "Oh no! The tornado ripped apart the log bridge and the rain flooded the river. How will we cross it now to reach the meadow?" Gazing at the devastated log bridge, Siba slumped down onto a rock and rubbed his temples. "I can't see Celine starving. Now, how will I prevent Uncle from selling her to the butcher?" he sniffled.

Rouble sympathized, "Don't lose your heart, I know someone who can help you. Follow me."

"Who? Where?" wiping his tears, Siba asked.

"Shhh! You ask too many questions. Just follow me quietly." Rouble flew from Siba's shoulder and began flying in front of him.

Siba looked around. "But where? I don't see any other way."

"There! Do you see that deer trail?" Rouble said, pointing toward a very narrow opening in the thick undergrowth, and began flying toward it. Siba and Limpoo followed Rouble, and they resumed their journey into a dense forest.

- CHAPTER 2 -

THE GREAT FOREST

After marching through the dense undergrowth for quite some time, the deer trail ended at the edge of a large pond. Siba stopped at the edge and shouted at Rouble who was flying above the pond, "Rouble! Where are you taking us? We can't fly across this pond like you. Do you want us to swim through it?"

"You don't have to. Wait there," Rouble replied loudly. He flew to the middle of the pond and whistled.

Several black, dome-shaped rocks rose to the surface of the pond and began floating toward Siba. He became scared and shouted in a trembling voice, "What's going on Rouble? What are those rocks?"

"Loch Ness Monster!" Rouble giggled. "They are ferry turtles. They will ferry you across the pond." As those floating rocks reached near the edge, their submerged bodies became more visible.

"Uff!" Siba took a sigh of relief. "Yeah! They are turtles. They scared the hell out of me."

Rouble chuckled, "Don't worry. They won't cause any harm to you. They are my friends. Whenever you want to cross this pond, you can whistle and take the help of ferry turtles."

The ferry turtles huddled together, forming a floating raft.

Rouble instructed Siba, "Stand on the turtle raft along with Limpoo. They will ferry you across to the other side."

Siba nervously placed his right foot on the turtle raft. It was very stable, just like a boat. He climbed onto it and then, called Limpoo. Limpoo also followed his master and jumped onto the floating raft. The ferry turtles swam smoothly across the pond and dropped them on the other side. Rouble whistled and the turtles sank back under the surface of the pond.

This side of the forest was completely different than the other side. In fact, unlike any other forest, it was more like a forest garden. Towering tree trunks rose high and formed a thick canopy, containing all kinds of fruits, nuts, flowers, and leaves. No two trees were similar. They all were different and unique. All trunks and branches were covered with flowering vines. Their beautiful flowers were hanging down from the branches giving it a romantic hanging garden look. There was very little undergrowth but various kinds of fruit bushes were adorning the forest floor at regular intervals, offering all sorts of juicy berries to snack on. Fragrances of different flowers filled the air, offering each breath a uniquely calming and rejuvenating experience.

Siba was amazed to see this heavenly garden. While lowering the banana leaf from top of his head, he stared wide-eyed at the canopy and wondered, "Wow! What is this magical place?"

Rouble replied in exhilaration, "This is my home - The Great Forest."

Enticed by the enchanting forest and still staring at the fascinating beauty of the fabulous forest, Siba asked, "Why have you never told me about this magical place? I always thought our village was your only home. I never knew you belong to this fairy world."

Rouble blushed, "Yeah, I belong to the Great Forest, but I live with you in your village as you are my best friend. I do visit this place sometimes when you are at school and meet my friends and family."

"Looking at all these exotic fruits, I am feeling absolutely famished." Siba swallowed.

"Yeah, of course! After such a long trek, you must be really hungry. Let me grab something for you." Rouble fluttered and perched on a high branch. He whispered something and returned back with a yellow-colored mushroom. "Eat this. It's a gift from the Great Forest."

Siba held that mushroom and stared at it suspiciously. "This doesn't look right. A mushroom, that is too brightly yellow-colored! Are you sure about this?"

"Yep! Eat it. After that you can eat whatever fruit you like," Rouble smirked.

Siba hesitantly placed that mushroom in his mouth and began chewing it. It had a very weird taste. Siba looked at Rouble nervously.

"Swallow it," Rouble chuckled.

Just as Siba swallowed that mushroom, his head began spinning, and he started hallucinating. Suddenly, he started hearing strange voices. Holding his head, Siba shouted, "Rouble! What have you done to me? What's happening to me? I thought we were friends. What are these eerie voices?"

Rouble laughed and replied, "Relax! Close your eyes for a minute and take deep breaths."

Still feeling dizzy, Siba closed his eyes and took deep breaths. Soon he became normal again. "What was that? What happened just now?" he asked, opening his eyes.

A heavy, resounding voice echoed, "You ate my fruit of connectivity. Now you can hear my voice."

Upon hearing a ghostly voice, Siba became scared. He moved back, pressing himself against a trunk. "Who's this?" he shouted with quivering lips.

"It's me, this forest - the Great Forest," the eerie voice echoed again.

Siba, trembling with fear, whispered, "Rouble, there's a ghost around us. We're going to die."

"Oh, no! It's the Great Forest. Didn't you hear him say 'It's me, this forest - The Great Forest?' " Rouble teased him, mimicking the heavy, resounding voice.

"I don't see anyone here." Siba panicked. "Rouble! What did you do to me? Am I dead or am I dreaming?"

"You are not dead, and this is not a dream," the voice echoed. Siba watchfully looked around and above him. "I'm this forest - the Great Forest. Even now, you are staring at my canopy. Rouble told me that you wanted to learn the language of the forest, so I offered you the fruit of connectivity. Now you can communicate with all the forest-dwellers by using the forest language."

"You mean I can talk to animals. Let me see," Siba spoke nervously. "Bow-wow! Grrr!" he barked at Limpoo. But the dog didn't give any response. "Oh yeah! Mr. Great Forest, did you see that? Limpoo just said that he didn't understand even a single word that I said," Siba taunted, looking at the canopy.

"Only forest-dwellers can understand the forest language. This dog doesn't belong in my forest. He lives with humans. He doesn't understand the forest language, just like humans don't," the Great Forest replied calmly.

"So, how Rouble was able to communicate with Limpoo?" Siba asked curiously.

"You little, inquisitive animal! You ask a lot of questions. Ask your parrot how he did that?" The Great Forest added fuel to Siba's burning curiosity. Siba stared at Rouble.

"Oh! Me? Thank you, Great Forest, for honoring me." Rouble cleared his throat and explained, "A word is a symbol - a particular sound associated with something to represent it and to communicate it to others. If you know what that sound symbol is associated with, you can understands it, otherwise it has no meaning for you.

"The basic sounds like crying, laughter, and howling that are produced under the emotions like pain, joy, grief, and excitement are generally similar among animals. Whereas, sounds linked to the other things vary from language to language.

"When you hear a sound, if your mind recognizes the object it represents, it creates that image in your mind. While the fruit of connectivity recognizes all sounds and directly creates the images in your mind. When different animals talk, I visualize the underlying images and correlate them with the sounds they make. That's how I learned different languages. Since I've lived in the human world for so long, I correlated and remembered human's and their pets' languages as well. That's how I communicated with Limpoo.

"You can also visualize and understand the forest language now, but you can't respond back yet. You can learn to do so by linking and remembering the images that the fruit of connectivity will create in your mind with the speaker's sounds, expressions, and actions. That's why Limpoo couldn't understand your meaningless barking," Rouble giggled.

"You, silly bird! Are you making fun of me?" Siba smiled. "Jokes apart, but that knowledge was enlightening. Thank you, Great Forest, for gifting me the fruit of connectivity.

I'll practice remembering animal sounds and communicating with them, just like Rouble does. But I haven't seen you yet. Where are you hiding in these trees?" Siba's big brown eyes searched for the source of the mysterious voice.

"O little animal! Look beyond what you see. I've told you already. I'm this forest. All these trunks that you see around you, they are my roots," the voice echoed again.

Siba became more confused. He asked, "How can trunks be roots? Shouldn't each trunk be a different tree by itself?"

"Let me tell you my story from the beginning. This whole forest that you see around you is only one tree. This tree doesn't have a trunk but only aerial roots. The aerial roots are so old and thick that they appear to be different trees. They are connected to each other by a network of special connector branches. These branches, serving as a link, keep the entire forest intact as one. The connector branches produce special fruits on my will which are found nowhere else on the earth, just like the fruit of connectivity.

"Each aerial root is unique and corresponds to a unique tree. Like any other tree, all aerial roots have normal branches that don't connect with other aerial roots. The normal branches belonging to one aerial root produce only one kind of leaves, flowers, and fruits. As you can see apples, mangoes, guavas, and so on, are growing on these branches. Their seeds are then spread across the entire world, where they grow into different trees and give nourishment to all life forms. I hope you understand it now."

Siba visualized the whole narration as an animated story in his mind. He shook his head affirmatively. "Oh yes! I understood every bit of it," he smirked.

"That's great!" Rouble spoke, shaking water off his feathers. "Now, will you please request the Great Forest to help you out with crossing the river, so you can collect grass for Celine. It will be dark soon. And surprisingly, the rain has slowed down too. We should get going."

"Oh! I completely forgot about everything else." Siba folded his hands and requested, "The Great Forest! Can you please help me with crossing the flooded river? I need to go to the forest meadow to collect grass for my sheep."

The Great Forest echoed, "The other side of the river doesn't fall under me, and it's not safe for children. Didn't your parents warn you about that?"

Suddenly, Siba's gaze dropped, and he became sad. The Great Forest asked, "What happened?"

Rouble told the Great Forest, "He doesn't have parents."

"I am sorry!" the Great Forest echoed sympathetically. "You don't have to go to the other side. Take these broad-toothed leaves from the vines on your left. All herbivores love these leaves way more than grass. Your sheep will also eat them happily." The Great Forest lowered the vines till Siba could reach them.

"Thank you, Great Forest! You solved my problem. Now, there's no need for me to go to the other side." As Siba plucked the leaves, Limpoo limped behind him. The voice echoed again, "What happened to your dog? Why is he limping?"

Siba sympathetically looked at Limpoo's leg. "His leg is hurt. A big thorn was stuck in his paw."

The Great Forest dropped a dark red-colored mushroom from a connector branch and echoed, "Squeeze this fruit of healing and apply its juice on his wound. He'll be fine."

Siba did as instructed and the wound healed immediately. Limpoo began jumping happily. "Wow! That's magic! Thank you, forest! Oh, sorry! The Great Forest! I really appreciate all of your help."

"You are welcome. I told you my secrets, but you didn't tell me your name."

"Oh, sorry! I forgot to introduce myself. My name is Siba."

"Siba! I am glad you visited me. You must be very hungry. Take some of my delicious fruits too and spread their seeds in your village."

"Thank you! We were so busy talking that I completely forgot how hungry I am." Siba plucked some apples and mangoes and packed them along with the leaves in his blanket and placed them on Limpoo's back. "I will definitely plant the seeds in my backyard."

Limpoo barked. Siba stared at the dog and said, "Rouble, I understood what Limpoo asked, but I don't know the sounds to respond yet. Can you please tell him that yes, he will have to carry those leaves, as his leg is fine now?"

"Ok, I'll tell him." Rouble barked, "Bow- Bow!"

Siba picked one avocado and took a bite. "Yummy! It tastes so good." He picked one more avocado and gave the second sandwich to Limpoo. The dog ate it cheerfully.

"Goodbye, the Great Forest! I will visit you soon. I should leave now."

"Yes! It's getting dark. You should leave now. But remember, no other human knows about this place. You must keep this secret hidden from the rest of the world," the Great Forest echoed.

"Yes, I will." Picking up the banana leaf, Siba smiled, and they left for the village.

With the help of the ferry turtles, they crossed the pool and began their journey back home through the narrow deer trail. Darkness and chirping of crickets kept growing with their every step. By the time they reached near their village, the drizzle stopped completely and the twilight had turned into night.

"Thank God! The clouds are taking a vacation. After so many days, the stars are twinkling again. I'm glad the drizzle died down. Now I don't have to carry this banana leaf anymore." Siba threw the leaf with relief.

On arriving near his house, Siba lifted the blanket filled with leaves from Limpoo's back and placed it on his own head. He patted the dog and said, "You go now. I'll meet you tomorrow." He headed toward his house, but Limpoo still followed him and sat down on the roadside, next to the main door of his house.

After carefully inspecting the patio, Siba rushed into the stable and hid his stock under his bed. Then he turned toward his flock to look for Celine, but she was not there. All other nine sheep were present, but only Celine was missing. He panicked and ran out at once, looking for her.

Rouble, perched on the clothesline, squawked, "What happened?"

"Celine is not in the stable," Siba yelled in panic.

"What? Where did she go?"

"I don't know." Siba ran to the backyard, looking for her, but she wasn't there. He searched the entire house but couldn't find her. Then he knocked on the half-open door of his uncle's room, but no one responded. The room was completely dark. He hesitantly entered and turned the lights on. But his uncle wasn't there as well. Siba walked out onto the porch, petrified.

Rouble fluttered and perched on Siba's shoulder. "Where can she go at night?"

Tears rolled down from Siba's eyes. "She didn't go anywhere. Uncle must have sold her to the butcher." He began weeping.

Rouble, not sure of what to do, blurted, "No! That can't happen. How can Uncle do that?"

Siba moved his arm closer to his shoulder. Rouble hopped onto his arm. Bringing his arm in front of him, Siba stared into the parrot's eyes with teary eyes. "Yes, he did that. He sold my Celine to the butcher." Tears kept rolling down incessantly from Siba's eyes.

"Siba, control yourself. I'm going to look for her and Uncle. Let me find out what's going on. You don't go anywhere. Do you understand? Just stay here until I return." Rouble fluttered and flew out into the village.

Siba couldn't take it. He ran into the stable and jumped onto his bed, crying.

- Chapter 3 -

Lurking Danger

"Siba! Come here." Rouble's voice came from outside the stable.

Siba sprang from his bed and rushed outside. "Did you find out?" Siba, teary-eyed, stared at the parrot fluttering over the road.

Rouble chuckled, staring toward the house next door, "Come here."

Siba moved out on the road. He looked where Rouble was looking. Celine was grazing flowers in the neighbor's front yard garden. Upon seeing her grazing happily, Siba's joy knew no bounds. He ran to her and hugged her tight. "I told you to stay inside. Do you even know how scared I was? I could have never forgiven myself, had anything happened to you."

Celine kept munching innocently as if nothing had happened.

"Let's go back before anyone sees us. Else, they will complain to Uncle. And you know that won't be nice," Rouble whispered, fluttering above them.

Siba brought Celine back to the stable. "Don't worry now. You won't have to starve anymore. I got enough food for you. You can share it with your sisters." He spread half of the leaves in front of them. Watching them eating voraciously, he jumped onto his bed and got lost in the dreams of the magical forest.

Ω

"Siba! Wake up! Soon your friends will be here," Rouble shouted, fluttering his wings on Siba's face.

"Stop! Stop! I'm up! Stop that." Siba pushed Rouble away from his face and got up from his bed. While sliding his feet inside the leather slippers, he complained, "They are not here yet! You could have waited for a few more minutes. I was in the middle of this wonderful dream. I was running over the branches of the Great Forest, eating delicious fruits. I was just about to try lychee when you woke me up."

"If you want, you can go there today and eat lychee for real. Now you are friends with the Great Forest. Who is stopping you? Don't blame me for your dream," Rouble frowned and fluttered away.

"Don't get mad. I was just joking," Siba giggled. "But you are right. I wanna go there again. Let's visit that amazing forest." Filled with enthusiasm, he began getting ready.

"Look! Mr. Lazy is already ready today," peeping through the stable's half-torn curtain, Robby remarked.

Masai added quickly, "Yeah! Someone is trying to catch up for yesterday. But why aren't you wearing our school uniform?"

"Hi," Siba stuttered. "Today I have to go with my uncle to meet his relatives in a distant village. I'll go to school tomorrow," Siba replied hesitatingly.

"Your uncle's relatives? In a distant village? Ok! But you never told us about them before. Perhaps! Alright! Anyway, this rice pudding is for you. When my mom came to know about your sickness, she made your favorite dish. You can have it later," Robby said, offering a lunch box.

"Oh! No, thank you! My uncle said that we'll eat at his relative's wedding feast. You share it with Nubina and Yasmine." Siba slid the box back into Robby's bag.

"Well, as you wish! But tomorrow, you must not miss school. Yesterday, our principal announced that our school's team for annual games will be selected tomorrow. You are one of our best players. Don't miss the selection process," Robby said, holding Siba's hand firmly.

"Of course, I'll come tomorrow," Siba assured the boys with a polite smile.

As soon as his friends left, Siba spread the remaining leaves in front of the sheep and folded his blanket to take with him. With excitement on his face, he said, "Let's go, Rouble. I'm curious to know more about that amazing place." Rouble perched on his shoulder right away.

They had crossed only a few houses when the big black dog sprinted toward them. "Limpoo, my boy! Look at you. You look hale and hearty. Do you want to come with us to the forest?" Siba asked while moving his hand across the dog's body. The exuberant dog wagged his tail, and the three of them marched together on the grassy trail.

Throughout the journey, Rouble displayed his skills of communicating with the forest-dwellers. Siba observed him keenly and practiced correlating and remembering different sounds of the forest-dwellers with the images that appeared in his mind. After some time, he was able to start simple conversations with the sparrows and doves.

"The Fruit of Connectivity is amazing. I can clearly see the images that different sounds are meant to convey. But it's difficult for me to remember so many different sounds. I still can't make the appropriate sounds to express myself fully," Siba expressed his concerns.

"It will come slowly with more practice. Don't expect to be an expert on day one. Remember, the more difficult the task is, the more effort you need to put in. At first, everything seems difficult. But if a task looks too big, break it into smaller parts and work on them one by one. Soon, you'll notice that you're making progress," Rouble advised.

"Hmm! It's a long way to go," a dejected reply came from Siba after a long pause.

"You have skills, which no other human has. You can understand at least. The only thing you need to do is to practice the other half – the expression." Rouble encouraged him.

Siba's eyes twinkled with a rekindled excitement. "Yeah! That's true. No one else can do what I can do. You watch! I am going to listen and master the forest language."

Siba carefully listened to the forest sounds, and at the same time, produced them to communicate with the forest-dwellers. To his greatest surprise, the birds and animals not only responded back but also approached him curiously. Pretty soon, he mixed with the wild animals and felt as if he was one of them.

"This is so much fun! I can't believe I'm actually doing it," excited Siba squealed with his arms spread out like a scarecrow. To his amazement, pairs of lovely love birds perched on his arms. A young chipmunk jumped from a nearby tree over his head and made his messy hair a cushion to rest on. Hummingbirds droned around him like tiny bodyguards. A group of rabbits hopped in front of him like escorts. Siba sang and played with those wonderful creatures all along the way until they arrived at the pond.

With the help of the ferry turtles, they crossed the pond. Super-excited about his new magical experience, Siba dashed and clung to one big aerial root of the Great Forest. "Thank you!" He kissed the thick, dark-brown bark. "Thank you very much, for the special gift. I can't believe I can talk to the wild animals. It's like a dream."

"Calm down, Bumblebee. There are more surprises waiting for you. Climb on my branches. Lychees are waiting for you," the deep resounding voice of the Great Forest echoed from every corner.

"Hold on for a second!" astonished Siba twitched. "How do you know about my dream that I wanted to eat lychees?"

The Great Forest's loud laughter filled the air. "O little animal! Have you never heard of the dream painters?"

Suddenly, Siba frowned. "No!" He responded in a disgruntled tone, "How could I know? I don't live here. And I am not an animal. Stop calling me that. I'm a human – a human child."

Rouble, enraged at his rude behavior, scolded him loudly, "Siba! Don't behave like a nasty brat. Apologize to the Great Forest. You should be grateful to him for agreeing to meet you and share his gifts and greatness with you. No other animal could even dream of disrespecting the Great Forest. It's because of the Great Forest that you see all those plants and trees in the world. If the Great Forest stops spreading his seeds across the planet, the life on earth won't exist at all."

The Great Forest said calmly, "Don't worry, pretty bird. He's only a baby and doesn't know how life works. He doesn't even know about himself yet. I can't be disrespected if someone says harsh words to me. His words hold no value until I give them value by accepting them and responding back. Nothing can disturb my inner peace until I allow it to get disturbed. His reaction only indicates that his inner peace is disturbed, and he needs our help. Also, I can smell arrogance simmering inside him. Alas! Those seeds of arrogance were planted by me a long time ago. Oh! That was agonizing. I shouldn't even think about that." After a long pause, he resumed, "This little child has to learn a lot in life. All he needs is a good mentor."

Siba realized his mistake. Filled with remorse and head hanging down, he apologized, "Please forgive me the Great Forest. I got carried away. I didn't mean to disrespect you. You have been calling me an animal since we met. I'm not an animal. I'm a human. Humans are superior to animals. So I got hurt by that remark."

The Great Forest echoed loudly, "No life form is inferior or superior. But don't expect all life forms to be the same or equal as well. Every creature, big or small, is unique and has a specific purpose in this world. Life is not about equality or superiority but specialty and uniqueness. Look around you. The plants have the ability to transform the sun's energy into food. The birds fly in the air. In the same manner, the honey bees transform flower juices into honey, and the ants carry loads many times heavier than their own body weights. You name any creature – fish, worms, elephants, snakes, fungi, even humans. All are unique and gifted with special powers, none matching with others. Appreciate their uniqueness."

After shedding light on Siba's ignorance, the Great Forest brought the spotlight back on the canker that irritated him in the very first place. "And if you didn't like being called an animal, you should have pointed it out at the very first time. Why did you wait for it to grow bigger inside you and then, burst like a volcano?"

Siba replied innocently, "I didn't realize it earlier. I only felt a little uncomfortable about that remark. So, I didn't pay any attention to it."

"Hmm! It's the Evil Bud," the Great Forest pointed. "Evil Bud is growing inside you."

Upon hearing the spooky name, a sudden rush of panic jolted Siba. "Evil Bud! What's that? Am I possessed by some demon?"

"Not demon, but you definitely need an exorcism. You must get rid of this tiny monster before it could do some serious damage. Do you see those pink flowers behind you?"

Trembling with fear, Siba twisted and looked at an overhanging branch. "You mean those ones with big petals?" he stuttered.

"Yep! Pluck one of them and keep it on your chest, close to your heart. Hold it there until the Evil Bud leaves you. It will hurt a bit, but stay strong. I know you are a strong boy."

Siba jumped and plucked one flower and held it next to his chest. Within seconds, he experienced a shooting pain in his heart. It felt like something was crawling under his shirt. Scared as hell, he lifted his shirt. Just like some horror movie, a tiny tendril was whirling and crawling out of his chest. He shivered and screamed in panic.

The Great Forest squeaked, "Don't move. Hold the flower for a few more minutes."

Siba stuttered in horror, "What's this thing coming out of my body? Is it a worm or forest demon?" The tiny vine tendril whirled and twined around the flower. In the next few minutes, the entire vine, roughly the size of Siba's index finger, crawled out from his chest and curled around the flower, leaving behind a tiny bloodless wound.

"This is the Evil Bud. It was growing inside your heart since the first time you heard me calling you an animal. You didn't realize it earlier, as it was too small to be noticed. You might have experienced it as a little uncomfortable feeling. That's why you ignored it.

"Whenever someone says or does something wrong to you, that very moment, Evil Bud develops in your heart. The more you ignore it or try to suppress it by not taking any corrective measures, the more it develops into a full-fledged vine, eventually engulfing your entire heart. Then it starts consuming your self-confidence and self-esteem and develops an inferiority complex in you," the Great Forest expounded in great detail.

Siba pondered over it and asked, "How can I fight with this little devil?"

The Great Forest echoed, "Well, let me put it this way. Everyone has a self-made image of themselves in their minds. I call it – Self-Image. You expect others to behave and treat you in accordance with your self-image. Sometimes, others' behavior, either intentional or unintentional, belittles your self-image. If you don't take any action to correct it due to self-interest, weakness, respect, and so forth, then this loss and damage to your self-image develops an Evil Bud inside your heart. That's why, the wise people say – nip the evil in the bud.

"Thus, you should retaliate or warn others at the very first instance when your self-image is hurt, but in a positive way. Politely express your concerns about the unacceptable behavior or comment toward you. If you don't express your limits, others would perceive their encroachment as acceptable to you, and from that point onwards, it would become their new normal behavior toward you. Therefore, you must take some action the very first time. If you don't take any preventive and defensive action, the Evil Bud grows quickly inside your heart and weans away your self-confidence and self-esteem. You begin to consider others' unacceptable behavior as acceptable. Gradually, it ruins your self-respect and morale. Finally, a shrunk and degenerated self-image is left. It makes you a very helpless and miserable person, unable to stand up for yourself against any unjust atrocities."

Silence prevailed, and it seemed as if time stood still. Breaking the silence, the Great Forest echoed again, "Next time, if you don't like anything, say it to me right away. Don't keep it inside and let the little devil consume you." Still imbibing that deep knowledge, Siba nodded his head in agreement. "But it doesn't mean you are not an animal. Now you belong here. So for me, you are the same as all other amazing creatures," the Great Forest conveyed his intentions in a light, amusing manner.

"Of course," Siba grinned. Still pondering over the lengthy elucidation, he asked, "At the beginning, you mentioned the seeds of arrogance. What are those?"

"Oh, Bumblebee! You are not ready for that yet. At the right time, you'll come to know about it. You still need to work on perfecting your communication skills," the Great Forest diverted Siba's curiosity.

"I'm already working on it. I practiced forest language earlier, while I was coming here. Now, I can talk with the forest-dwellers," Siba said with conviction.

Rouble sniggered, "Sure, you can."

The Great Forest revealed, "Sound is just one form of communication. You still have to work on touch, smell, taste, vision, and most importantly – body language. You should master these skills too. I have no doubt about your capabilities."

"I can seek help from Rouble." Siba twisted his head to look at the scarlet macaw, but he was not there. "Where did he vanish? He was just there a few moments ago."

"He's with his family. Follow the stone trail alongside the stream, and you'll find him," the Great Forest told Siba.

"Come Limpoo, let's find Rouble." Siba left his blanket there, and both marched over the wet, slippery stone trail flanked by wildflowers and berry bushes. After covering some distance, their search operation halted abruptly. The trail and the Great Forest were inundated by the swollen river. Unable to proceed further, they got stuck. He called for help, "Hello! Is there anyone around?" But no one replied. He shouted again, "I'm looking for Rouble, a scarlet macaw. Does anyone know where he is?"

Someone whispered from the canopy, "Shhh! Don't shout!"

"Rouble, is that you?" Siba mumbled, scanning the canopy.

"Yes, it's me. Move away from the water and climb up the trunk," Rouble whispered.

Siba climbed high into the canopy. There, he saw Rouble perched on a thick branch with several other birds. They were holding some secret discussion. Siba inquired, "Is this your family?" All birds slightly bent their necks sideways and stared at him. Siba chuckled nervously, "Hi! I am Siba - friend of Rouble."

A big, grayish-brown tiger owl, presiding over the meeting, stared into Siba's eyes. "All birds and animals of the Great Forest are family. Woody the Owl welcomes you into our family." Woody's big, penetrating, yellow eyes, feathery horns, large sharp talons, and pointed black beak presented a scary sight.

Siba nervously smiled and stuttered, "Thank you! Did I disturb you? I was looking for Rouble. He left without informing me, so I was a little worried."

Woody hooted, "Oh, I see! I sent him a message to attend a quick huddle. Our forest is in danger. Soon, all forest-dwellers are meeting at the Old Rock, and we were planning to go there to put forth our concerns. You may also join us. In fact, since the Great Forest has accepted you as a part of our forest family, everyone is curious to meet you."

Siba asked hesitatingly, "May I know what that danger is?"

"Flood! Can't you see all that water?" Woody the Owl blinked and bobbed, "You'll know the rest when you reach the Old Rock. We don't have time. We must leave now before we are late for the emergency meeting. Don't get down in the flood water. It's not safe. Follow us on these branches." Woody left the fire of curiosity burning inside Siba and fluttered deeper into the forest.

Siba instructed from the top, "Limpoo, you stay here and wait for me. I'll be back soon."

"Bow-wow." Limpoo hopped twice.

Hopping from branch to branch, as they ventured deeper inside the forest, more flocks of animals and birds joined them. Siba overheard their murmurs and chatters.

"Is he the human child, the Great Forest was telling us about?"

"Is he going to live in the forest now? Fox was telling me that he'll live in the eagle's nest."

"Oh damn! Why is he moving so slowly? I heard he's very fast, faster than a cheetah."

"Can he speak forest language? Can he understand us?"

Siba enjoyed listening to the rumors about him while pretending as if he didn't understand a single word. Rouble interrupted his entertainment, "Siba, we have reached the Old Rock. We are out of the danger zone. You can get down now."

Grasping a vine, Siba climbed down from the canopy. Rouble glided down as well and perched on his shoulder. It was a vast circular clearance in the middle of the Great Forest. Its edges gently sloped down toward the middle, where a giant tree stump stood high above the ground like a stage. The stump was so big that an enormous elephant was standing on its top, and still, there was enough space to accommodate a few more animals. Sparsely covered with grass, this place resembled an amphitheater. The only difference was that instead of humans, forest-dwellers were encircling the giant stump. All kinds of animals, birds, rodents, reptiles, even insects were present, and more were joining.

After checking out the location, Siba inquired, "Where is the rock? I don't see any rock here."

"Didn't you hear properly? It's not a rock. It's Old Rock." Rouble pointed with his wing to the middle, "Do you see that big tree stump?"

Siba stood on his toes and peered through the crowd. "Yeah!"

"That's Old Rock," Rouble squawked.

"Who did that?" Siba wondered, "The Great Forest told us earlier that no human knows about this place. It's a secret. Moreover, not even a single tree was damaged or chopped in the entire forest. Then how did this happen?"

Rouble shrugged, "Forest-dwellers don't know about that. All we know is it's been there for eternity, perhaps the Great Forest knows something about it."

Suddenly, a thundering trumpet silenced everyone. From the top of the tree stump, the elephant roared, "Hello forest-dwellers! Thank you for coming at such short notice. As you all are aware of the grave dangers that floods bring to our Great Forest, once again our lives are under threat. Several of our friends have already died. But this time, the tornado has made the flood situation worse. Our usual path of migration is blocked by the damaged trees. Fulfilling my duty as your king, I stand by the laws of the Great Forest. Tomorrow morning, with the first ray of light, I'll lead you to a safe sanctuary by a different path. Inform others as well who couldn't make it here. Suggestions to tackle this problem are welcomed." Raising his huge trunk, the elephant trumpeted again. His gaze fell upon Siba who was tiptoed looking at him. "Is that a human cub?" The elephant shouted, "Come here, Cub."

Every wild eye turned to Siba in surprise. Siba walked toward the elephant amid showering awestruck gazes. Upon arriving at the Old Rock, Siba had a closer look at the mighty beast. The agape boy looked up at the giant's long trunk that was swinging like a pendulum and long, smooth tusks, which were pointed at him like cannons. Siba's head almost touched his back when he tried to look into the eyes of the world's biggest beast. He immediately lowered his gaze and bowed before the mighty king in humbleness and amazement.

The elephant raised his trunk and flapping his giant fan-like ears, said, "I'm Huzo – the King of the Great Forest. I welcome you to my kingdom. So you are the one who's on everyone's lips. Are you aware that this is not a good time for you to be here? The danger is lurking all around the forest."

"O King of the Great Forest! What is this danger that everyone is talking about? Maybe I can offer some help," Siba asked restlessly.

King Huzo exhaled, "Hmmm! You must be aware of the heavy rains that lasted several days. The river passing through our forest swelled and flooded most of its parts."

Siba nodded, "Yeah, I know. I saw water everywhere on my way."

"But what you couldn't see are the giant alligators hidden under the muddy water. They are wreaking havoc on forest life. No one is safe from those monsters. Originally they lived in Emerald Lake. But every time, when the river floods, they sneak into our forest along with the flood water and feast upon the innocent lives," King Huzo expressed his dismay in a helpless tone and lowered his gaze.

Siba couldn't think of how to respond. All he could offer was an instinctive sympathetic look.

Huzo resumed, "Early this morning, they attacked Bison. He was a good friend of mine." A tear rolled down from the king's eye. "We must move to the higher grounds until the water recedes."

Siba suggested, "You should seek the Great Forest's help. Won't they listen to him?"

"These monsters don't belong here. They don't follow the golden rules of the Great Forest."

"Hmmm!" Siba murmured while pondering, "It's a serious issue. They don't belong here, but they trespass every time when the river gets flooded. The rain has stopped, and the water will recede in a few days. They need water to hide, feed, and live. So they will go back to the lake when the water recedes. What if they can't go back and get trapped." Upon conceiving this idea, Siba jumped in excitement. "Yahoo! That's it! They'll be trapped."

"Trapped? What?" Huzo didn't understand what happened to Siba.

"Yes, trapped! We will build a dam on the narrowest part of the river and cut their water supply from the lake. In the next few days, when the water recedes, the river will dry out. They won't be able to swim back and will get trapped on land. Then, they will have to follow the golden rules of the Great Forest, or they will perish forever," Siba revealed his plan to tackle the menace.

"Build a dam!" Rouble, perched on Siba's shoulder, exclaimed.

King looked at him as if he was speaking a foreign language. "What are you saying, Cub?"

With a twinkle in his eye, Siba spoke, "Trust me. This plan will work. But I need help from all of you. Together, all of us can make them kneel down."

"Hmmm, I see what you mean. Come here and announce your plan to everyone," the elephant moved a step back on the Old Rock to make space for Siba.

Siba clambered on the giant tree stump and spoke loudly, "Hello, my name is Siba. I have a plan to put an end to the danger that you are facing. You won't have to run or hide anymore. But as per the wise saying: 'Unity is Strength,' I need help from all of you. First we'll take the babies, as well as the old and the infirm, to a safe place. They can take refuge there. Then, the strong ones will march along the swollen river until we find an ideal location to build a dam."

An old wild-boar, standing in front of the crowd, snorted. "Dam! What's that?"

A beaver, with chisel-like buck teeth, squealed from the middle of the crowd, "I know dam. That's my home. I call it my log nest."

Siba raised his brow, "Exactly! You have the skills to build a dam. You guide us, and we'll construct one to seal the river."

The beaver cheered, "Sure, let's do it and teach those monsters a big lesson."

Huzo ordered a big condor, "Find the narrowest part of the river, and tomorrow, lead us there."

With her body covered in black plumage and white, feathery ruff around her neck, the condor resembled some princess from the Elizabethan Era. Right away, she flapped her large half-black, half-white wings and flew to the sky, leaving behind tiny dust devils.

Huzo turned to Siba. "It's going to be dark soon. You should return to your village and join us at dawn."

An elk with large antlers came forward and offered, "The forest is not safe, and it will be dark before you get there. Allow me to take you to the boundary of the Great Forest."

Siba looked at Rouble for approval. Rouble blinked. "Alright!"

Elk asked, "Are you excited to ride me?"

"Super-excited! It would be fun to ride on your back, Mr. Elk." Excited Siba hopped onto the kneeled elk.

"Goodbye, King Huzo! I'll see you with the first ray of light." Siba waved his hand.

"I'll be waiting for you. Be safe," the elephant trumpeted with raised trunk.

Siba lightly kicked the elk, and it zoomed toward the human settlement. Limpoo, waiting on the side of the stone trail, twitched his ears on hearing approaching Siba. "Come Limpoo, let's go home. Follow us," Siba shouted. Limpoo chased Elk until they arrived near the end of the Great Forest.

Siba signaled Elk to stop near his blanket. When he was getting down from the elk, Rouble reminded him, "Don't forget to request leaves from the Great Forest. Your flock must be hungry."

"Oh! Thanks, Rouble for reminding me. I almost forgot about leaves and also about lychees."

The very next moment, a vine with big leaves lowered down, and the deep voice of the Great Forest echoed, "Be quick. It's getting dark."

"Were you listening to our conversation?" the astounded boy asked.

"Obviously, you are under my cover. I can hear you all the time."

"Then why did you never say anything throughout the whole time?"

"You never asked me anything. If I start poking into every conversation I hear, then I'd be blabbering all day long. I stay silent and intervene only when it's important."

"Hmmm! Anyway, thanks again for the leaves. My sheep really like your leaves more than grass."

"Take some lychees with you too." A branch full of exotic fruit lowered down. Siba packed leaves and lychees in his blanket and balanced it on top of Limpoo.

Elk offered, "It's too dark now. I can drop you at your village."

"Ok! That would be great." Siba placed his blanket on Elk and rode it till they arrived at the village boundary. Rouble and Limpoo followed them closely. On arriving near the village, Siba bid adieu to Elk and walked to his home.

"Good night, Limpoo. You stay here, near the main door. I will see you later." Siba patted the dog and carefully sneaked inside his house and dashed to the stable. He grinned and hugged Celine who was waiting for him and quickly spread leaves in front of her. Celine bleated in excitement on getting more leaves to gorge on.

- Chapter 4 -

Dam in the Wilderness

Early in the morning, holding an oil lamp in his hand, Siba sneaked out of the stable and tiptoed to the clothesline where Rouble was sleeping. He whispered in the bird's ear, "Wake up, Rouble. We have to leave."

The scarlet macaw yawned, "Why are you up so early, even before me? It never happened before." Under the dim light of the lamp, he noticed that Siba was ready to leave. "Where are you going so early in the morning?" Rouble yawned.

"Have you forgotten or are you still sleeping? We have to meet Huzo. Now, get up. Don't be lazy."

"I remember, but what about your school? You already missed it twice. What will happen when Robby and Masai won't find you here? Your uncle will beat the hell out of you if he finds out what you have been doing."

"Oops! I didn't think about that. Let's go to Robby's house first and inform him about my plans."

"Have you gone nuts? You are not supposed to reveal the secrets of the Great Forest to anyone. Don't you remember that?"

"Oh, hell no! I'll make up a story."

"Hmmm, story? Like what?"

"Like I'm going to take my uncle to the city."

"Going to the city for what?"

Siba twitched his lips, "Ok, check this out. My uncle slipped and broke his leg. I'm going to take him to the city hospital. How's that?"

"Think twice. If your lie is caught, you'll be in big trouble."

"I need to help the forest-dwellers. I don't have a choice."

Rouble thought for some time and nodded his head, "Alright!"

They went to Robby's house and knocked on the big wooden door. An old lady responded, "Who's knocking on the door this early in the morning?"

"Granny, it's me. Siba," Siba shouted.

The front lights of the house turned on, and an old lady in a loose, white gown opened the door. Braiding her gray hair, she asked, "Come in, son. You are up so early! Is everything ok?"

Rouble fluttered and perched on a nearby utility pole. Siba entered the courtyard and requested, "I'm fine. Can you wake Robby up? I need to talk to him."

"What's so important that you couldn't wait until sunrise?" She covered her head with a white scarf, looking into his eyes.

"It's urgent and personal. I can't tell you. Can you wake him up? Please," Siba pleaded.

"Oh my little boy, what's so urgent and personal that you can't tell me? You're not supposed to hide anything from your granny. You can tell me. I promise I won't tell anyone."

Hesitantly, Siba told her that his uncle broke his leg, and he couldn't go to school. He was here to tell Robby not to pick him up for school.

Granny grew suspicious. "Oh! Robby told me that you were sick on Wednesday, and yesterday, you went with your uncle to another village. Today again you can't go to school?

I know your uncle very well. He doesn't have any relatives. What's going on? If there's something wrong, you should tell me. Always speak the truth, my child. I promise I'll help you out with whatever you are going through. I know it's hard to live without parents. And your drunkard old man," she turned silent for a moment. "Uff! Leave that. I'm going to the temple. I don't want to talk about him in the morning." She looked at him sympathetically.

Siba asked innocently, "Promise me, you won't tell anyone."

Granny smiled gently, "I promise."

Siba spoke slowly, "I'm going to the forest to help the forest animals. They are in danger."

"Forest animals? In danger? I heard the forest is flooded. It's not safe to go there. Moreover, you are too young to go to the forest by yourself." With raised brows, she touched Siba's face.

"I won Huntzman Trophy last year, and I'm not going alone. Rouble is going with me."

"What can that bird do if some wild animal attacks you? And winning that trophy doesn't mean you are ready for the forest." Granny stared into Siba's eyes and asked, "Son, tell me the truth."

"This is the truth, Granny. I swear. I went to the forest. The forest spoke to me. I became friends with the forest animals. Due to the flood, their life is in danger, and I'm going to help them out," Siba blurted out in one breath.

The old lady shook her head, "Wait a minute! What did you just say? Forest spoke to you! And the wild animals became your friends! Am I dreaming or have you lost your mind?"

"I know. It's hard to believe, but this is true. I'll explain the rest later. I have to leave now. The animals are waiting for me. Please don't tell this to anyone. But please tell Robby that my uncle broke his leg, and I'm taking him to the hospital. So that he doesn't come to my house." Siba left the old lady behind, confused and concerned.

"I'll tell him. But make sure you are ok." The dumbfounded old lady waved her hand.

Siba strode down the grassy trail. Rouble hovered above him. The cool morning breeze was very refreshing, but it was still very dark, and the stars were twinkling brightly. As he entered deeper into the woods, thick trees blocked the moonlight, making it hard for him to see his path. Sporadic croaks of frogs and shrill whistles of other bugs sent chills down his spine. Feeling a little scared in the wilderness, he avoided looking back. Suddenly, the crackling of leaves alarmed them. Someone was following them and moving closer. Siba trembled in fear.

Was it Uncle or did Granny tell someone about him? Might it be alligators or some other wild beast? A pandora's box of dark fears opened and all hidden bogeymen were let loose in his tiny mind. But to his surprise, Elk stepped out of the bushes and said, "Ah! There you are."

Siba gasped, "Oh! You scared the hell out of me."

"Me too." Rouble also sighed with relief.

Elk sniggered, "I didn't mean to scare you. King Huzo told me to pick you up."

Siba said, "Ok! That's fine."

Elk kneeled. "Hop on and hold my antlers. King is waiting for you at the Old Rock."

Fulfilling his promise, Siba arrived at the Old Rock with the first ray of sunlight. On top of the big tree stump, Huzo was discussing something with Beaver and Condor. All forest-dwellers were sitting around them, waiting for their king's command.

On seeing Siba getting down from Elk, Huzo welcomed him cheerfully, "Welcome, my friend. You made it right on time. Everyone is here, ready to proceed. Condor found a good site for building the dam – a narrow gorge. She'll lead us there."

With a pleasant smile, Siba cheered, "Sounds good!" He asked Condor, "How far is that spot?"

Condor spoke in her peculiar shrill voice, "Water is almost everywhere in the forest, except near the foothills of Rocky Hills. Only that region is dry and free from alligators. We can go to Rocky Hills. It's not that far. And from thereon, we can proceed on trails along its edges till we reach the narrow gorge. According to my estimation, the narrowest part of the river should be the best site for building a dam."

Beaver approved, "Yep! That should be a perfect location for building a beaver's nest."

King Huzo trumpeted, "Awesome! Let's do it."

Condor led the evacuation through the dry part of the Great Forest. Huzo and Siba walked in front of the convoy. The birds flew, encircling the migrating caravan to keep a vigil on the hidden dangers. Rouble and Woody the Owl perched on both shoulders of Siba and briefed him about the golden rules of the Great Forest. Around noon, just outside the Great Forest, they arrived at the foothills of a small rocky hill range. Tall fir trees lined its boundary. Dotted with fruit trees and bushes, it offered a delightful view and a safe refuge to rest.

King Huzo stopped at the base of a hill. After analyzing the area carefully, he announced, "This place looks safe and out of reach of those scaly monsters. It also has plenty of food for all of us. From this elevation, we can keep an eye on our forest as well. From this point onwards, only the strong ones who can contribute to building the dam will proceed with me. The rest will stay here until the Great Forest is safe once again." All animals cheered his decision.

The robust healthy animals and birds resumed, while the weak, young, and old stayed behind. The journey ahead was treacherous. The slippery, moist, and mossy rocky trails demanded extra focus and tenacity to climb. Several landslides from the recent rains constantly blocked their way. But they kept on overcoming every obstacle with coordination and determination.

Ω

Meanwhile in the village, while returning from school Robby and Masai found Siba's uncle lying unconscious on the roadside. Robby tried to lift him up. "Yuck! He smells so bad all the time. I wonder how many years ago he took his last bath?"

"Must be before my birth," Masai chuckled, offering his skinny hand. But the old man didn't get up despite their efforts. "What happened to him? Is he dead?" he uttered in worry.

"No, dummy! He must be drunk and might have passed out. But Siba told Granny that he was taking him to the city hospital. Then how come he's here?" Robby became suspicious.

"You are right. Where is Siba? In that case, he should be here with his uncle," Masai too became skeptical.

"Maybe he went to ask for help from someone." Robby tried to stay optimistic.

"Hmmm, maybe or maybe not. What shall we do now? We can't leave him in this condition," Masai expressed his concerns.

"Look! The village head is coming in his horse wagon. We should ask him for help. Maybe he can drop this stinking old pig to his pen," Robby suggested. The village head was generous and dropped all of them at Siba's house. After laying the unconscious old man in his bed, both boys searched for Siba. But he was nowhere to be found.

Angry and worried, Masai kicked a pebble on his way back to his house. "This is not fair. We are his best friends, and he lied to us."

Robby tried to calm him down by exploring the other possibilities. "He might be in trouble or what if he's kidnapped. Until we know for sure, we shouldn't come to a conclusion. I have full faith in him. There must be a reason behind all this."

But furious Masai was not ready to forgive Siba. He yelled, "No, can't you see? His uncle's legs were fine. He lied to your grandmother. And stop taking his side. You always defend him, even if, it's his mistake."

Robby got annoyed. "Alright! Don't fight with me. I didn't lie to anybody. I'm more concerned about the fact that he's missing, instead of being angry over his lie. I think we should talk about this to Granny."

"Ok!" Masai agreed.

Pushing aside the big wooden door of his house, Robby shouted, "Grandma, where are you? We want to talk to you. It's very urgent."

Robby's mom screamed from the kitchen, "What happened? Why are you shouting? She's not at home. She has gone to the temple for evening prayer."

"Nothing mom," Robby spoke in a lower tone. He whispered to Masai, "Let's wait here until she returns." They sat on the porch stairs, waiting for the old lady.

Ω

Meanwhile, in the forest, after crossing several obstacles Siba and his determined convoy arrived at the narrowest part of the river toward the end of the day. King Huzo ordered Beaver to survey the location. The buck-toothed rodent climbed a tall rock to get an overview of the site. He scanned the area and commented, "It's really a good spot for building a giant beaver's nest." The very next second, he dove into the river and traversed across its depth and breadth. After emerging from the river, he reported worriedly, "O King, I inspected the on-site conditions. The water current is very strong, and depth is more than my building skills."

"Don't worry about your skills. You are not going to build it by yourself. Just tell me, if we all can build it together or not?" the king inquired.

Beaver clicked, "Oh yeah! This current doesn't stand a chance in front of your mighty strength. With the combined effort of everyone, it shouldn't take us long to accomplish this feat."

King Huzo announced, "We'll begin building the dam tomorrow. Find a spot to sleep before we lose sunlight. And Woody, you watch for dangers throughout the night."

Woody the Owl muttered, "I'm not a watchman."

King Huzo asked angrily, "What did you say?"

Woody stuttered, "I will be your watchman, my king."

Rouble chuckled, "Don't worry. I'll give you company, Woody the watchman."

Woody glared at Rouble and whispered, "I want to contribute to building the dam, not in watching them sleeping and snoring."

Rouble giggled, "Can't you see? It's a major contribution. We are in alligator territory. What if they attack us tonight?"

"Hmmm, I didn't think about that." Woody scratched his beak with his talon.

After the sunset, the birds perched on the trees and the animals sought refuge in the hilly caves and cracks. Siba laid down next to Huzo and slept with his arm wrapped around the giant's trunk. Woody and Rouble took turns in hovering over the area, monitoring every suspicious moment.

Ω

At Robby's house, both boys were still waiting for the old lady. She returned from the temple with flowers and holy water. She noticed both boys sitting on the porch stairs under a flickering bulb. She understood at once that something was wrong.

"Come here, my little muffins. Give your granny a big hug. Are you waiting for your bedtime story?" she asked, offering holy water to them.

Masai spoke, "No, Grandma. We don't want to hear any story." She frowned.

Robby asked, "Do you know what happened today?"

"No?" Granny pretended to be clueless.

Robby informed her, "We found Siba's uncle unconscious on the road."

Masai added quickly, "And Siba is missing. We looked for him everywhere. But he's nowhere to be found."

Robby expressed his concern, "Maybe, he's in trouble. Are you sure about what he told you this morning because his uncle's legs are perfectly fine?"

Granny pretended to be entirely unaware of that fact. "How's that possible? That's what he told me. He was going to take his uncle to the city hospital."

Masai glowered at Robby, "I told you, he lied to us. I will never ever talk to him again. We are his best friends. How can he hide things from us?"

The old lady hugged Masai and kissed his forehead, "O my sunshine! You will talk to him. You are angry because you care for him. Don't worry. He will be back very soon."

Robby became suspicious about Granny's lack of concern for the missing boy. Her assurance that he'd be back soon made him intuitively feel that she was hiding something. "Grandma, aren't you worried that Siba is missing? Or do you know where he is? If you know about him, please tell us. We are not only his friends but more like brothers. We promise we won't let anyone know that you told us about him. We are only worried about him."

Masai also strengthened Robby's request. "Yes, Granny. We promise we won't tell anyone."

"Alright, my muffins! I can't see your little brains worried unnecessarily. But, even if I tell you what Siba told me, you won't believe that either. Anyway, I'll tell you. He told me that he was going to the forest to help his friends – the wild animals," Granny revealed.

The baffled boys stared at each other and blurted, "Wild animals! His friends?"

"I told you, it's hard to believe. I don't believe that either. Siba told me that and left in a hurry. I don't know if he's ok or not. He told me not to tell you about this. So, if you see him, don't talk about that. However, if he's not back yet, then that's a real matter of concern." The worried old woman stared at them. "Masai, you should go home. It's too late. You need to get up early for school."

Masai replied, "We don't have school for the next two days. Did you forget? It's the weekend."

"Oh yes! For me, every day is a holiday. How can I remember which day is which?" She smiled. "You can sleep here, in Robby's room. Let's go inside. Dinner should be ready. Tomorrow, we'll figure out what's happening with Siba."

Robby told Masai excitedly, "Great! Let's go to my room. I'll show you my new pet – clownfish."

Granny said, "First, have your dinner. Then you can play with her for the whole night." She removed her sandals and entered the dining room with both boys.

Ω

At daybreak, Huzo checked the river for any signs of alligators. The water in the gorge was deep but not deep enough for the mighty beast. As he waded through the deepest sections, his head and back were still above the water. After a thorough inspection, he gathered everyone on the bank for discussing the next plan of action. He sniggered, "They must be looking for us inside the forest, and we are here, inside their kingdom. Fools! Anyway, let's chalk out our plan and finish it fast before they sniff our presence. Ducks and geese, you'll swim around us, and if you sense any danger, give us alarm calls. Beaver, you'll give directions to everyone related to building the dam. Siba, you'll stay on the river bank and observe if things are working out or not. Everyone else, follow Beaver's instructions. Any doubts?"

The crowd shouted out loud, "No."

"No questions. Then, let's do it," the elephant trumpeted.

Beaver requested, "My king, the water is too deep in the middle. First, I need your help in leveling the river bed."

Huzo asked, "What do you want me to do?"

Contemplating over the problem, Beaver replied, "I don't know. That's what I'm thinking as well."

Siba came up with a smart solution. He pointed to a nearby landslide and proposed, "We can use those big rocks. They won't float and will sit at the bottom." Staring at the elephant, he said, "You should be able to lift them with your brawny trunk and level the river bed."

The conceited pachyderm boasted, "Ahem! That's a piece of cake for me."

"Bingo! Here we go," Beaver exclaimed. "My king, you can finish this heavy task. In the meantime, others can collect logs and branches from the nearby trees and pile them on the bank. My brothers and I will stack them watertight to block the flow of water."

Huzo lifted a big boulder and moved to the middle of the river. "Should I place it here?" he asked Beaver.

Beaver dived to the bottom for inspection and instructed, "A little further upstream." The elephant moved to the guided spot and dropped the boulder. After a few rounds of dumping, the river bed rose to the desired level.

Beaver signaled, "That would be enough, my king." In the meantime, birds and animals had gathered enough material for the beavers to begin. From higher ground, Siba and Huzo watched them build the structure. Throughout the day, wood gatherers kept on bringing all sorts of logs and branches that they could find. Like accomplished craftsmen, beavers chiseled logs with their powerful jaws and sharp teeth to integrate them perfectly into the rising structure. The water flow slowed down with each new layer of timber. Everyone worked tirelessly throughout the day, and just before the sunset, the dam was ready.

"The water flow stopped completely, and the dam wall is high enough for anyone to pass; especially, for those crawling monsters," King Huzo remarked in triumph.

Siba responded, "Now all we need to do is to wait until the water level goes down in the forest. Then we shall see, how they'll beg for mercy."

Rouble reminded Siba, "Good job! Should we return home? You were not there last night as well. I'm sure your old man will be waiting for you with his cane."

Siba looked at the sun. It was about to hide behind the hills. He gasped in panic, "Oh geez! I completely forgot about him. I'll tell him that I slept at Robby's place last night as we were working together on our home assignment."

Siba twisted his head toward Elk and requested, "I know you must be very tired. But can you please give me a ride back home? We are too far away. I won't be able to reach there on time by myself."

Elk obliged, "Siba, you are helping us during our worst times. It'd be my pleasure to assist you with whatever I can. Don't worry. I'll run like the wind. You'll be at your home on time."

Huzo spoke, "Go Siba. Don't be late. Each inhabitant of the Great Forest is grateful to you. We'll wait on these hills until the flood water recedes. I'll send Condor to inform you when things get better. Then we can decide our next plan of action."

Siba hopped on the kneeled elk and waved at Huzo, "I'll eagerly wait for your message."

"Hold my antlers." Elk whizzed through the forest and dropped him at the periphery of the village; just when the stars started appearing in the twilight sky. Rouble almost dropped dead chasing the superfast Elk.

Siba sniggered at the out-of-breath parrot, "I thought you forgot your way back home."

Panting heavily, Rouble scowled, "Grrr."

- Chapter 5 -

Taste of Sadness

Upon arriving near his house, Siba saw Limpoo sitting right in front of his main door. "Limpoo, my boy! Did you miss me?" Siba hugged him tightly. "My uncle must be very upset with me. If he sees me with you, he'll become more furious. You stay here. I'll see you in the morning."

He quietly entered the house. As he stepped onto the porch, he saw his uncle's cane on the floor. He lifted the cane and whispered to Rouble, "How's he gonna walk without his cane?"

The scarlet macaw sniggered, "I thought you were going to say – 'How's he gonna beat me without his cane?' "

"Shut up! You silly bird," Siba whispered. He stealthily headed toward his uncle's room to return his cane next to his bed. Suddenly, his gaze fell upon a beer bottle. It was broken and its pieces were scattered all over the floor. He became anxious. He swiftly opened the door, and inside the dark room, found his uncle fallen on the floor, unconscious.

Siba got scared. He shook the old man. "Uncle, what happened to you? Open your eyes! Talk to me!" But the unconscious man didn't show any sign of life. He got more scared and cried in panic, "Get up, Uncle. I'll never go anywhere without telling you. I promise. Please open your eyes. I'll always do whatever you say. Please get up."

Rouble suggested, "He's not breathing. Call someone for help."

Siba didn't know what happened to his uncle. His mind had stopped working. Wiping off the tears rolling down his cheek, he asked, "Whom should I call?"

Rouble suggested, "Robby's or Masai's parents. Who else?"

Siba at once ran to Masai's house. "Masai! Masai!" he yelled banging the main door, "Please open the door."

"Hold on! Wait a minute!" Masai's father shouted loudly from the inside. On opening the main door, he found Siba sniveling. He inquired, "Siba! What happened? Is everything ok?"

Siba sniffled, "My uncle! He's not moving!" That's all he could say before breaking into tears again.

"O Siba! He must be drunk. Don't worry. He'll be up by tomorrow. Wash your face and go to sleep," the middle-aged, tall, skinny man consoled the weeping boy.

"No! No!" Siba whimpered, "He's not breathing. Please come and see him."

"Don't cry, son. Let's go. Just a second, let me get my torch." He went inside the house and fetched his torch.

They almost ran through the dark, empty streets to get to Siba's house. When they reached there, Masai's father placed his index finger in front of the unconscious old man's nostrils. "You are right. He's not breathing." Right away, he held the old man's wrist to check his pulse. But there was no pulse. He placed his ear on Uncle's chest. "Heart is not beating," he said worriedly. He thought for a minute and said, "You go and sleep at Robby's house tonight. Masai is there too. I'll take Uncle to the city hospital."

"No, I won't leave him again. I'll go with you." Siba refused to leave his uncle.

"Fine! I'm going to bring the village head's horse wagon to carry Uncle. In the meantime, you go and tell Robby's father that we need his help and bring him here."

Siba wasted no time. Within twenty minutes, Robby, Robby's father, Masai, and Granny were at Siba's house to check Uncle's condition. After another ten minutes, riding on a horse wagon, the village head and Masai's father arrived there too. Right away, the three men took the unconscious old man to the hospital. The three kids went with Granny to her house.

After performing the medical check-up, the doctor told them that the old man was dead, and he died from alcohol poisoning.

The next day, the villagers gathered at Siba's house to mourn the old man. Masai's father shared his worry, "Who will take care of Siba now? How will he live by himself?"

Robby's grandmother, rearranging her scarf, willingly offered to take Siba's responsibility, "Until I'm alive, no one needs to worry about Siba. In fact, I wanted to adopt him from the day the old man found him abandoned in the forest. But he insisted to keep the infant to quell his loneliness. I suppressed my desires and allowed him to keep the baby."

Masai's father exclaimed, "Siba was found in the forest!" Everyone's jaws dropped with shock.

Robby's father asked the old lady, "What are you saying, mother? Isn't Siba his distant nephew's son? That's what he used to tell everyone."

"No son, only we two shared this secret. One day, while grazing his flock of sheep in the forest, the old man found a newborn baby near the river. Now he's no more, and I can fulfill my long-standing wish." The old lady's eyes shone with contentment. "But don't tell Siba about this secret. I don't want him to face two shocks at the same time."

Siba, drenched in tears, performed the last rites of his uncle. Granny embraced him, "My little muffin!" She stared into his tear-laden eyes, "Be strong, son. Death is part of life. Old leaves give place to new ones. Everything that has a beginning has to come to an end one day. This is the law of nature. No one can escape from it. Not your uncle, nor me, and not even you. One day, everyone has to leave. Wipe your tears. From now on, you will stay with me. I'll take care of you, just like Robby."

Granny brought Siba to her house. But the young boy, unfamiliar with this harsh reality of life, got overwhelmed by the enormous grief of sudden death. That devastating blow completely shattered his tiny little world. The unbearable pain and grief kept on oozing from his eyes in the form of tears.

Granny, wiping Siba's tears, consoled, "Everyone knows, he was not a good man. He never took good care of you. Do you remember how many times he lashed you with his cane?"

Siba sniffled, "I never saw my parents. I don't know how they would have treated me. Even though he was abusive sometimes, he was my only family."

The old lady couldn't say anything. She stayed quiet. After some time, she spoke, "Wash your face. I'm cooking your favorite dish – rice pudding. I made your bed next to Robby's. He must be tired of sleeping next to his clownfish. After having dinner, you sleep there."

Ω

Flying ahead of running Siba, Rouble shouted, "Look! Look! Our sheep are grazing there." He pointed toward the flooded side of the Great Forest.

Panting heavily, Siba halted. "Where?"

"There! Just behind that bamboo grove," Rouble signaled.

Siba looked there. "Only nine sheep are here. Where is Celine?" he asked worriedly.

Suddenly, they heard Celine bleating for help. Siba chased her screams and to his horror, found her surrounded by alligators. Without a second thought, he picked a stick and charged toward them. But when he raised the stick to fend them off, to his utter dismay, he realized it was not a stick but a snake. He screamed in panic and woke up.

Robby's sleep broke by the loud scream. "Siba, what happened? Nightmare?"

"Celine must be very hungry. I completely forgot about her. I must go and feed her."

"In the middle of the night? Can't she wait till morning?" Robby consoled and persuaded him to go back to sleep.

Siba laid down and covered his face with the blanket but couldn't sleep for a long time. The next morning, when he woke up, he found Robby's bed was already made. He thought that Robby always wakes up early, so he should also get up early if he was going to be his roommate. He yawned and walked out to the porch.

Robby's father was sitting there, reading a newspaper with sips of warm tea. "Robby told me that you had a nightmare. Don't worry about your sheep. Today, I'll buy fodder for them. You just focus on your studies." Just then, Robby walked out of the washroom. His father resumed, "Well, Robby took a shower. You should also get ready for school. It will help in coping with your grief. And breakfast will be ready by then." He gave Siba a reassuring smile and carried on with his newspaper.

At school, Nubina and Yasmine asked Siba about his uncle's sudden death. He couldn't utter a single word. Deep down in his heart, he was feeling guilty for not being there when his uncle was struggling for his life. Recollecting those tragic memories, his eyes brimmed with tears. Yasmine solaced him, "You are not alone. We are with you. We are your family."

Nubina pulled a colorful mermaid doll out of her bag. "Siba, keep my princess with you. Whenever you feel sad or lonely, she will make you happy." She handed it to him.

Siba reluctantly held the toy. "But it's your favorite doll. You like her so much."

"Her name is Care. She stays with those who need care, not with those who like her. She was with my mother when she was small, then with Yasmine for some time. After her, she came to me. Now, you need more care than I do. So, I pass it to you. When you feel someone else needs more care than you, give it to them," she grinned.

Little dimples formed on Siba's wet cheeks as he smiled. "Thank you. I'll always keep her close to my heart."

In the meantime, Miss Sony entered the classroom. All the students exclaimed, "Good morning, miss!"

"Good morning, students! You look fresh after the weekend, huh?" Her eyes scanned the students but got fixed on Siba. She asked him, "You missed school for three days. Robby told me that you were sick. How are you feeling now?" Siba couldn't raise his head.

Yasmine stood up and spoke on Siba's behalf, "Miss, Siba's uncle passed away."

Miss Sony walked to him and sympathized, "I'm so sorry. How can God do that to you?" She paused and suggested, "You should divert your attention to move out of this painful situation. I'll request our principal to select you for the Annual Huntzman Games. The list was finalized last week, but I'm sure the principal won't mind adding the name of last year's champion. It'll keep you busy and divert your mind from painful thoughts."

Siba looked up and said, "Thank you, Miss!"

"After your classes, meet me where the great minds live." Miss Sony smiled and walked to her desk. She opened her book and scribed "ENERGY" on the blackboard. "Today, we will learn about energy. Everything you see around you is energy – sun, moon, earth, plants, animals, you, me, everything. Everything is made up of energy. It can neither be created nor be destroyed. It can only be transformed from one form to another. Like this matchstick." She picked one matchstick and ignited it. "Watch it carefully." When it burned completely, she asked, "Where's the matchstick?"

One student leaning over the front desk replied, "It became ash."

Another student sitting next to him argued, "No, stupid! It became fire."

The third one shouted, "Miss, it's in the air as smoke."

The teacher explained, "All of you are correct, but partially. Matchstick was one form of energy that got converted into fire, smoke, and ash. Do you understand now, how one form of energy is transformed into three different forms?"

"Did my uncle also transform into some other form of energy?" Siba asked innocently.

The whole class silenced. After some time, the teacher spoke, "Your uncle became a star. When someone dies, they become a star." She lowered her gaze and picked up her stuff. "Today's class is over. Tomorrow, we'll learn more about energy." She left in a hurry, avoiding eye contact with Siba.

After his classes, Siba went to meet Miss Sony in the library. At the entrance of the library, there was a big sign – "Great minds live here."

Miss Sony smiled upon seeing him. "Congratulations! The principal agreed to our request. I'm sure you'll bring glory to our school. Good luck!"

"Thank you, miss. I'll give my best." He left the library and strode back toward his classroom where Robby and Masai were waiting for him. While passing through the corridor, he heard someone shouting his name. He turned around. A tall boy was chasing him.

Siba waved, "Hi Nick."

Nick shouted with a bright grin, "Congrats! Our champ is back. I was so worried about this year's games. But when I saw Miss Sony talking to the principal about you, my joy knew no bounds. I heard about your uncle as well. I extend my deepest sympathies to you."

A budding smile on Siba's face melted into a sad frown. "Even though he died, I hope I can find him in the night sky. Maybe I can find my parents as well somewhere among the stars."

Nick chuckled, "Did Miss Sony tell you about that star crap?"

Siba asked, "Yes. Did she tell you the same when your father died?"

Nick scoffed, "Not when my father passed away, but last year, when my puppy died."

Siba inquired eagerly, "Did you find your puppy among the stars?"

"No. But my mother gifted me another one on my birthday. I don't believe in it, but I look at Pole Star when I miss my father, as Pole Star is always there for me," Nick replied nostalgically. "Tomorrow after your classes, meet me at the ring. Mr. Drock is our coach again. You know how he is. So better be on time for the practice session. We'll practice hard every day and before the end of the month, we should be ready for the games."

"Sure Nick! I'll be there right after school. I don't want Drock to croak. By the way, are you going to be our team's captain again?"

Nick scratched his chin. "I'm not sure. You are last year's champion, so you should lead our team. Your name was not on the list, that's why everyone was considering me. But now, you are in. So it should be you."

Robby and Masai, walking toward them, spoke together, "Mr. NOT is here, and we searched for him everywhere."

Siba twisted, "Oh sorry! I was just coming there."

Masai teased Siba, "Why would he care if someone is waiting? He's now part of the most prestigious team."

Siba became embarrassed. "I said sorry."

Nick chuckled, "Blame me, guys. I borrowed your friend."

Robby and Masai laughed out loud. "We know. We were just teasing him," Robby said.

The three boys walked back to their village. On the way, they talked about Siba's excellent performance in last year's games. When they arrived near Masai's house, Siba said, "I'll see you in a little while. I'm going to my home to check my flock."

Robby said, "No, we all will go together. What if you disappear again?"

Siba agreed, "Alright!"

At his house, Siba was delighted to see a big heap of fresh-cut grass. All sheep were happily chewing their cud. He didn't disturb them and moved out. He hugged Robby with contentment. "Thank you, Robby! It should be enough for the entire week."

Robby placed his hand on Siba's shoulder and said, "Oh! Don't thank me. Let's go to my home and thank my father. On seeing your sheep eating, I'm also feeling very hungry."

Siba moved his arm toward the scarlet macaw, perched on the clothesline. "Come Rouble, let's go." The bird hopped on his arm and walked to his shoulder.

- Chapter 6 -

Days to Remember

The next day at school, a tall, lanky man in a black suit walked into the classroom. He fixed his tie and walked to the teacher's desk. He placed his brown bag on one side of the desk and stepped to the front of the room. Scanning the entire class, he instructed, "Today, we'll study gravity. Open your books to page number seventy-six."

The students replied in unison, "Gravity, Mr. Nobel!"

"That's correct, gravity. Gravity is the reason why we are stuck on the ground. Else we would be floating and hitting everywhere." Mr. Nobel took a ball out of his bag. "What will happen if I throw it in the air?"

One boy answered, "It will hit the roof."

"Ahem! What if I throw it in an open field?" Mr. Nobel asked.

"It will fall back on the ground," Yasmine replied.

"That's my smart girl. Do you know why?"

She thought for a while and replied, "Once, I fell from a ladder. My mother told me that whatever goes up falls down later." All students laughed.

"Silence! Silence!" Mr. Nobel knocked the desk with a duster and explained, "All objects pull each other closer to them by an invisible force. This force is called gravity. The bigger the object, the more gravitational force it exerts. Now, the earth is bigger than this ball. So, the earth pulls it toward itself." He dropped the ball and it hit the floor. Everyone got confused. Yasmine raised her hand to ask a question.

"Yes Yasmine, what's your question?" Mr. Nobel asked.

"I'm bigger than Nubina. It means I have more gravity than her. But why won't her candies and toys fall on me?" Yasmine asked innocently. The whole class burst into laughter again.

"Keep quiet!" the teacher said loudly. "It doesn't work like that. Gravitational force is very weak at our level. You see its effect on the planetary level. Like the way the moon revolves around the earth or the way the planets revolve around the sun. Do you remember the planets of our solar system that we studied in the last class?"

Yasmine replied, "Yes, Mr. Nobel. Mercury, Venus, Earth, Mars, Jupiter."

"That's fine. I didn't ask the names. But if you remember, I told you that in our solar system the sun is the biggest object. So it has maximum gravity. Yasmine, you tell me now. Which planet should have the next highest gravity."

Masai shouted, "Jupiter."

Mr. Nobel rebuked Masai, "Is your name Yasmine?" Everyone laughed.

Robby raised his arm. Mr. Nobel asked, "Yes Robby, what's your question?"

"What about birds and clouds? How do they fly? Is their gravity bigger than earth's gravity?"

"Birds fly in the air just like fish swim in the water. Clouds fly because they're lighter than the air. I'll teach you that next year. It's not part of your syllabus. Any more questions?"

Siba asked, "Does that mean nothing can ever move away from the earth?"

Mr. Nobel stared at him. "It's possible. If you move at a very high speed, faster than the force that pulls you back, like rockets." He smiled. "I'll teach you that next year too." He pulled out a big chart of the solar system from his bag and hung it next to the blackboard. "I'm going to explain another aspect of gravity. Do you see the moon and sun in the sky?"

Everyone said, "Yes."

"Good!" Pointing to the chart, he said, "Do you see here, the earth is bigger than the moon? So the earth pulls the moon toward it, as it has more gravity. Similarly, the sun is bigger than the earth. Thus, it pulls the earth toward it along with the moon encircling our planet. You must be thinking, then why don't they fall into the sun?" He glanced at students, who looked completely puzzled. He chuckled, "It's because they fly around the sun at the same speed with which they are being pulled. Thus, instead of falling into or flying away, they keep on revolving around our star in a particular orbit. So Siba, if you fly at a speed fast enough to beat earth's gravitational force, then you can escape into space. Oh! I answered your question now itself."

Bell rang.

"Well, time's up. We'll continue in our next class." Mr. Nobel packed his bag and left.

Nick was waiting outside Siba's class. As soon as the teacher moved out, he sprang into the class. Siba lifted his bag and said hurriedly, "I was just coming to see you."

Nick responded promptly, "That's fine. I know Mr. Nobel. He never leaves the class before time. I got free early, so thought of picking you up. Are you ready for practice, captain?"

"What do you mean? I'm the captain?" Siba stumbled.

"Don't you know? The whole school knows that. In today's meeting, you have been selected to lead our school's team. Mr. Drock himself recommended your name. We must rush to him now, else you know what will happen."

They dashed through the side door of the ring. A hoarse voice thundered, "You are five minutes twenty-seven seconds late." A bald, beefy man, staring at his stopwatch, roared, "I don't expect this kind of undisciplined behavior from the captain of our team."

Siba stuttered, "Sorry, Mr. Drock."

Mr. Drock shouted, "I don't want you to set a bad example on the very first day of the practice session. Two rounds!"

Nick chuckled. The coach pulled his brows together and shouted again, "Two rounds of the track, both of you. Shoot!"

After two rounds of the race track, they almost crashed in front of the coach. "Did you get your second wind?" Mr. Drock rumbled.

The panting boys groaned, "Yes, coach."

"Hmmm! Delicious!" The coach roared, "Two more rounds! Everyone!"

By the time, all six team members completed two rounds, Siba and Nick nearly fainted.

Mr. Drock addressed six panting players in his peculiar loud hoarse tone, "You six are here because you outperformed other contestants. But that was just the beginning. Your real journey begins, now. In Annual Huntzman Games, you'll be tested for your survival skills. Today, I'll explain to you the outlay of the arena and the rules that must be followed throughout the relic hunt. Everyone to that table," he pointed to a big table placed in one corner of the ring.

All players surrounded the big table containing a miniature replica of the Annual Huntzman Games arena. With a long pointer stick, Mr. Drock tapped a hill in the middle of the model. "For the first-timers, this hill in the middle is the Victory Hill. Judges and spectators will watch each player's movement from here. Four main schools in our county participate in these games every year. Each team has its own color. Our color is blue. Out of six players, four will play, while two will be substitutes, in case someone gets hurt."

A brawny boy interrupted, "Which two will be substitutes?"

"Did I finish Harry?" the coach growled.

Harry quivered, "Sorry, Mr. Drock."

"If anyone interrupts me again, he'll be the first substitute. Got it? What was I telling?"

Nick reminded him in a shivering tone, "The different sections of the arena."

"Oh yes, arena! It's divided into four sections. This one, in front of Siba, is the marsh. And this dam separates the marsh from the river. There will be four canoes tied next to this dam, one for each team. Only one player can go into the marsh by using their team's canoe. Next to the marsh is the grassland. This is the easiest section to explore. Adjacent to it is this woodland with big trees. This section is the most challenging one. You must keep your eyes not only on the ground but more importantly, on the trees. Siba, you should explore this area. Last year, you surprised everyone with your agility and the swift manner in which you climbed the trees and explored that area."

Siba blushed, "Thank you, Mr. Drock! I'll try my best."

The coach pointed to the last section and resumed in his usual hoarse tone, "This is the last segment of the arena – our ancient ruins. You need to be extra careful here. Don't cause any damage to our heritage. Place every step very carefully. Some rocks may be unstable. And one last thing, this stone wall surrounding the entire area marks the boundary of the arena. Now you may ask questions if something is not clear." He stared at Harry. Harry lowered his gaze.

A girl with two long braids asked, "Excuse me! What about this river? It's touching the edge of the marsh and then, passes through the side of the grassland. Is it also a part of the arena?"

"Good question, Terry! I forgot to tell you about this river. Even though this river falls inside the arena, don't worry about it. A long time ago, it used to be a part of the games. Because of several casualties that happened there, it was removed from the challenge. You should focus only on the four sections. That small area of the grassland, on the other side of the river, is still part of your challenge. Make sure you don't go too close to the river as alligators prowl those waters. Be safe. Always use the footbridge to cross it. Any more questions or should I proceed?"

Everyone remained silent.

"No questions? Alright! I'll explain the rules. There will be four relics for each team, one for each section, disguised and hidden. Our team's color is blue, so our relics will be blue as well. Whenever you find a relic, take it to the judges on the top of Victory Hill. They will raise your team's flag on the watch tower corresponding to the side of the relic found. The team who is first to have all four flags raised on each side of the hill wins the game. You should always keep an eye on the flags to be aware of the progress of the other teams. That should be enough for today. Tomorrow when we meet, we'll discuss different strategies."

Right after the practice session, Siba raced to his house. A few of his sheep were sleeping while others were munching. In one corner, Rouble was playing with Celine. He asked Rouble, "Did you hear anything from Condor?"

"No. But I saw her flying all over the forest. Maybe she was inspecting the flood-affected areas," the scarlet macaw replied.

"Well, let's wait until Huzo sends a message. I'm going to Robby's house. You keep an eye on our flock." Siba winked with a smirk and left.

The next morning was very hot and humid. The sun was showering fire from the sky. The three boys on their way to school tried to avoid the bright sunlight as much as they could. They ran and took cover under the shade of trees. But still, they couldn't help getting drenched in sweat.

Siba cursed the hot weather, "Damn! It's so hot today. How will I practice for the games?"

"I'm sweating like a pig. We should stop at the temple and pray to God for the wind to blow," Robby suggested.

"Last time, when I prayed with you at the temple for passing the math exam, you know what happened. I'm not praying with you again," Masai rebuffed spontaneously. Recollecting that Masai got zero in that exam, Siba burst out laughing.

Robby's face turned red with a sudden surge of anger. He yelled, "Don't make fun of God. If you don't pray with your heart, don't blame God for your misfortune."

Controlling his laughter, Siba suggested, "Ok! Don't pray. But we can drink cold water at the temple, take some rest, and then, move ahead. I'm going there. I'm dying of thirst."

Robby cheered, "Yes, let's go there."

After reaching there, they quenched their thirst with cold water. Masai poured some cold water over his head and face. "It's so refreshing. Thanks, Robby. It was a good idea."

Robby grinned, "I know, right."

The priest, opening the doors of the main hall, noticed them and asked, "Siba, come in son. Have a seat." The three boys entered the main hall. "I hope your friends are helping you in recovering from grief," the priest spoke, placing his hand over Siba's shoulder.

Robby said, "Yes, we are. Siba is staying with me in my house."

The priest smiled and told Siba, "I know you are a strong boy. God's wish is beyond our comprehension. Always have trust in him. He must be having some divine plans for you. Surrender your mind, body, and soul to God. He never abandons his true devotees. And whenever you feel low, close your eyes and pray. Lord always responds to sincere prayers."

Siba smiled and nodded.

Looking at his watch, Masai spoke worriedly, "We better start moving. I don't want to be late for class."

The priest gave them holy water, and they ran to the school.

Ω

"Can someone help me?" a shrill voice came floating through the classroom door. All students huddled toward the door. A skinny young lady, squatting outside the classroom, was pushing a big wooden box. She squeaked, "Oops! Hi! I can't push this. Will you help me? Please! Thanks!" Two hefty boys took over and pushed the box inside the classroom. Pressing and twisting her wrist, she sighed. "Phew! I'm Sisi, your new teacher," she giggled nervously.

Everyone stood up, "Good morning, Miss Sisi!"

She opened the box and clumsily pulled out a big cream-colored skeleton. She gave it a jerk and hung it on a hook adjacent to the blackboard. Watching the weird expressions on students' faces, she chuckled, "Don't be scared. It won't hurt you. It's only a plastic toy."

The students settled down calmly.

"I will teach you, how our body works. Let's begin with bones. At birth, a baby has 270 bones. As we grow, some bones fuse together and the number goes down to 206." She lifted one arm of the skeleton and said, "The skeleton forms the foundation of our body by providing rigidity and strength. Muscles cover these bones and control their movements. On top of muscles, lies the covering of skin. The skin protects our body from the outside environment."

Sisi took out a poster from the wooden box and hung it on the wall. Pointing to the pictures of different organs on the poster, she resumed, "This is a brain. It controls the functioning of the whole body. This one is a heart. It pumps blood." She went on explaining the other body organs while Siba got lost in his own dream world.

"Do you have any questions?" Sisi shook Siba, bringing him back from his imaginary world.

"Village priest told us that we are made up of body, mind, and soul. I'm confused about mind and soul. Can you please explain to me where they are located inside my body?" Siba asked with an innocent face.

Baffled by his innocent question, Sisi froze for a moment. After a short pause she spoke, "Science has not yet discovered mind and soul. Perhaps one day you'll discover it and explain it to the world," she replied with a sparkle in her eyes and an optimistic smile on her face. Just then, the bell rang. She trembled and stumbled back to the hanging skeleton. Still thinking about Siba's question, she haphazardly packed her stuff and left the class in a hurry. Those two hefty boys followed her, carrying her big wooden box.

- Chapter 7 -

The Dark Cave

By the end of the month, the flood water receded completely inside the Great Forest. With no additional flow due to the blockade by the dam, the river nearly dried up, leaving behind small muddy pools along its length. The alligators vacated the drying lands and marched back toward their lake. But their belly-crawl walk toward their safe haven soon came to an abrupt standstill. The mighty dam wall, soaring high above the dried river bed, blocked their way.

The desperate reptiles strived hard to crawl up against the high wall, but it was in vain. The higher they climbed, the harder they fell upon others behind them. With each passing day, more and more alligators piled up in the drying mud holes before the dam wall. After countless futile attempts, the muddy site turned into a gruesome congregation of exhausted, injured, and dying reptiles. Their endless groans and painful grunts echoed throughout the hills as their wounded bodies squirmed and writhed in mud, red with their own blood. Unable to see their agonizing sufferings, Huzo took pity on them. He sent a message to Siba via Condor. He also ordered Elk to bring him safely.

The next morning, Siba and Rouble rode Elk to the dam's location. Siba watched the pathetic condition of the writhing monsters, begging for mercy. He told Huzo, "Now they will listen to you and follow the golden rules of the Great Forest, unless they are willing to suffer their gruesome fate."

"Well done, Siba!" Huzo cheered. The forest-dwellers praised and cheered Siba for bringing those hideous creatures to their doomsday.

Siba turned to the groaning alligators and shouted loudly, "All of you will die here, and the Great Forest will be safe forever."

One giant alligator crawled over his fellows' dead bodies and pleaded before Siba in a very humble and painful voice, "O King of Land! I am Gator – the King of Water. I beg for your mercy. We have committed uncountable atrocities and unleashed an endless reign of terror against the innocent lives who were already enduring the wrath of nature. We were bound by our savage nature. But for the first time, we experienced their pain, their plight. We realized how it feels to be stranded in the middle of hopelessness and helplessness. We went through the same trauma and brutality that we inflicted upon others. We are extremely shameful of our wicked and nefarious sins. On the behalf of my suffering brothers and sisters, I beg your forgiveness. Please allow us to return to our lake. We promise we will never again cause any harm to the peace-loving animals of the Great Forest."

Siba thundered, "Not only animals but humans and their livestock as well. You live in water, so feed on fish. Why do you kill other animals? If you ever enter the Great Forest again and attack any of its residents, you will not get a second chance." He gave them a final warning.

"We will never harm anyone again. We promise," all alligators took an oath.

Siba signaled Huzo to break the dam wall. With his powerful tusks, the mighty beast blasted the wall as if it was made of twigs and feathers. Life-giving water gushed into the river once again. Lifeless alligators twitched their thick scaly tails, and within minutes, the river was once again teeming with their floating log-like bodies.

Gator, wagging his tail, belly-crawled toward Siba. "Thank you for your generosity. Sit on my back. As a token of my appreciation, I want to take you for a ride in the Emerald Lake."

Siba became scared with the idea of riding an alligator, especially the one he had just brought to his knees. He looked at Huzo seeking his opinion.

The elephant blinked his eyes and spoke with a smile, "Go ahead. Alligators are not humans. They are animals. Don't worry. He won't go back on his word."

Siba straddled the giant monster hesitatingly and clasped his thick rough scales. The very next moment, Siba was inside the river, riding the most fearsome beast like his best pal. Gator took him to the Emerald Lake and showed him its serene majestic beauty. With crystal clear water and lush green surroundings, it was a paradise hidden from the world. His new friend showed him the most elusive and scenic views. The jaw-dropping beauty of the colorful fish and the giant lotus flowers left him mesmerized. After the exciting pleasure ride, Gator dropped Siba safely in the Great Forest.

"This day marks the beginning of our friendship. I'm very grateful to you for letting us go. I'll personally make a round of the river every day to make sure that all alligators adhere to the commitment. If anyone breaks the rules, I'll bring him before you for punishment." The giant alligator waded back into the water and disappeared under its calm surface.

Siba jubilantly narrated his adventurous experience to Huzo, "The lake is so big and its water so pure! Unbelievably so! Colorful fish, giant conifers, and the reflection of clouds and hills on its serene surface. That's just amazing! And the ride, I can't even tell you. With my legs dipped in cold water, I felt like I was a duck, going up and down all across the lake."

"Sweet! Looks like you had a lot of fun with your new friend," Huzo said nostalgically.

"Oh yeah! But what happened to you? Is everything fine?"

"Everything is ok. I just got lost in my calf-hood memories. When I was young like you, I had lots of friends – Giraffe, Rhino, Cheetah, Panther, Chimpanzee, and Tiger. But with time, things changed. Some passed away, some moved away, and Tiger." Huzo became silent and his face turned gloomy.

"What happened to Tiger?" Siba asked curiously. "Tell me about him."

Huzo took a deep breath, "He was powerful, very handsome, and proud of his strength. But his ego came between our friendship, and he left the Great Forest. Since then, I've been all alone."

Siba furrowed his brows. "All alone? I don't get it. You are a good king. All animals love you. They follow your every command without any question or doubt. Moreover, if Tiger left the Great Forest, we can go and request him to come back. Masai and I have always fought, but after a few days, we become friends again," Siba suggested.

Huzo wrapped his trunk around Siba and said smilingly, "It's not that simple when you grow up. Moreover, I don't know where he went." He looked inside the boy's confused eyes and elucidated, "When you are a kid, your heart is pure. You mix up with everyone without hierarchy, without expectations, and without reservations. You fight one day, forgive the next day. But when you grow up, things change."

Siba became more confused, "I don't understand. What changes when you grow up?"

Huzo explained, "Friendship is possible only when both friends listen, understand, argue, and respect each other's ideas and values. They should have the freedom to agree or disagree. This is possible when both consider each other to be equal in some way. When you are small, you don't know your and others' potential. That's why you consider everyone to be similar and equal. This equality is lost when you grow up, as you recognize your true potential and understand your place in the social hierarchy.

"Now look at my situation from this point of view. You mentioned earlier that these animals treat me as their king and follow my command. It's because I'm the biggest and strongest, and they consider me to be superior to them. When someone follows another person, then there's a follower and a leader relationship, but no friendship. The leader may or may not give importance to the follower's emotions, ideas, and desires. Whereas the follower thinks the leader is superior and right, and he should follow the leader's command all the time. That's why they follow my every command without any question or doubt. Therefore my friend, as I told you earlier, friendship can happen only between equals because only they can understand each other's problems and situations properly. That's why I just have followers but no friends."

Huzo furrowed his brows and looked into Siba's eyes. "You tell me now, who in this forest is strong enough or equal to me in stature to be my friend? To whom can I share my problems and feelings?"

"I got your point," Siba pressed his lips and pondered. "But if you and Tiger were friends, then what went wrong?"

"Tiger was a small cub when humans killed his parents. My father adopted him and raised him like my brother. We grew up together as best friends. Not only was he more powerful than me but way more handsome as well. With those charismatic orange and black stripes all over his shining coat, he was a formidable beast to be reckoned with. The forest-dwellers always debated who would become the next king after my father, Tiger or me. The widespread rumor was that Tiger would take my father's position. But one day, he left the Great Forest without telling anyone. Since then, no one knows where he is." Huzo closed his tear-laden eyes.

Baffled Siba shrieked, "He left? He can't leave just like that! There must be some reason."

"My little friend, this is the law of nature. There can never be two rulers in one kingdom. I never realized such a big storm was brewing inside him. He should have talked to me at least. Now, the only thing that I'm left with other than his memories is this." Huzo picked a big, sharp claw from a tree hollow with his trunk.

"What's this?" Siba inquired.

"This is his claw. He used to travel to distant places just by himself. Perhaps, to run away and find peace from the burning hate and anger that he had for humans. Any news about humans or even the word – human, would provoke the demon inside him. After returning from one such journey, he told me that he broke it while hunting a yak. He said to me that I should give it to someone who has the same courage as him. For all these years, I kept it with me, close to my heart. Now, I give it to you because I see the same courage in your eyes." Huzo placed it on Siba's palm.

Siba grasped the smooth object in his hand and plucked a silkworm's cocoon from a nearby mulberry branch, spinning one strong thread from its silk. He tied Tiger's claw to it and hung it around his neck like a necklace. Holding it tight, he said, "I'll always keep it with me."

A crashing in a nearby bush made them both turn. "There you are! I searched for you everywhere," tired Rouble spoke while walking out of the bush, shaking leaves off his wings.

"After Gator's ride, I got busy listening to King Huzo's story," Siba replied, hiding his chuckle.

"Who cares for a parrot now that you have friendships with the King of the Great Forest and the King of the Water?" Rouble taunted him.

"It's not like that," Siba quirked.

Huzo said, "Don't worry Siba. I smell something burning. Oh! It's you, Rouble." Both laughed at Rouble. "You should stay here tonight. It's already very dark, and we'll celebrate your achievement," the king requested.

Siba accepted the king's invitation, "Sounds like fun!"

Siba and Rouble stayed there. Along with the other forest-dwellers, they feasted upon the Great Forest's most exotic fruits collection and relished the special delicacy – the magic mushrooms. After savoring the dripping flower juices and sparkling wild honey, Siba slept on a low-lying branch, hanging just above Huzo.

Ω

It was late afternoon and Siba was running late for Mr. Drock's practice session. By the time he arrived at the ring, other players were already running on the track.

Mr. Drock yelled, "Where were you? Partying the whole time? Do you think everyone else is free? You never value time, either yours or others. Today, I will teach you a lesson that you will never forget." Coach, burning red with anger, dragged him to the rear side of the ring. Next to the ring, there was an open field, and its owner had set the stubble on fire. "If you want to stay in the games, then cross this field, barefoot," Drock snorted with a wrinkled nose.

Scared and panicked Siba pleaded before him, "Sorry, coach. I will always be on time. I promise I will never be late again. Please forgive me this time."

Mr. Drock maintained his notorious reputation for showing no mercy. "No, you never listen. Don't waste further time. Cross this burning field, right now."

The sobbing boy removed his leather sandals and entered the field barefoot. As he ran through the burning spine-like stubble, his soft, little feet got punctured with them. Unable to bear the pain, he fell from the branch on Huzo's back.

"The sky is falling. The sky is falling," Huzo screamed, waking up from his dream as well.

At the same time, Siba tumbled down to the ground from the giant's back and yelled, "Help! Save me from the fire." Both stared at each other and realized that they were just dreaming.

"Ouch! Ouch!" Siba's feet were red and swollen. Lots of fire ants were biting and stinging his feet. "Ouch!"

Huzo looked at the pathetic condition of Siba's swollen feet. "Oh, Cub! It seems that last night, you dropped fruit juices on your feet and didn't wash them before sleeping. That's why these poisonous ants are biting you. Wash your feet quickly and get rid of them before the swelling spreads upwards to your legs. Only the leaves of the sambar tree can reduce the pain and swelling from a fire ant bite. You stay here. I'll bring those leaves for you." He left the wailing boy behind and after some time, returned with a big branch, full of tiny, elliptical leaves. "Pluck these leaves and chew them. Then apply the paste on your feet."

Siba followed his instructions and immediately got some relief from the burning sensations. He asked, "Why did you bring such a big branch? I only needed a few leaves."

Huzo replied innocently, "I don't know. This is how I do it."

After getting complete relief from inflammation, Siba asked, "Why were you shouting – 'The sky is falling?' "

"I was dreaming."

Siba giggled. While applying another layer of paste, he asked, "I always wonder about the mystery behind dreams. The Great Forest once mentioned the dream painters, but before he could reveal that secret, I screwed it up. Do you know about that?"

"No one knows how many mysteries the Great Forest is hiding inside his roots. Well, I don't know about it, but we can make a request. I'm sure the Great Forest is generous enough to share it with us."

Huzo, raising his trunk, requested, "O Great Forest! This humble servant of yours is requesting before you to enlighten us about the mysteries of dreams."

Siba whispered, "Ahem! Dream painters."

"And dream painters," Huzo added.

In his usual deep resounding voice, the Great Forest spoke, "It was pleasing to see Siba and forest animals enjoying together last night. It reminded me of that era when humans and animals used to dwell together happily under my shade. It was one big family. I liked when you slept on my branch. And I was expecting this question since I saw dream painters entering your noses when both of you were sleeping and snoring."

Huzo jumped and snorted, "What do you mean? Did something enter my nose? Don't you remember my great grandfather got killed by an ant that entered his trunk when he was sleeping? Please save me. Help! Help me!" Siba and the Great Forest burst into laughter.

"Do you need these sambar leaves? Now I know why you brought such a big branch earlier." Siba jokingly offered him a few leaves.

The Great Forest chuckled, "I never knew, the mighty king is scared of a tiny ant. Don't worry. Dream painters don't hurt you unless they paint a nightmare." Siba laughed again.

"That was not a joke. It's a matter of life and death for me," Huzo said angrily.

The Great Forest echoed, "Last time, when I started telling about the dream painters, Siba got angry. This time it's you. It seems like I should keep this secret only to myself."

"Sorry! I apologize for that. Please reveal the mystery," Siba requested.

"Sure, but you can't see dream painters with your eyes. For that, you need a special vision – Ultravision. You must go to the Dark Cave. Inside that cave, you will find Master Sung Tzu. Only he can give you Ultravision."

Huzo expressed his concerns, "But no one goes inside the Dark Cave. It's darker than night. Anyone, who went inside that dark labyrinth, never returned back."

Siba intervened, "Don't worry about darkness. We can use a torch. But what will happen after we get Ultravision?"

"Once you can see the dream painters, you can ask them how they paint dreams. I don't know their secrets. You better hurry up, so you can meet Master Sung Tzu before evening," the Great Forest echoed.

"Thank you!" Siba and Huzo spoke together.

Siba climbed on Huzo's back and left for the Dark Cave. Rouble perched on the pachyderm's huge tusk.

After arriving at the Dark Cave, Siba made a fire by rubbing two dry sticks and lit one piece of wood. He raised the burning torch and entered the cave. He looked back at Huzo and Rouble. They were still at the same spot. "Come on, don't you wanna go? Are you scared?"

Both replied, "You go ahead. We are not interested in dream painters anymore."

"I know why you are not interested. I'll go by myself," Siba scoffed and went into the cave. The scary dead silence of the cave was sporadically broken by the water drops dripping down from the roof. The only other things that he could hear were his own footsteps and the flame.

Unable to see much, except the black, moist rocky walls, Siba stuttered nervously, "Hello! Is there anyone here? Hello!" But no one replied. He mustered his courage and kept on going deeper and deeper inside the dark labyrinth. After coming across a few bones and skulls, he swallowed and tried calling one more time. "Master Sung Tzu, can you hear me?"

A squeaky voice echoed, "Who dared to enter this cave without my permission?"

Siba began shivering in fear. He firmly clinched his torch with shaking hands and lifted it to see what lay ahead. But no one was there. He swallowed and spoke in a trembling voice, "It's me, Siba. The Great Forest told me that Master Sung Tzu lives here. I've come to meet him."

"That's alright. Please lower your fire. Do you want to burn Master alive?" the same squeaky voice came from the top of Siba. At once, he lowered his burning stick and moved back. Then, he carefully looked above. A big, shining, brown ball of fur was hanging from the roof. Before he could guess anything, the furry ball unfurled its membranous wings and opened up into an old brown bat with long white whiskers.

"I am Master Sung Tzu. How's my old friend - the Great Forest?" the old bat asked.

Siba relaxed and took a deep breath. "The Great Forest is great as usual. Why do you live in this dark place? You should stay in the Great Forest with all the other amazing creatures."

"Long time ago, I used to live there, but no one liked me. No one would even talk to me. I had no friends, except for the Great Forest. Everyone used to make fun of me that I'm neither an animal nor a bird. They never allowed me to enter their groups. In the middle of the forest teeming with wildlife, I was just one lone bat. One day, I decided to move away and gain supernatural powers so that no one could laugh at me anymore. I made this cave my home, as everyone was scared to enter in. After a long struggle and practice, I mastered meditation and acquired supernatural powers. Finally, I attained what I needed the most."

Siba anxiously asked, "And what was it?"

Master Sung Tzu closed his eyes and spoke in a very calming voice, "Inner peace. Now I live in peace. I don't need anything else." Peace and tranquility spread across the cave. Master opened his eyes and said, "You didn't tell me your reason for coming here."

"Oh, me? I came here for Ultravision. I want to see the dream painters."

Under the flickering light of the torch, with his eyes eerily affixed on Siba, the upside-down hanging Master replied, "When you meet the sun, don't ask for light. Ask how to shine." Siba swallowed. The old bat continued, "Anyway, it took me five years of deep meditation to attain Ultravision. Are you ready for that?"

"Five years?" blurted the shocked boy. His enthusiasm vanished into thin air.

Master Sung Tzu smilingly stared at the demoralized boy. "Don't worry. The Great Forest has sent you to the right place. I'll help you. Close your eyes and tell me what you see?"

Siba closed his eyes and replied, "I don't see anything. It's just dark and black."

"Try harder. Try to see what's going on in your body, in your mind, in your thoughts."

"No, Master. I still don't see anything."

"You can't see because you are not focused. Let's say, focus on a dog. Do you see it now?"

"Yes, Master. I see Limpoo."

"Limpoo? What's Limpoo? I said dog."

"Limpoo is my dog. I see him running toward me."

"Oh! Ok! Where is he running? On the road or the ground? Where?"

"Nowhere. He's just running on a black background. There's nothing else, only him."

"That's enough. Open your eyes. That black background is your mind's eye and part of it formed the colorful moving image of the dog. Some say, it's the third eye. You can visualize anything in that eye. In fact, whatever your two eyes see, their image is actually formed in your mind's eye. Not only the eyes but the processing of information from your other senses also takes place there. Your sensory organs are just tools to collect outside information. It's the mind's eye, which actually sees, smells, tastes, hears, and feels."

Siba asked gleefully, “Is that Ultravision? Would I be able to see the dream painters now?”

“Not yet. I told you about the mind’s eye because dreams form there. Have you forgotten? It took me five years of vigorous mind-focus training to develop Ultravision.”

Siba’s rekindled excitement dissipated once again. “Does that mean I can never see dream painters?”

“I didn’t say that.” Master Sung Tzu smilingly offered an ochre-colored strip of cloth. “Tie this around your forehead, covering your eyes and ears.”

Siba held it carefully and curiously looking at it under the waving flame, asked, “What’s that?”

“This is what you came for – The Ultravision.”

“This is it? A piece of cloth!”

“Yeah! What were you thinking, glowing glasses? This is Ultravision.”

Siba tied it around his forehead, covering his eyes and ears. “How am I supposed to see with my eyes closed?” he asked, moving his arms around like a blind person.

Master said slowly, “Look beyond what you see, beyond the darkness. Not through your eyes but through your mind’s eye.”

Siba did accordingly. To his wonder, he could see everything with his eyes closed – the cave, dripping drops of water, slippery floor, and Master dangling upside down from the roof by one leg. Everything was glittering and shining. He couldn’t believe his eyes. “Is it real or a dream?” He couldn’t hold back his excitement. He went ahead and touched the moist walls and jumped in the water puddles.

“Slow down, kiddo! It’s for you. You can play with it later.”

Siba asked, "If I take it, then how will you see in this dark cave?"

"I don't need it. I can see without it."

Siba got confused. "Sorry Master, I don't get it. Do you mean you can see in darkness?"

Master explained smilingly, "Long time ago, my spiritual guru tore this strip from his robe, infused supernatural powers in it, and gave it to me. Later, progressing toward awakening, I found the same power of Ultravision sleeping inside me. With my guru's teachings and higher meditation techniques, I awakened it. Before leaving, my guru instructed me – 'One day, someone who deserves it, will come to you looking for it. You must give it to him.' Finally, my long wait for five hundred years is over."

After knowing all that, Siba became more puzzled and ambitious. "Do I also have that ability inside me? Can I also develop it with practice?"

"Yes, of course. Why not? But that will require a special kind of training. Your mind should be completely focused and free of thoughts. Then you can explore a plethora of mystical treasures hidden inside you. A time will come when you won't need eyes to see. But now, it's time for you to leave." Master Sung Tzu silenced. He closed his eyes, folded his wings, and turned back into a big, brown ball of fur.

"Thank you, Master." Siba bowed before the hanging brown ball.

"Look within to know beyond," Master spoke and entered into a trance.

Siba doused his burning torch by dipping it in a water puddle and came out of the Dark Cave. After stepping out, he removed Ultravision and ran happily toward Huzo and

Rouble. They also became happy on seeing him come out alive.

"What took you so long? I was about to die from an anxiety attack," Rouble gasped.

"I'm fine." Siba held the bird and kissed him. "There was nothing to worry about."

Huzo warmly wrapped his trunk around Siba. "I'm glad to see you again. Did you meet the Master and get that Ul, Ultra, what was it?"

"Ultravision," Siba reminded him.

"Yeah, whatever it is!"

Siba showed them the strip of cloth. "This is Ultravision. It will do for the time being."

"What do you mean by the time being? Does it have an expiration date?" Rouble questioned.

"No," Siba giggled. "We should move back to the Great Forest. I'll tell you the rest on the way." He climbed the elephant and on the way back, narrated the whole incident.

- Chapter 8 -

The Secret World of Dreams

After listening to Siba's enlightening interaction with Master, Huzo regretted his decision. "I should have listened to you. I should have also gone into the cave."

Rouble added quickly, "Me too."

Siba chuckled, "I told you so. Have faith in yourself, not in rumors."

"Here comes the Great Forest. Show us now, how this piece of cloth works," Huzo said anxiously. He raised his trunk for Siba to grasp it and then, brought him down safely.

Siba tied the strip of cloth around his eyes. To his surprise, the forest appeared to be teeming with a whole new world of magical creatures. "Wow! Am I in a fairyland? Look! Look! What are those mystical creatures?" Siba said, pointing to his right.

Perplexed Huzo and Rouble looked in that direction. "What? Where? I don't see anything strange there," Huzo exclaimed.

Siba pointed again. "There! Right there!"

"I am the king of this forest. I should better be aware of who is trespassing into my territory. Tell me Siba, what are they doing? Are they causing any damage?" Huzo asked worriedly.

"I don't know." Siba asked the Great Forest, "O Great Forest! What are these weird creatures that I'm seeing with Ultravision? Some of them are like ribbons, meandering freely through the air; while some are like spiky pulsating balls, sparkling colorful lights. Those red ones disappear and then appear at different locations. I'm very confused. There are too many of them, and they're everywhere. Look! These glowing drops are going up toward the sky. Geez! Those ones are entering into the animals and plants. And what are those fairy-like creatures with long pointed ears that are jumping from branch to branch? Wait! Are they talking to leaves?"

"Hold on, Bumblebee. From where do you get so many questions all the time," Great Forest's heavy voice echoed, "I wasn't aware that Ultravision can reveal my secret world to you. These hidden creatures were always there. You used to feel them. Now you can see them as well. Those floating ribbons are songs of birds, pulsating spheres are fragrances of flowers, and glowing drops are evaporated vapors of water."

"Which of them are the dream painters? Are they the fairy-like creatures?" Siba inquired anxiously.

"No, they are the messengers of seasons. You'll have to wait until someone sleeps. Dream painters are very elusive. They appear only when someone is about to dream. Why don't you wait until Huzo sleeps? It will be easy for you to catch them when they'll sneak into his long trunk," the Great Forest suggested.

Huzo got scared.

Siba looked at Huzo and laughed gently. "Don't be scared. They are not ants."

Huzo turned his head away, thought for a minute, and then, looked at Siba. "Ok, I'm in. But don't ask them to reveal my secret dreams."

"Don't worry. I won't peek into your crazy, weird dreams of falling skies." Siba grinned and clutched his swaying trunk, "Thank you!"

The twilight turned into a full moon night. Sitting next to the calmly flowing river, Siba and Huzo gazed at the lone clouds wandering through the star-studded sky. Soon the dark riverfront woods came alive with the synchronous blinking dance of fireflies. The flashes of yellow-green lights transformed the dark forest into some mystical fairyland.

Huzo jokingly expressed his worry, "I'm a little nervous. Please don't chop off my nose when the dream painters enter into it."

"Don't worry. I won't." Siba laughed.

Within no time, Huzo slept and started snoring. Siba, with Ultravision around his eyes, fixed his gaze on Huzo's quivering trunk. He waited patiently, trying hard not to fall asleep. Around the middle of the night, tiny rat-like creatures emerged from the ground. Their bodies were glowing with different colors. They had tiny wings that were fluttering rapidly like hummingbird wings and long hairy tails like paint brushes. Out of curiosity, Siba moved closer to them. They got scared and disappeared into the ground. He moved back and holding his breath, sat as still as a rock.

After some time, one head popped out of the ground and quickly scanned the surroundings for any danger. Upon noticing no movement, the rat-like creature emerged again and whistled. Right away, its entire team emerged from the ground, and they raced toward Huzo's trunk. Just when they entered into it, Siba leaped and pressed the trunk close to the elephant's head to block them from entering into his head. The sleeping beast sneezed, and those mysterious creatures went flying out of his trunk. Siba quickly grabbed one pink-colored creature. The tiny creature panicked.

Siba spoke in a very soft voice, "Aww! Don't be scared. I'm not going to hurt you." The tiny creature calmed down a little. "I'm Siba. I want to be your friend. What's your name?"

The rat-like creature opened its eyes very slowly and gazed at Siba for some time. Then, in a very faint voice, replied, "Tina."

Siba loosened his grip and opened his hands. The creature stood upright on his palm. "Tina – the dream painter?" Siba asked excitedly.

"Hmm! You can call me that. I along with my family paint dreams."

Siba's eyes shone with excitement. "Wow! I can't believe I'm actually talking to a dream painter. Painting a dream must be very adventurous. Isn't it?"

"Not that much. This is what we do all the time. We paint whatever the captain wants us to paint. We only follow his command," Tina replied.

"No, Wait! Captain? Now who is this captain? Don't you paint dreams in the mind's eye? That's what I heard about you?" the puzzled boy asked.

"Of course, we do paint in the mind's eye. But I'm surprised, how come you are not aware of the captain; the one who controls everything inside you?"

"What do you mean? Don't I control myself? Is there someone else inside me who controls me? Is this what you are trying to say?" Siba didn't understand what Tina was trying to tell him.

"Really! You don't know what goes on inside you?"

"I thought, I knew. But now, I feel like I don't know anything. Please talk to me in layman's language. I don't understand your riddles."

Tina giggled. "All I know is that you are like a sailor who enjoys the journey called life in the ship of your body, and this ship is controlled by the captain."

"According to what you said, it looks like the mind is the captain," Siba interrupted.

"I don't know that. I just take orders from the captain and do my job."

"Ok, no problem. I'll figure it out later. You just tell me what you know."

Tina continued, "Captain is responsible for all your activities. He's the one who processes information, understands, thinks, and keeps records of your data. Even when you go to sleep, the captain stays up and keeps on working on important issues. When you are sleeping, your eyes are closed. So, the captain doesn't receive input from them but your other senses keep on sending information continuously."

"So many things happen during my sleep, and I'm completely unaware of all that," Siba wondered.

"Not only that, this information also triggers positive and negative responses inside you. The positive responses generate desires, while negative ones generate aversions, fears, and phobias. When you are sleeping, the captain is relieved from the major task of processing outer information received by your senses. So he diverts his full attention to your inner issues like healing your body and mind, problems that you are facing, and unresolved desires, fears, and phobias. To show you what the captain is working on, he calls us to paint a dream in your mind's eye. That's when we jump into the picture. Like last night, when the captain felt the burning sensations on your feet, he called us to paint a dream of fire."

Siba exclaimed, "But there was no fire."

Tina twitched, "Of course, there was no fire. But the captain couldn't see as your eyes were closed. He could only feel the burning sensation on your feet and looked for something familiar from his stored data to correlate with. And he correlated that sensation to fire."

"Wow! Do you mean the captain was trying to protect me in my sleep by giving me a warning signal? That's amazing! Hold on. Once I had a dream about lychees and the Great Forest knew about it. How's that possible? How could he know about my dream?" Siba recalled.

"It's because it was the Great Forest who told me to paint that dream," Tina twitched. "Sometimes we carry messages as well, but that's very rare. We do it only for those who are very closely attached to each other by strong emotions."

Siba got lost in thoughts. His face turned serious.

Tina inquired, "What happened to you?"

"Oh, nothing. I appreciate you for sharing your secrets about dreams. But your secrets arouse new questions in me. I was thinking about this captain that controls me. Why can't I control myself?" Siba revealed the question that was troubling him.

Tina giggled, "You are funny. To solve a smaller problem, you jumped into a bigger one. That's why a few things are best hidden. The more you explore a problem, the bigger it grows."

Siba frowned, "Don't laugh at me. Just tell me, can I bring myself under my control or not?"

"Yes, you can. But to bring anything under your control, you must first understand it. If you don't know it, how can you control it? But don't ask me how to do that. I'm only a dream painter," Tina replied innocently.

Siba cleared his throat, "Of course! You've already taught me so many things. Thank you. The night is about to come to an end. I'm sorry for taking up too much of your time. You must have so many dreams pending to paint."

"Yep, plenty of work left. Pretty soon, I'll see you in your sleep, when I come to paint your dream," Tina grinned.

Siba said smilingly, "Sure, I'll be waiting." He lowered his hand. Tina jumped from his palm and disappeared into the ground. He removed the strip of cloth and laid down next to Huzo. He pondered wearily about the conversation and fell asleep without even realizing it.

At dawn, Rouble fluttered his wings on the sleeping boy's face. "Get up Siba. Wake up." Siba woke up, pushing the bird aside. Huzo also woke up with a loud yawn. Rouble reminded him, "We have to go back. Today is your final practice day for the games."

Siba stood up in a hurry. "O, my Lord! I almost forgot that." He gave Rouble a nervous glance. "Even if we start now, I won't be able to make it to school on time." After thinking for some time, he said, "Why don't I skip the school and directly go to the practice session. Nobody will know. Moreover, I have a few questions that I can ask from the Great Forest."

"Hmm, I don't know. If you think so," the unsure bird replied.

"Which questions?" Huzo got suspicious, "And what happened last night? I dreamed someone was trying to choke me in my sleep."

Siba chuckled, "It was me. I squeezed your trunk to catch a dream painter."

Huzo and Rouble gasped, "For real?"

"Don't you trust me?" Siba said with a serious expression on his face.

Both looked at Siba in awe and nodded, "We do."

Siba pressed his lips and exhaled, "But she left me more confused than ever before."

"What happened, Siba?" Huzo inquired. Siba told them everything about his interaction with Tina. They also got confused.

Huzo exhaled, "Hmmm, you are right. I also want to know who else is in me, other than me. Let's ask the Great Forest about this captain."

Siba, staring up at the canopy, spoke in a loud voice, "O Great Forest! I know you'll say, I ask too many questions. But this time, I'm really filled with a lot of them."

Huzo added, "Me too."

Rouble shouted as well, "Me three."

Siba resumed, "The dream painter told me about the captain. Who's this captain inside me?"

The Great Forest echoed, "I'm glad, Bumblebee. This time, you are asking the right question, but you are asking the wrong person."

"What do you mean?" the confused boy asked.

"The student is ready, and his teacher has appeared. It would be better if you ask your teacher this question," the Great Forest replied.

Siba pulled his brows and asked, "Do you mean, Master Sung Tzu?"

"Yes," the Great Forest replied pleasantly.

"Good idea. Thank you, for showing me the way." Siba said, "Rouble, let's get back to school before the practice session begins."

Huzo raised his trunk and waved. Siba and Rouble returned to their village.

- CHAPTER 9 -

THE HUNTZMAN GAMES

On seeing Siba entering the ring, the coach asked him angrily, "Where were you for the last two days? You didn't even inform anyone. You know, the opportunity knocks on your door only once. If you don't grab it, it moves to the next door." He bent down and looked straight into Siba's eyes. "Tell me, are you serious or should I remove your name from the final four players list?"

Siba was expecting this. He replied right away, "I apologize for my absence. I got caught up in a very important task."

Mr. Drock smirked, "Wow! Very important task for a twelve-year-old! Interesting! Would you mind sharing it with us?"

"I went inside the forest to fulfill my deceased uncle's last wish to drop his belongings in the Emerald Lake," Siba presented his excuse nervously.

Mr. Drock's jaw dropped upon hearing that. "Emerald Lake! Do you mean the Emerald Lake? The one deep inside the hills?"

Siba asked suspiciously, "Yes, that one. Why? Anything wrong with that?"

Mr. Drock kneeled and held Siba's shoulders. "O boy! That lake and the surrounding forest are possessed by evil spirits and demons. It's forbidden to go there. Don't you know that?"

Siba replied with an innocent face, "No. No one told me that."

Mr. Drock continued, "Anyone who went there, never returned. I'm surprised, how you came back alive. Don't even think of that place ever again. Perhaps that old drunkard wanted you to die. That's why he must have told you to go there. Discuss with some adults before doing anything crazy like that. Ok, go now and practice one last time before the games. Tomorrow, all eyes will be on you." He patted Siba's shoulder with a smile.

After finishing the practice session, Siba went to Robby's house. Robby's whole family was very worried about him. On seeing him, Robby's father glowered at him, "Where the hell were you? There's not even a single place left where we didn't look for you. Do you even care? Listen, boy! This is not your uncle's house. If you want to live here, you will have to follow the rules of this house."

"You don't have to worry about me. I can take care of myself. I don't need anyone's help," Siba shouted angrily and walked out of their house.

Robby and his grandmother tried to calm him down and asked him to at least have dinner with them. But Siba didn't listen and ran back to his house. Holding back tears, he hugged Celine and slept next to her.

The next morning, he woke up very early. He dressed hurriedly and raced to the ring. Mr. Drock was already there, talking to the coaches of other schools. On seeing Siba, the excited coach asked, "My boy! Are you ready for the big game?"

"Yes, coach," Siba replied nervously.

"Alright! Pick your team's T-shirt – the blue one and go to the main arena. Wait for your team members on Victory Hill. I'll meet you there shortly," Mr. Drock smiled cheerfully.

Siba climbed to the flat top of Victory Hill. Terry was already there, waiting for other team members. On seeing him, she said excitedly, "Hey! See, I told you. You can't arrive before me, Mr. NOT - Never On Time."

Siba said breathlessly, "I come from another village, whereas you live right next to our school. I got up early, but it wasn't enough. It doesn't matter how hard I try, I can never beat you."

Picking up her binoculars, Terry giggled, "That's why I told you yesterday, don't mess with girls."

"Alright, I accept my defeat. When did you get those binoculars?"

Terry replied, "I borrowed them from my cousin to get an overview of the arena. He purchased them recently for his bird-watching tour. By the way, what do you think should be our strategy?"

Siba borrowed her binoculars and analyzed the arena very carefully. "I think, this year we should form our strategy based on our strengths, rather than the structure of the arena. Last year, we divided different sections among ourselves and barely made it before the City School's team. I must warn you. They are not only smart and skilled but extremely shrewd at the same time. We must be extra careful of them, especially of their team leader – Bingalo. He's wicked and can go to any extent to snatch the trophy back."

"Look at our captain, Harry! He's in such a hurry to win the trophy that he forgot half of his team," Nick's loud voice fell upon Siba and Terry's ears. They turned around. Nick and Harry were standing there, laughing.

"It's not like that. I was just," Siba threw a quick excuse.

"Don't worry, captain. We were just teasing you. For the first time, you're not the last, Mr. NOT. The other two players are also on their way. In the meantime, tell us our roles," Harry said.

Siba resumed, "I was just telling Terry about the last year's game. The way we hardly managed to win and about the City School's team leader Bingalo."

Nick became infuriated upon hearing that name. "Bingalo! That mean, little creep! Today, if he repeats something nasty like last year, I promise I'll break his nose."

"Hold that anger. Use it to win the trophy instead." Siba calmed him down. "Now, focus on our strategy. This is what I think should be the best plan. Terry, you're good at rowing and swimming. You should explore the marsh. Nick and Harry, both of you should search the ruins. I'm good at climbing trees, so I'll explore the woodland like last year. Grassland is the easiest one. Whenever we find a relic in our section, we should move to the grassland and search there. How does that sound?"

Everyone cheered, "Sounds perfect!"

Nick added, "Also, keep an eye on the flags to check the progress of the other teams. And when you explore, check every blue-colored thing. Be it an animal, bird, fruit, or any other item. Relics can be of any shape. We must not waste time searching the same area again. Do it right, the very first time." He winked and gave the thumbs up.

Meanwhile, other teams and their coaches, judges, local media, and spectators arrived as well. Shortly, the city mayor arrived with great pomp and show. Young school kids greeted him with flowers and a special welcome song. Others welcomed him with whistles and a standing ovation. Teachers showered flower petals on him till he reached the podium. He greeted the crowd and unfurled a piece of paper to deliver his speech, "Are you excited?"

The crowd cheered loudly.

"That's the spirit," the mayor resumed. "Welcome everyone to our Annual Huntzman Games. These games stretch our abilities as human beings. They inspire us to become stronger, faster, smarter, and most importantly, to unite us as a team, as a society, and as a human race. These games connect us to our roots, our environment, and our past.

"A long time ago, our ancestors lived in these forests. They ruled these hills, rivers, and forests. They hunted animals and lived a nomadic life. But slowly, they understood the secrets of nature and settled here as farmers. These ruins were once their homes. In this place, they established their first settlement. This very hill witnessed the victory of the human race over nature. That's why, every year, we celebrate these games to remember our heritage and to connect to our past.

"These ruins are like milestones that help us to keep track of our journey since we left the forest. These games will keep on inspiring and motivating our future generations to grow and prosper. Without holding you back any further, I'm going to light the Spirit of the Annual Huntzman Games." He lit a big cauldron on the stage. "Let the games begin!"

Sounds of drums, bugles, and the cheering crowd filled the air. The players of the four participating school teams came forward, and the city mayor wished them good luck.

Bingalo, wearing a red T-shirt, motivated his teammates, "Give your best, guys. Let's get our trophy back from these country apes."

Nick's face turned red with anger on hearing that. "Who are you calling apes? You, city skunk! If you utter a single word again, I swear, I'll rip your tongue."

Siba jumped between them. "Stop, Nick. Pretty soon, he'll know who'll be keeping the trophy."

On seeing Delta School's coach in a purple T-shirt coming toward them, they became quiet. The coach pulled out a starter pistol from his pocket and strolled around them. He roared, "Are you ready to set this place on fire?"

All players shouted, "Yes, sir."

"Alright, I'll count to three and fire the starting shot. Any doubts?" he thundered.

A player from Army School in a yellow T-shirt shouted, "No, Sir."

"Ready! One, two, three." The Delta School's coach fired his pistol.

Sixteen players, from four teams, raced down the slopes to different sections of the arena. The five judges took their respective seats and picked up their binoculars to observe the movements of each team.

Terry raced to the dam that controlled the water level between the marsh and the river. She hurriedly untied the blue canoe and rowed into the marsh.

After arriving at the stone wall that ran through the middle of the ruins, Nick instructed Harry, "You explore the citadel, pyramid, and temple complex. I'll search toward the right side of this stone wall. Those stone houses demand extra caution. Their old walls and roofs can crumble any moment." Harry gave thumbs up and dashed toward the ruins of the temple.

Siba began his exploration from the farthest end of the woodland. Bingalo, along with one other teammate, was also searching the same area of the woodland.

Rowing slowly and calmly amidst the duckweeds and water lilies, Terry carefully scanned for any blue-colored item. She became a little nervous when nearby frogs, basking on the floating leaves of water lilies, jumped into the water. Upon seeing her approaching, the ducks hid their ducklings in the dense cattail plants. As her canoe disturbed the still water, dragonflies flew and hovered over her like tiny patrolling helicopters.

Meanwhile, in the ruins, Harry and two other players in yellow T-shirts were searching the temple complex. Suddenly, Harry heard a loud cry of triumph from the fireplace. He looked there and saw those two players holding a fire opal and jumping in joy. Right away, one of them raced toward the Victory Hill to hand it over to judges, whereas the other player ran toward the woodland. Harry became anxious and moved to the pyramid. On the other side of the ruins, Nick was carefully inspecting the broken walls and collapsed roofs of the old houses.

In the woodland, Siba was carefully listening to the birds' songs for any clue. While probing for relics with a long wooden stick, he found a yellow-colored abandoned beehive. He realized at once that it was the relic of the Army School. He did not touch it and continued ahead with his search. A little while later, he saw a Delta School player, terrified and crying. Siba moved closer to him and asked, "Why are you crying?"

The player in a purple T-shirt replied, "I saw a snake, right there!"

Siba laughed. "What else do you expect in the wilderness?"

"I'm scared of snakes. I wanted grassland, but my captain picked it for herself," he sniffled.

Siba consoled him, "Don't worry. Come with me. They won't harm you if you don't harm them." Both of them began exploring together.

Bingalo climbed a tree to get a better view. Looking at the hill, he shouted to his teammate on the ground, "We better hurry up. The yellow flag on ruin's side is already up." Then he saw Siba with a player from a different team. After checking the surrounding area, he climbed down wondering why they were together.

In the marsh, Terry rowed into an open pool teeming with lotus flowers. Several geese and a pair of swans were also swimming there. Just then, her gaze fell upon the hill, and she saw a purple flag on the grassland side going up. She said to herself, "Terry, chop-chop!" Toward the edge of the lotus pool, hidden among the exotic flowers, a purple gallinule bird caught her eye. She noticed that the bird was not moving. Out of curiosity, she went closer to check. As she advanced, the bird still didn't swim away. It was only when she lifted the bird she realized that it was just a toy. "Terry, don't waste time in finding relics of others," she scolded herself. She placed it back and rowed ahead.

Bingalo's teammate saw a red apple on a faraway tree. He said, "Look, apple!"

Bingalo scoffed, "Stupid! Apples don't grow in this season." When they went closer, they found that it was a real apple but tied by a thread. Bingalo kissed his teammate's cheek in excitement. "You are awesome! This is our relic. Hurry up! Take it to judges and help our friend in ruins. I don't know why marsh is taking so long. Anyway, I'll search the grassland." When the boy took the apple to the hill, Bingalo, instead of going to the grassland, secretly followed Siba to find out why the two were together.

Meanwhile, Nick found a blood-red ruby inside an old, cracked clay vase. He secretly hid it inside his pocket. He murmured, "Let's see now, how Bingalo will win?" But, before leaving that ruined house, his father's last words rang in his ears, "Why should you become bad if someone else is bad? If you change yourself because of another person's wrongdoing, then you've already lost. Kill another's wickedness with your goodness, not by becoming like them." He went back to the vase and placed the ruby inside it. He moved out of the house and looked toward the hill. The red flags on the woodland and marsh sides were raised. "God, please help me," he prayed with closed eyes and entered the next house.

Siba climbed a dead tree to get a broader view. He spotted another Delta School player – a girl in a purple T-shirt, chasing butterflies. He shouted to advise her, "Those butterflies are alive. They are not your relic." The girl halted and twisted her neck to see who yelled. Siba shouted again, "Here! On this dead tree." He waved at her. She saw him and went there. The boy from the Delta School became happy upon seeing his captain. From the top, Siba spotted a purple-colored eggplant.

The girl told her teammate with excitement, "I found a purple toy bird in the grassland."

The boy asked, "Which bird was it?"

She replied, "I don't know. It was our relic. That's all I cared."

Siba climbed down. Pointing toward the direction where the eggplant was, he said, "I think your relic is that way."

The boy requested, "Please come with me."

Siba replied with a smile, "You have your captain. Now you shouldn't be scared. I can't help you anymore. After all, we are competitors, and I have to find my relic too. You both go that way, and I'll go this way."

The boy appreciated, "Thanks a lot for your help." They shook hands and moved on their paths. Bingalo watched them while hiding behind a tree and became more confused.

Near the cattail plants, Terry found an abandoned goose nest. It contained one blue-colored egg. She told herself, "That's odd! Goose eggs are creamy white. There's something fishy going on here." On touching it, she found it to be made of wood. "Hurray! I found it."

Meanwhile, Nick finished searching his side of the ruins and moved to the other side to help Harry. On meeting him, Nick inquired, "Which portions are left?"

A swift reply came from Harry, "Only this part of the citadel. I've covered the rest."

Nick appreciated, "Awesome! Let's finish it up quickly."

Siba was carefully listening to the birds and in between, talking to them. The more Bingalo stalked Siba, the more puzzled he became. Suddenly, he saw Siba coming toward him. He tried to hide behind a big tree, but it didn't work. "You found your relic a long time ago. What are you doing here?" Siba asked.

Bingalo couldn't say anything and became nervous.

Siba asked him again, "Are you stalking me?"

Bingalo pushed him down and ran away toward the grassland.

Siba got up from the ground and shaking the dirt off his clothes, shouted, "Bloody rascal!"

Marching ahead, Siba saw a blue jay, perched on a dead fallen tree. He whistled, but the bird didn't respond. He threw a stone at it, but it didn't move. "Woo-hoo!" Siba whistled with excitement. He picked up his relic and rushed to the hill.

After handing it over to the judges, he entered the grassland, where Terry was already searching for another relic.

Terry said, "I just saw our flag going up. You are the best."

Siba blushed, "No, you found yours before me. You are the best."

"I am. I just wanted to hear that from you," Terry smirked. "I already covered the area next to the woods. Only the portion of the grassland near the river is left. It shouldn't take long for the two of us."

"What are we waiting for? Let's finish it up."

Just then, a red flag on the ruin's side and a yellow flag on the woodland's side went up. Looking at those flags, Terry said, "Yeah! Let's finish it up quickly."

In the ruins, Nick and Harry finished the citadel but couldn't find their relic. Disappointed Nick asked Harry, "Did we miss anything?"

Harry replied anxiously, "No."

Nick became upset. "Then, where is it? I checked each and every inch of my section. It has to be on your side. Think again, in case you missed something."

Harry thought for some time and then, replied worriedly, "I think temple. When the Army School's team found their relic in the fireplace, I thought there won't be any other relic in the temple and moved to the pyramid. It must be in that unfinished section."

Nick scolded him, "Are you stupid? This is not your school exam that only one question will come from each chapter."

They sprinted to the temple complex. Within a few minutes, Harry shouted, "I found it! I found it!"

Nick ran to the fireplace. Harry was holding a blue sapphire in his hand. Nick said, "Good job! Give it to the judges and meet me in the grassland."

Bingalo was also searching in the grassland area adjacent to the river. He found a blue-colored golf ball near a bush. He didn't touch it and moved ahead. He had gone only a few steps further when he saw the third blue flag going up. He panicked and turned his head toward the dam. The purple and yellow canoes were still not there. He breathed out a sigh of relief. But then, he saw Siba and Terry coming toward the bush from one side and Nick from the other side. It wasn't hard for him to guess that the three of them would find the golf ball in no time. But before they could find the ball, Bingalo picked it up and threw it into the river. All three got enraged at Bingalo's nefarious deed.

Nick charged at Bingalo and punched his nose. Terry fell to her knees, wailing. Siba couldn't believe what just happened. His brain froze at that moment and couldn't think how to react.

All of a sudden, Siba zoomed toward the river and dived into it. Terry, Nick, and Bingalo with a bleeding nose arrived near the river bank. They shouted and called for help. Soon, the crowd from the Victory Hill also arrived there. But there was no sign of Siba. And because of alligators, no one dared to enter the water. Holding their breath, everyone stared at the river like mute spectators. All they could do was pray to God for a miracle to happen and to save Siba from the notorious river.

After some time, Siba emerged in the middle of the river, sitting on top of a giant alligator and with several other smaller alligators escorting him. He cheerfully raised his hand to show the golf ball. But the people on the river bank panicked and moved back. The alligators dropped Siba in the shallow water and submerged back into the river.

Everyone was shocked on seeing Siba alive and unscratched. No one knew what to say. Like stone statues, they watched him walking toward them. He smugly handed the ball to one judge. But the judge trembled and threw it away. Looking at the agape faces of his team members, Siba cheered, "Hurray! We won the Huntzman Trophy."

To Siba's horror, instead of cheering or celebrating, his team members screamed in fear. He was appalled at his friends' strange behavior. The crowd suddenly became agitated. People began whispering and pointing at Siba in panic. Someone from the crowd shouted, "He's a demon!"

Another voice came, "Devil!"

Suddenly, the entire crowd was shouting and calling him evil. Upon hearing evil slogans against him and looking at their horrible expressions, Siba got scared to his core.

"He's possessed. He went to the Forbidden Forest and the Ghost Lake. Stay away from him," someone shouted from the crowd. Instantly, everyone moved away from Siba in fear and horror. Siba recognized that voice very well. It was his coach – Mr. Drock. On hearing that, Siba's eyes filled with tears. He wiped his tears and ran toward his village. He didn't even look back to see if someone was following him or not. He neither stopped running nor crying until he reached his home. Limpoo was sitting in front of his house. Siba hugged him tightly and sobbed, "I'm not evil."

Robby and Masai were chasing him closely. Soon they arrived there. "We know you are not possessed," Masai said consolingly.

"Grandma told us that you made wild animals your friends. We know you, and we trust you. Did you forget that we are friends forever?" Robby revealed. "Now stop crying like a baby."

Siba wrapped his arms around both of them.

Rouble flew there from inside the stable. "What happened? Did you lose the game?"

Masai said, "Nothing happened. You go back and watch your flock." The parrot flew and perched on a nearby tree.

"Forget what happened today. Let's go to my home. My mother cooked your favorite rice pudding. You haven't even eaten anything since yesterday," Robby persuaded. Siba nodded his head while wiping his tears. The three walked toward Robby's house.

Robby's father was sitting on the porch. On seeing Siba entering his house, he yelled, "Stop! Stop right there! Robby, don't you dare bring this evil boy into my house. I'm warning you, once and for all. Don't ever meet him again."

Robby revolted, "What are you saying, dad? He's my best friend."

Robby's father stomped toward them. "You don't know, son. He was found inside the Forbidden Forest, abandoned. No one knows his real parents. When he disappeared earlier, his uncle died. Now, when we were taking care of him, he disappeared again. And you saw yourself what happened today. Did you hear what his coach said? He went to the Ghost Lake. I'm warning you, this kid is pure evil. Stay away from him. You don't know what misfortune he'll bring upon you."

Siba again broke into tears and ran back to his house. Robby tried to go after him, but his father held his arm and pulled him inside the house. Masai couldn't understand what to do. He ran to the temple to look for granny.

- Chapter 10 -

The Feral Shepherd

Siba jumped on his bed and cried out loud. Celine went close to him and licked his tears. He hugged her and cried his heart out, "Celine, you are the only one who believes in me."

Rouble said, "I believe in you too. But will you at least tell me what happened?"

Siba wiped his tears and picked himself up. "I'm leaving this fake world of humans filled with stupid idiots."

Rouble asked, "Where will you go?"

"I'm going to live in the Great Forest," Siba sniffled. He took his blanket, bag of clothes, and his flock of sheep with him. Rouble and Limpoo also supported his decision and moved to the forest along with him.

They traveled in a group for several hours until they arrived at the gateway of the forest. After crossing the pond on the turtle raft, as they entered the Great Forest, Siba shouted out emotionally, "O Great Forest, your little animal is seeking your sanctuary. I've left the human world, and I'm here to live under your benevolent canopy."

The Great Forest's voice echoed, "Welcome, Bumblebee! Welcome home."

Rouble asked Siba, "Where shall we stay in this vast forest?"

Siba dropped his bag under a branch laden with cherries and replied, “I don’t know. We’ll see that tomorrow. I’m too tired to walk. My whole body is hurting like hell. For tonight, let’s just sleep here.” He spread his blanket on the ground and crashed on it, allowing sleep to take over him.

Ω

The next morning, they gorged themselves on juicy mangoes and black grapes. After filling their tummies, they embarked on their quest to find new shelter. Siba checked several spots and found an interesting tree hollow. But as he entered inside it, a sparrow shouted, “You better not enter into raccoon’s home. He doesn’t like strangers.”

Siba backed off quickly. “I’m sorry.”

After wandering for a long time and making several other unsuccessful attempts, he finally found a big sycamore tree. Its hollow looked completely empty. He looked around and saw one squirrel collecting nuts. He asked her, “Does anyone live here?”

With her mouth full of nuts, the squirrel barely muttered, “No.” Suddenly, all the nuts she was holding in her mouth dropped onto the ground. She picked them up again and hopped away throwing a nasty look back at Siba.

Siba giggled and happily went inside. “This one is big enough for me. I can lie down here comfortably,” he told Rouble.

“Nice! You stay here and take some rest. In the mean-time, I’ll go see Woody.” Rouble said, flying away.

Siba, feeling contented, spread his blanket inside the semi-enclosed cavity of the tree and laid down on it. His flock began grazing around that tree, while Limpoo started playing with the butterflies. Barely half an hour had passed when he heard someone knocking outside. Siba stuck his head out of the tree hollow but no one was there. He scoffed and laid down again. But after some time, another knocking sound disturbed his peaceful sleep. He got very annoyed and clambered out to see who was spoiling his dreams. He looked around angrily, but no one was there. Suddenly, the knocking sound came again from above. He looked up. A woodpecker was pecking on the mottled bark of the sycamore trunk.

Siba pursed his lips and pulled his brow together. "Geez! No wonder, no one lives here!" He packed his stuff and said to his flock, "Well, we're back on the road." Along with his dog and flock of sheep, Siba marched toward Woody to look for Rouble and a better shelter.

Meanwhile, wandering through his territory, Huzo heard bleats. He followed the unfamiliar voices to find the intruders. Upon seeing Siba with his livestock, he cheerfully trumpeted, "Hey, Siba! It's a pleasure to see you again."

The flock became frightened on beholding the beast and cowered behind Siba. He turned toward his flock and spoke, "Don't be scared. Huzo is the king of this forest. He's very gentle. He won't harm you." He twisted his head toward the elephant and waved, "Hey, Huzo. You scared my sheep."

"Oh! These fluffy things are your friends? I'm sorry. I didn't mean to scare them." Huzo walked toward Siba with his trunk swinging like a pendulum. "I heard some rumors about you. Are they true?" the king inquired. Siba told him everything that happened in the village. Huzo consoled him, "This is your home. We're your family. We'll be more than happy to have you here with us. And don't worry about a place to stay. You pick a spot that you like. I'll get it vacated for you."

Siba replied, "No, no, no! I don't want to steal someone's home. Is there any other place that's already vacant?"

After thinking for a while, Huzo replied, "Yes, there is one. Follow me." He took them to a small hill at the edge of the Great Forest. With his long trunk, the elephant pointed to a big crack in the hill, "Do you see that den?"

"Yes," Siba replied curiously.

"You can stay there. No one lives there."

"It's a big den. How come it's empty? I mean, why no one lives there?"

With his gaze fixed on the den, Huzo replied, "Because, that was Tiger's den. After he left, no one goes there. If you'll live there, I'll feel my long-lost friend has returned."

"Thank you!" Siba hugged Huzo's trunk and happily moved his stuff inside the den.

"Celine, how's this place? Better? Here you can graze all day long," Siba spoke, rubbing her thick fur.

Celine bleated happily, "Baaa."

Later, when Siba was resting on the den's floor, his gaze fell upon an ancient rock painting on the roof. Most of the painting was damaged but a few human-like figures holding red-colored spears in their hands and a chopped tree were still visible. He stared curiously at the painting until night covered it under a sheet of darkness. But he still kept wondering about its mystery.

The next morning, Siba ordered Rouble and Limpoo to watch over the grazing flock, and he went looking for Huzo. Upon finding the elephant rolling in mud, he spoke hastily in one breath, "I found a painting inside the den. Do you know anything about that? Did Tiger paint it?"

Huzo was taking a mud bath. Raising his trunk smeared in mud, he replied, "Hold on, Cub! Don't you know you should respect others' privacy, especially when they are taking shower?"

Siba asked with a puzzled expression, "Shower? But there's no water here."

Huzo sprayed a trunk load of mud on Siba and giggled, "We don't need water."

Siba got fully covered in mud. He coughed and sneezed, "Achoo!" He removed mud from his face and hurled it back at the beast. "If that was some kind of joke, I didn't like it."

Huzo laughed. "I'm sorry. I was just kidding. Here, we take showers with water as well as mud. Get used to new bathing habits. It'll help you to adapt to your new neighborhood."

Siba, shaking off the mud, frowned, "Thank you for the demonstration. But I'm good with just a water bath."

Huzo giggled, "Ok, don't be mad. Let's go to the river. I'll give you a shower there with water." At the river, Huzo sprayed water on Siba with his trunk. Both played in the river and cleaned the mud from their bodies. After coming out of the river, Huzo asked, "Oh, I completely forgot. You were telling me about some paintings. What was it?"

"Yeah! It has a few humans with red spears and a chopped tree. Do you know who made it?"

"No. We should ask the Great Forest. He knows everything about the trees," Huzo suggested.

Siba replied appreciatively, "Good idea! He must know about that."

Siba and Huzo discussed the issue with the Great Forest. After listening to their story, the majestic entity revealed, "As I told you before, a long time ago, humans lived here comfortably with other forest dwellers. Everyone followed my golden rules. One day, I thought of spreading my rules beyond my boundaries. As I cannot move, I chose humans to be my messengers. In order to equip them for this task, I offered them the fruit of intelligence. But along with the fruit, they ate its seeds as well. And those were the seeds of arrogance."

Siba interrupted, "Are these the same seeds that you told me about once?"

Huzo got irritated, "Siba, don't speak in the middle. Hold your questions till the end."

"I'm sorry," Siba apologized. "What happened after that?"

The Great Forest echoed, "You asked another question, so hear its answer first. Yes, these are the same seeds that I talked about earlier. Now hear the story. With better intelligence, their knowledge began to rise. But with more knowledge, their arrogance increased many fold. By understanding the laws of nature, they tamed fire and developed tools and weapons. They began to consider themselves superior to everyone else. They burned the forests and brutally massacred the other animals. They seized the free lands and made their homes on them from stones and mud. Later, they began planting their own food.

"It took me some time to realize the blunder I made. To do justice to other forest dwellers, I decided to offer the fruit of intelligence to all other creatures. But somehow humans came to know about my plan, and they chopped my trunk so that I could never produce that fruit again. This heinous crime of cutting down my trunk acted as a tipping point and all forest-dwellers came together to fight against humans. But humans ran away and never returned. The Old Rock in the middle of the forest was my trunk. Now I'm left with aerial roots only."

Upon hearing the heart-rending story of the Great Forest, Siba and Huzo became very sad. Their eyes filled with tears of pain. Siba said painfully, "Humans don't care for other humans, not even their children. Why would they care for trees and animals? It's them who are evil – the real evil. I feel ashamed to be a human."

The Great Forest spoke, "Don't be ashamed of yourself. It doesn't matter if you have a body of a human, but you are not like them. You have a pure heart that cares for everyone. Indeed, you should be proud of yourself. You protected my residents by building a dam and also spread my golden rules to those barbaric alligators."

Siba expressed his worry, "But if I feel proud, it will lead to arrogance, and I may do something evil like my ancestors. Please save me from that."

The Great Forest spoke, "Wisdom is the cure for arrogance. But only my trunk could have produced the fruit of wisdom. Sorry, Bumblebee! I won't be able to provide you wisdom."

Siba thought for a moment and asked, "Is there any way to bring your trunk back to life?"

After a long silence, the Great Forest replied, "Only the elixir of life can bring it back, but there's no more elixir left on earth."

Huzo spoke, "O Great Forest, if you can't give Siba the fruit of wisdom, then at least you can share your wisdom with him. It may help Siba in controlling arrogance."

The Great Forest's voice echoed, "Yes, you are right! I didn't think about that. Although I can't give you the fruit of wisdom, you will eventually gain wisdom with time and experience. For the time being, I can teach you the law of characteristics. That should be enough to keep arrogance suppressed, but it will demand a higher level of awareness."

Siba's face cheered up. "I'm ready for it."

"There are numerous abilities and qualities that are required for one's survival and growth, for example, strength, agility, size, courage, adaptability, stamina, and so on. These qualities are present in all creatures but with varying levels of expression. To understand it better, let's take the example of Huzo. He has more strength than a rabbit but is less loyal than a dog. Do you get it?"

Siba replied, "A little bit."

"Ok! The level of expression of these qualities determines one's character, and one's character dictates one's behavior and actions."

Siba raised his doubt, "You mean my behavior and actions are governed by my character?"

The Great Forest replied, "Yes. But when I'm saying something, don't take it personally."

Siba rebuked, "I didn't take it personally."

"Oh, Bumblebee! By personal I mean when someone tells you something, you shouldn't correlate it to yourself. You shouldn't imagine how you would respond in that situation, or how it is related to you or affects you. In other words, you shouldn't view it as the first person and start responding to that situation. Instead, you should look at it from the outside as a third person. Like an observer, observe and understand what the other person is trying to tell you. You should just focus on the picture that the other person is trying to show you.

"But, whenever I tell you something, instead of perceiving it as a piece of information, you become an active player. You start considering how it applies to you and deviate from what I want to convey. The negative part of doing that is, instead of understanding the concept, you just end up day-dreaming. Instead of viewing the whole picture, you end up admiring only those parts of the picture that you like and disliking other parts that you aren't fond of."

Siba at once realized his mistake. "I'm sorry. I understand what you mean. When you were giving Huzo's example, instead of focusing on what you were trying to teach me, I was thinking about whether I was more courageous and loyal than him or not. Later, when you explained that character dictates our behavior, then instead of understanding how it works, I was thinking how my character controls my behavior."

"Exactly! Do you see now? That's why you were not asking the right questions to help you understand the logic better. But you kept on asking questions about how that situation would apply to you."

"I got it," Siba smirked. "From now on, I'll always look from outside the box."

The Great Forest resumed explaining, "As I was telling you, one's behavior is controlled by one's character. You can bring your behavior under your control with a higher level of awareness. If by some means you can increase your awareness, then you can realize why you behave in a particular way. In fact, you can precisely pinpoint and regulate the expression of each quality. Based on how you want to respond to a situation, you can promote or suppress these qualities. But if you don't like any quality, don't lose it, because you never know when you'll need it in the future. Remember, whatever is there in nature, it's there for a purpose. Let me explain this aspect by giving another example of our king. His giant tusks – the overgrown teeth, are not used for eating. You may think if they don't help in eating then why do they exist. They exist because they serve a different purpose. He uses them when required, to attack and scare the enemy away. I have told you everything that you need to bring your behavior under your control. I think arrogance shouldn't trouble you anymore."

Siba replied smilingly, "I'll try my best."

With an innocent face, Huzo said, "I swear, I would never hurt anyone with my tusk. But I'm astonished to know that they are in fact teeth. I always wondered why I have horns on my face, instead of on my head."

Siba giggled.

"Siba, how will you raise your level of awareness?" Rouble's voice came from the top.

Siba and Huzo looked above. Rouble was sitting on a high branch.

Siba shouted angrily, "What are you doing here? I told you to look after our flock."

The scarlet macaw replied, "They will be fine. Who will harm them in the Great Forest? Moreover, Limpoo is there too."

"But why are you here?" Siba questioned.

"I wanted to know the mystery of the cave painting too." Rouble asked curiously, "You didn't answer my question. How will you raise your awareness?"

Siba smirked, "I know who can help me with that. Let's go to the Dark Cave." The three seekers bid adieu to the Great Forest and marched toward the Dark Cave.

- Chapter 11 -

Three Disciples of Master Sung Tzu

Before entering the Dark Cave, Siba lifted his shirt and untied the Ultravision wrapped around his waist. As he was about to tie the strip of cloth around his eyes, Rouble asked, "Why don't you light a torch, so we all can see?"

Siba mocked, "Aren't you afraid of going inside?" Rouble frowned.

Huzo said, "Leave the past behind. We both want to meet Master Sung Tzu."

Siba wrapped the ochre-colored strip back around his waist and lit a piece of wood. As they passed through the dark and slippery cavern, Huzo and Rouble followed Siba closely.

Suddenly, Master's voice echoed from the darkness, "Welcome to my dark world."

Siba stopped at once and raised his torch. Upon seeing a big brown ball of fur hanging in front of them, Huzo and Rouble screamed in fear. Siba giggled at them.

Unfurling his membranous wings, Master asked, "Have you never seen a bat before?"

Siba told his scared friends, "Meet Master Sung Tzu."

Huzo and Rouble greeted in a shaky voice, "Hello Master!"

Master asked, "How are you?"

"I'm good, but I'm not sure about my friends," Siba chuckled.

Rouble responded quickly, "I'm good too. It's just my eyes. They are taking some time to adjust to this darkness."

Siba joked, "If your eyes are giving you trouble, do you want me to turn down this light?"

Huzo shrieked, "No!" Others burst into laughter.

Master asked Siba, "Did you meet the dream painters?"

Siba replied, "Yes Master, I met one dream painter. She told me that there's a captain inside me who controls my every activity. Can you please tell me how to get rid of this captain? I want to bring myself under my control."

Master replied with a smile, "What they call a captain, is actually who you really are." All three looked completely lost.

Siba requested, "Master, please tell us in layman's terms."

Master smiled broadly. "Ok! First, let me tell you what's inside your mind. Then it'll be easy for you to understand. Like your body has different organs for different tasks, in the same way, your mind too has different parts. For example, you must be familiar with memory."

All replied enthusiastically, "Yes!"

Master continued, "Good. Memory is the storehouse of information. It stores the outside information that enters the mind through senses as well as the information that the mind generates. Each stored memory has two components – the factual component and the emotional component."

Rouble asked, "Master, I don't understand these components."

"Ok, let me show you. Everyone, close your eyes and imagine your favorite fruit." Master paused for a few seconds and then asked, "Now, one by one, tell me what are you seeing and how you feel after imagining it."

Rouble responded at once, "I see nuts. I feel like cracking them."

Huzo spoke next, "I see bananas. They are yummy."

After that Siba said, "I see mangoes. They are juicy and delicious."

"Good job!" Master gave them another task. "Now imagine a watermelon and tell me how you feel about it."

This time, Siba spoke first, "I love watermelons. They are so refreshing."

Huzo said, "They are good for playing. I feel like crushing them under my feet."

At last, Rouble responded, "I don't like watermelons. Can I imagine something else?"

Master said, "Open your eyes. Did you notice the difference?"

The three confused disciples asked, "What difference?"

Master explained, "In the first case when you had the freedom to pick your favorite fruit, your mind selected the ones that you like. So your fruits were different but the feelings were similar that you liked them and wanted to eat them. Whereas in the second case, the object – watermelon was the same but you experienced different feelings about it. Does that make sense to you?"

Nodding his head, Siba replied, "Yes, Master. The image of an object in mind is the factual component, whereas how we feel about it, is the emotional component. Am I correct?"

Master answered with a smile, "Absolutely correct. The details about the object that you perceive through senses like color, shape, texture, smell, and so on, are plain facts. These details form the factual component. While the emotional component is based upon the emotions it triggers inside you. Both these components combine together to form the memory of that object. When different individuals see the same thing, the factual component remains the same for everyone but the emotional component varies based upon an individual's perception and beliefs."

Siba inquired, "But Master, if the object is the same, then how it can trigger different emotions in different people?"

"It's because everyone perceives differently. Perception is dependent upon an individual's mindset and his outside situation. And generally, everyone's mindset and situations are different when they perceive any item. So, when the same object is perceived differently by different individuals, it triggers different emotions in them," Master answered.

Huzo asked, "One silly question! When I imagined bananas, why did I feel so good?"

"When you imagine or focus on a particular memory, your mind retrieves its factual and emotional components. So you visualize the stored image as well as feel the emotions attached to it. Not only that, the first memory of an object forms the base of its factual and emotional components. After that, whenever you see or imagine that object again, its previously stored facts and emotions automatically get attached to its subsequent images. That's why they say – the first impression is the last impression. Because once the factual component is attached to the emotional component, it's extremely difficult to separate them," Master explained.

Siba inquired, "Is it possible to separate the two components?"

Master answered, "Yes, by delinking both components. But it requires higher mental techniques. Anyway, are you clear with memory?"

The three disciples nodded together, "Yes, Master."

"Ok, the next part of the mind is intellect. Intellect processes information to understand and conceptualize how things work. Better understanding of the world helps an individual to live better. As the perceived and stored information have two components, so they are processed in two different ways –reasoning and intuition. Reasoning processes the factual components, while intuition processes the emotional components. Just like the fruit example, reasoning based on facts leads to similar concepts and conclusions in different individuals, while results based on intuition vary from person to person. Even within an individual the final results from reasoning and intuition can contradict each other, and one may end up in a dilemma," Master explained in detail.

Siba asked, "Is there any method to overcome this dilemma?"

Master replied smilingly, "Yes, my child. Here, the third part of the mind, judgment, comes to your rescue. Using your set of beliefs as a yardstick, judgment compares both results against those beliefs. Whichever result is closer to your beliefs, it picks that one. That's why it's very important to build your beliefs carefully. And remember, once beliefs are established, don't take them for granted. You must always keep on re-verifying and updating your beliefs based on new and better information.

"Further, the final decision also depends upon an individual's orientation, whether one is inclined toward intuition or reasoning. Most of the time, while processing information, the emotions become hyperactive and overpower a person's mind, then the individual goes ahead with intuition. But at the bottom of his heart, he always knows what is right. Later on, that person may repent but then, nothing can be done. So you must be careful. Don't let emotions hijack your mental faculties," Master spoke, staring into their eyes.

The confused elephant asked, "When judgment is hijacked by emotions, then how can one make the right decision?"

Right away, a crispy reply came from Siba, "Wisdom!"

Master appreciated Siba, "Awesome! From where did you learn that?"

"The Great Forest," Siba replied. "But he said that it comes with time and experience. So, until I grow old and gain enough experience, I cannot become wise?"

Master replied smilingly, "Wisdom is the true antidote for ignorance. You can become wise through your own experience or by observing and learning from others' experiences. But there's one shortcut – intelligence!"

Siba got confused. "Master, aren't wisdom and intelligence the same?"

"Well, they are very similar. In fact, overlapping but not the same. Intelligence gathers information and knowledge related to a particular problem from outside and based on that, it finds a solution. On the other hand, wisdom, along with the gathered knowledge, also uses previous knowledge and experience to make a better decision. Intelligence is based on reasoning and logic. Wisdom, on top of that, also includes emotions, beliefs, and cultural factors. Thus, intelligence uses only reasoning, while wisdom uses both reasoning and intuition for decision-making.

"Intelligence focuses on gathering facts. On the other hand, wisdom also tries to read between the lines by hearing the unsaid and seeing the concealed. The scope of intelligence is limited only to finding the solution, while wisdom goes beyond that to find out why the problem arose and to foresee the long-lasting impact of the decision.

"Intelligence tries to make one better and superior. It tries to control nature and mold it according to one's wish. Wisdom aligns and syncs one to the ultimate truth. Intelligence focuses on how to win. Wisdom focuses on how to avoid conflict. Intelligence views each problem as unique and different, while wisdom sees everything as interconnected.

"Intelligence makes an individual a powerful thinker with strong intellectual capabilities. Wisdom makes a person able to discern right from wrong and helps one take morally correct decisions. So my boy, either you learn from others' mistakes or else life teaches you the hard way."

Huzo questioned, "Master, can I learn from your experience?"

"You can do that. But the conditions and circumstances under which I gained my experiences might not be the same as yours. That will lead you to assume many things. For taking care of these assumptions, you will need a higher intelligence. So, for learning from others' mistakes and experiences, you will have to first increase your intelligence level."

Thinking about decision-making, a past incident flashed in Siba's mind. He asked, "My village priest told us to base our decisions on religious beliefs and morals. But I found that each religion has different morals, teachings, and beliefs. Why are they so different?"

Master expounded, "Religions are the knowledge of ancient times. The ancient people observed nature and tried to explain its phenomena by forming their own theories. Those theories consist of two parts – facts and myths. The actual causes behind phenomena that they were able to understand, they explained logically. Those logical explanations became facts. Whereas, other phenomena which they experienced but couldn't understand, they explained them by using myths. So different religions are different theories of different times, based upon their level of understanding of nature. Facts, being the logical explanations, stood firm against the test of time, while religious preachers try to impose myths on the public under the name of faith. Thus, only facts should be used to develop your beliefs, but still, you must thoroughly test and verify them with your intelligence, observations, and experience."

"Thank you, Master," the three disciples said humbly.

Siba asked, "But Master, out of all these parts of the mind which one is the captain?"

Master stared into Siba's eyes and spoke, "Just like your heart never stops beating, similarly, your mind never stops working too, not even when you are asleep. But you consciously use only a tiny fraction of your vast mind at any given time. The rest of your mind still keeps on working, which you are not consciously aware of. That's called the subconscious mind. But it doesn't mean that you have two different minds – a conscious mind and a subconscious mind. There's only one mind, and I told you about its different parts earlier.

"Now, what you think of yourself to be as who you are, that is, your idea of yourself, is consciousness. But that's just a tiny fraction of your mind. It's the rest of your mind, which is not under your direct control that actually guides and controls you. That's what the dream painters call the captain."

Siba inhaled deeply, "Hmmm! It makes perfect sense now. My subconscious mind is not under my control, and it controls everything inside me. And when I'm sleeping, it directs Tina to paint its activity as dreams."

Upon hearing the last part of the conversation, Rouble became confused. He stared at Siba. "Did you get it, Siba? I am so confused." He expressed his doubts, "Now what is this consciousness?"

Master stared into Rouble's eyes and asked, "Who are you?"

The parrot replied, "I'm Rouble."

"Rouble is your name. But who are you?"

"Oh, sorry! I'm a bird – a scarlet macaw."

"That's what your body is. But who are you? Who is it inside you that said a scarlet macaw?"

Rouble frowned, "Master, are you playing a game with me? I don't know."

"Who is it that is expressing itself as I?"

The confused bird shouted, "It's me."

"Exactly! That thing inside you, which you consider to be yourself, is consciousness. Consciousness is formless and limitless. When you give this consciousness an identity by associating it with something; like your profession, relation, nation, culture, and so on, you put a boundary on it and limit its infinite scope of possibilities. You put limitations on what it can do, and what it can't do. In a way, you curb its freedom to express itself the way it is. When you dissociate yourself from all identities, whatever is left, that pure self is consciousness," Master explained calmly.

"That's true, Master. I'm the King of the Great Forest. I'm bound to do everything like a king; not the way I want to do it. Sometimes, I feel that I should escape somewhere else where I can do what I really want to do. Where I can be what I really want to be." Huzo asked, "Is there any way to break this identity?"

Master replied softly, "Be like water!"

All three disciples fixed their surprised gazes at Master and exclaimed, "Water?"

"Yes, water. Have you seen a drop of rain?"

"Yes, Master," all replied together.

"When that drop falls in the river, can you find it again?" Master asked.

Rouble scoffed, "How can we? It's impossible."

"Yep, it's impossible, because it loses its identity as a drop and becomes part of the river. The water inside a pond takes the shape of the pond. If it is inside a well, it takes the shape of the well. As water, it supports life. But if it takes the shape of a flood, cyclone, or tsunami, it destroys everything that comes in its way. As a cloud, it flies in heaven. As ice, it becomes hard like a rock. When you drink water, it even becomes you. In fact, sixty percent of your body is water. Therefore, my child, by losing your identity as a tiny speck of the universe, you become the universe itself. Learn to let go of whatever is yours, until only the true you is left. Then, learn to lose yourself, until only the self is left," Master sighed, "I lost myself to find self. After finding self, I became pure self."

King Huzo bowed before the bat, "Master, till today, I thought myself to be the king. All animals and birds followed my command. But now, I feel I was living in a big illusion. I feel I'm nothing, who has nothing, and who knows nothing. I don't even know who I am. I want to spend the rest of my life learning from you."

Master suggested, "Learn from self. Self is the supreme teacher. Explore yourself and find the self. Before asking me any question, ask yourself first. Perhaps, you won't even have to ask me after that."

Siba spoke, "Master, I came here to ask you just one question. But after listening to you, now I will try to find its answer myself first."

"You will find the answer when the time is right. And now, I think it's time for you to leave. It's dark outside. I don't want you to get lost in the darkness before you find yourself."

Surprised Rouble and Huzo asked Master, "How do you know it's dark outside?"

Siba spoke immediately, "Did you forget? Inner Ultravision!"

"Oh yeah!" Huzo remembered. "Thank you for enlightening us."

While curling back into a big brown furry ball, Master spoke, "Look within to know beyond."

- Chapter 12 -

Forbidden Forest

A melodious song of cuckoo permeating through the cool morning breeze fell upon Siba's sleeping ears. He yawned lazily and peeked out of his den. Rouble was staring at the beautiful bird. Siba mocked Rouble, "Are you taking singing lessons? Let me see how well you do."

Rouble irked, "Don't make fun of my voice."

Siba giggled, "I asked you to sing because today is my birthday."

Rouble recalled, "Geez! I completely forgot. Happy birthday, Siba! Now, you're officially a teenager." He gasped, "Time just flies. It feels like yesterday, when last year, your friends brought you gifts. We celebrated and had so much fun."

Siba sighed, "Yeah! Now I have new friends to celebrate with." He felt nostalgic about his school friends. Suddenly, he stood up and started looking for something in his bag.

Rouble asked, "What are you looking for?"

"Nubina gave me a toy. It's not in my bag. I think I forgot it in the stable."

Rouble suggested, "Let's go to our house and bring it back."

"Alright!" Siba instructed Limpoo to look after his flock and left for the village with Rouble. But when they arrived there, the village appeared to be unusually quiet and deserted.

There was no one on the roads and the houses were locked. Siba asked Rouble suspiciously, "That's strange! I've never seen this village so desolated."

"I don't know. All streets are empty. How come there's no one around?" Rouble wondered.

"You check what's going on here. I'm going to our house. Meet me there," Siba instructed.

When Siba reached closer to his house, he smelled a strong stinking stench in the air. Swarms of flies were buzzing all over the place. He coughed, "Eww! Who died here?" Unable to breathe in the rotting stench, he covered his nose and passed through the buzzing flies. When he opened the main door of his house, he was horrified to see a big heap of slaughtered alligators in front of his porch. The entire ground was red with blood as if red paint was splattered all over it. The scaly reptiles were so brutally butchered that their limbs were chopped off and their intestines were hanging out. After crossing the hellish scene, he entered the stable and looked for the toy. It was hiding in one corner under his bed. He grabbed it and dashed out of his house. Unable to take it anymore, he vomited on the street.

Before he could clean himself up, Rouble arrived there yelling, "Get out of here. Run back to the forest."

While controlling himself, Siba asked, "What's going on here?"

"Don't go near your house. The priest was telling the villagers to burn down your house along with everything that belongs to you to ward off evil. They are coming this way. If they see you, they'll burn you along with your house. Run!" the bird squawked.

Just then, the uproars of the approaching crowd fell upon their ears – "Burn the evil! Burn the evil!" They got very scared and raced back to the safety of the woods. From there, they watched the mob burn down their house. Black clouds of smoke soared above the village. Siba asked Rouble, "There were dead alligators in our house. Do you know what happened to them?"

Rouble told him, "I heard villagers saying that from the day you rode the alligator, they were behaving abnormally. They weren't attacking villagers or their cattle. The priest told them that the alligators were possessed too, just like you. So they killed them and are burning them along with your house."

Siba became angry and worried. "I'm going to see Gator. God knows how he is. You go and keep an eye on our flock. I'll meet you there."

After arriving at Emerald Lake, Siba shouted, "Gator! Gator! Are you here?"

Upon hearing Siba's call, the giant alligator slowly emerged out of the lake. Right away, a big slashed wound on his snout caught Siba's attention. Traumatized by the gruesome view, Siba screamed with pain, "I'm extremely sorry for this devilish act of humans."

Gator belly crawled toward Siba and groaned, "I and my alligators could have easily killed those bloody humans. Just because you took a promise from us, we didn't retaliate and tried to escape and hide. They dragged my friends and family out of the river like fish and slaughtered them in front of my eyes. I couldn't do anything except watch them getting butchered. Those ruthless barbarians didn't even leave their dead bodies behind." He gasped, "It's not them who killed my family. It's you, who killed them. You are responsible for this massacre. You should have allowed us to die on that day, instead of getting us killed like this. At least, I would have died along with my family without any regrets."

Holding himself responsible for the gruesome bloodshed, Siba's heart filled with remorse and sorrow. He couldn't bear it and ran away crying into the nearby hilly forest. Perhaps he was not running from Gator but from himself. Running and sobbing through the treacherous woods, he arrived near a small stream. Blood was oozing from the cuts on his legs left by the wild thorns. He climbed down a rocky bank and dipped his feet inside the cold flowing water, perhaps, to ease the pain, not of his wounds but of his heart. He sat there on a rock holding his sobbing face between his knees and contemplating his mistake. While he was still thinking, he heard some movement in the bushes behind him. He turned his head to look. A big tiger leaped over him, nabbing him under his paw.

Siba screamed while covering his face with his arm. The tiger lifted his paw from Siba's chest to slice him, but the necklace around the boy's neck got stuck in his claws. The tiger stared at the claw in awe and recognized it at once to be his own. He roared angrily, "From where did you steal this claw?"

While his arm was still hiding his face, Siba stuttered, "I didn't steal it. Huzo – the King of the Great Forest gave it to me."

The tiger moved back. He stared at Siba and scoffed, "In this whole world, he couldn't find anyone better than a human kid." He glared, "That too when he knows – I hate humans." The disappointed tiger turned and jumped on the rocky bank.

On seeing the tiger leaving, Siba shouted, "What? Did you change your plan? Am I not a meal anymore?"

The tiger jumped back from the top of the rocks. With an angry stare, he roared, "Huzo was supposed to give it to someone who has the same courage as me."

Siba curiously asked, "Are you Tiger – Huzo's childhood friend?"

The tiger again jumped away and replied nostalgically, "Yes!"

"Wait! I heard a lot about you."

Tiger twisted his head toward the boy and said, "Kiddo! Go back from where you came before I change my mind."

Climbing the rocks, Siba shouted, "I won't go without you. Do you know how much Huzo misses you? How could you leave him without letting him know?"

Tiger growled, "You don't know anything."

"What I do know is that his parent took care of you and how much Huzo still loves you."

Tiger thundered, "You want to know my story? Fine! Come with me." Under the star-studded sky, they climbed a nearby hill. From the top, Tiger pointed toward the plains. "Do you see those glowing lights?"

"Yes, that's my village. I mean, it was my village."

"Yeah, that human village," Tiger pointed, "And next to it, that giant woodlot. Then the next one – Huzo's Great Forest, that gorgeous Emerald Lake, and these hill forests. Once, my father ruled all of them. I was a small cub at that time. One day, my parents and I were passing through that woodlot. Near the river, the humans had dug a trench and laid down a trap to catch my family. My father was clever. He evaded the trap. But I was small. I fell straight into it.

"My parents tried to pull me out of that hole, but it was too deep. By that time, the humans arrived there and attacked us with stones and sharp weapons. My parents tried to protect me and fought back. On hearing the commotion, Huzo's father arrived there. My father was severely wounded. He told Huzo's father to take care of me and his kingdom until I grew up. Huzo's father promised and pulled me out of the hole with his long trunk. Suddenly, a stone hit me, and I fell unconscious. When I gained consciousness, I was inside the Great Forest. Huzo's father informed me that my parents were dead and humans took their dead bodies. That very moment, I promised myself, if any human ever enters my forest, then he would not return alive," Tiger said with burning eyes.

"What happened next?" Siba inquired curiously.

"Huzo's father became the king. He raised me like his own son – just like an elephant. But I'm not an elephant; I'm a tiger. The Great Forest was too small for me. Soon, I began feeling suffocated there. I started traveling to other forests to learn what it means to be a true tiger. After the sudden death of Huzo's father, everyone in the Great Forest was talking about who'd become the new king. Huzo's father had never told anyone about his promise to my father that after him, I should become the next king. As per the golden rules of the Great Forest, it's the king's son who should become the next king. So there was a strong feeling in the forest that Huzo should take over his father's place. He was my close friend and my brother. I knew he possessed all qualities to become a great king. So I didn't feel it was right to mention that promise to anyone and left the Great Forest on the night before the selection of the new king," Tiger revealed.

"Where did you go after that?" Siba asked curiously.

"I moved to these hilly forests around the Emerald Lake. Humans used to come here for hunting animals and to gather wood and wild honey. It was the perfect place to take my revenge. I killed every human who entered this forest," Tiger smirked, "Not even a single one managed to escape. The humans stopped coming here gradually, and the fire of vengeance inside me calmed down. After that, I decided to settle here and claimed these hilly forests as my kingdom. Now, I rule all these hills and the mountains beyond them. The Great Forest is not even a tiny fraction in front of my vast empire."

"You left Huzo for a bigger kingdom? That's disgusting!" Siba wrinkled his nose.

"You don't get my point. I didn't leave him for a bigger kingdom but for my own kingdom. Because that's what I am – a king, a born king."

"You are so arrogant. I never thought you'd be like this."

"Watch your tongue, kiddo! Where did you see arrogance in me? As it's the nature of flowers to bloom, birds to fly, and bees to sting; just like that, it's the nature of a tiger to rule. It's not arrogance. That's who I am – the king of the jungle. I have to do what I'm born to do."

Suddenly, Siba stood up. Placing his hand on his head, he said, "Oh, my God! I made a big blunder."

Tiger got confused. "What do you mean?"

"I understood the mistake I made. I forbade alligators to act according to their true nature." Siba told Tiger about what happened to the alligators.

After listening to Siba's story, Tiger responded, "True, it was a mistake. Attack and defense are two separate things. You should have told them not to attack innocent lives but allowed them to defend themselves when their lives are in danger. Moreover, their nature is to be aggressive. You should have allowed them to display their aggression. In that way, others would have been scared of them and wouldn't have harmed them."

"I understand that now. But I'm unable to cope with this burden. I don't know how to rectify my mistake. It will hound me for the rest of my life," Siba said remorsefully.

Tiger consoled and guided the sad boy calmly, "There are some moments in life when we feel we are stuck, and we don't see any ray of hope. It's because we are stuck in some problem, and we are looking at it from the inside. When we look at it from the inside, all we see is the problem and the suffering it's inflicting upon us. Whereas to find the solution, we must rise above the situation and look at it from the outside, the way a third person would look at it. We should imagine as if it's not our problem but someone else's, and we are trying to help him. Then you'll definitely find the solution."

Siba remembered that the Great Forest had told him something similar earlier about taking a third person's viewpoint while listening to others. He inhaled sharply. "Ok, let me try!" He closed his eyes and looked at the entire situation as a third person. After a few minutes, he opened his eyes and with a smile on his face, said, "Aha! I found it! Thank you, Tiger! What you told me, only a wise person could have said that. But still, I don't understand why you never returned to the Great Forest?"

Tiger sighed, "Alright, kiddo! Then listen. Now, even if I want to return, I can't do that. I rule a vast kingdom. With higher position and power, comes higher responsibility. It's my duty to take care of my kingdom, maintain its balance, guard it closely, and ensure that everyone in my kingdom leads a happy and fair life. If I leave this place, its balance will be disturbed and everything will turn into chaos. So I can't leave it now. Please don't tell Huzo about our meeting, or else, he'll feel bad about being the King of the Great Forest. No one else can take care of the Great Forest better than him."

"Don't worry about that. I won't tell anyone," Siba nodded and threw a reassuring smile.

Looking at the stars, Tiger resumed, "It's almost midnight. While talking to you, I didn't realize how fast the time passed by. Nights on hills are usually colder than on plains, and especially during these months, they start getting even colder. I will stay with you and protect you while you sleep. You can return to the Great Forest tomorrow." Siba slept next to him and placed Tiger's large paw on his shoulder for warmth.

The next morning, when Siba woke up, Tiger was not there. He got up and shouted, "Tiger!"

Tiger's voice came from a distance, "Coming! Wait a minute!" Tiger arrived there with some herbs and gave them to Siba. "Apply them to your friend's wounds. He will recover soon. Whenever I got injured by the sharp weapons of humans, these plants healed me quickly."

"I appreciate your help. But I'll still request you to meet Huzo, at least once. He misses you a lot," Siba requested.

"No, kiddo! I thought about it many times. I love him and miss him too. But some things are better left alone. Please make sure you keep our meeting a secret." With a warm smile, Tiger gently touched Siba's face with his paw and disappeared into the hilly forest.

Armed with herbs and hope, Siba raced to the Emerald Lake. He loudly called for Gator. The giant alligator's wounded snout emerged above the serene water of the lake. Sending tiny waves toward the shore, Gator floated toward Siba. After coming out of the water, the giant reptile said remorsefully, "Last night, I couldn't sleep. My previous deeds kept recurring in my mind. Perhaps, it was our karma. We killed uncountable humans and animals. Maybe it was our payback time, and I was left alive to witness the primordial law of nature – 'what goes around comes around!' I'm sorry for my harsh words."

"Don't be sorry. It's me who should be sorry. I realized my mistake. It's your nature to be aggressive and fearsome. So always pretend to attack the way you used to do earlier. But don't hurt anyone, just pretend it. That will maintain your fear in others, and they'll always treat you the way they should treat you – stay away from you. Self-defense is your right, and no one can take that right away from you. From now on, if someone attacks you, you are free to defend yourself."

Gator replied appreciatively, "Thanks! I hope it never happens again."

"If you will pretend to be aggressive, then it won't happen again for sure." Siba applied herbs on Gator's wounded snout and walked back to his den.

- Chapter 13 -

Mysterious Well

Leisurely walking under the warm afternoon sun, Siba finally arrived at his den. Rouble yelled at him angrily, "Where were you this whole time? We were so worried. I searched every single place, even in our village. We thought villagers killed you, if not, then the alligators for sure."

"I'm back. Don't worry about me. How's our flock?" Siba asked.

"Go, check yourself!" miffed Rouble yelled. "Wandering around like Woody for the whole night, I didn't even get a chance to sleep."

Siba looked at his flock. "Where is Celine?" he asked Rouble.

"Last time when I saw her, she was grazing. She must be around somewhere," tired Rouble replied.

"I don't see her. Let's find her."

Rouble yawned, "Are you kidding me? Look at me. I can't even keep my eyes open. Ask Limpoo. He does nothing other than playing with butterflies."

Siba spoke with furrowed brows, "Ok! Ok! Go and sleep." The scarlet macaw flew to a shady branch and slept.

Worried Siba waved at Limpoo. "Limpoo, where's Celine?" The dog stopped playing with butterflies and stared at him with puppy eyes. "Don't give me that look. Come, let's find her," Siba yelled anxiously.

Siba and Limpoo began searching for Celine. The dog sniffed and followed her scent. Toward the end of the day, following the scent trail, they arrived near an old abandoned well. Siba looked inside the well. It was dark and deep. He shouted, "Celine!" But only his echo returned. He chopped several long vines hanging from nearby trees and tied them together to form a rope. After securing it against a big rock, he slowly climbed down the well. The rope broke midway, and Siba fell on a heap of dry leaves at the bottom of the dry well. But there was no sign of Celine. After his eyes adjusted to the darkness, he found a narrow, dark passage on one side of the well. The curious boy entered the passage. It led him to an underground cavern of weird mineral formations and strange glowing plants. Their blinking bulb-shaped fruits were illuminating the cavern, and in the middle, Celine was munching their glowing leaves happily.

"Phew! There you are!" Siba hugged her. Suddenly, he heard a faint sound. They both followed the sound through the cave and arrived at an underground waterfall falling into a small pool. Above the pool, a huge chandelier with colorful flames was hanging by a grapevine. "Chandelier? Why would that be here?" Siba asked himself curiously. He yelled suspiciously, "Is anybody here?"

From the opposite side of the pool, a soft voice responded, "How did you get here? No one is supposed to be here."

Siba couldn't see anyone on the other side of the pool. He tied Ultravision around his eyes and looked there again. A white orb-like apparition appeared out of the waterfall and hovered above the pool. Siba got scared upon seeing the ghost. He stammered, "My well fell! Brrr! My sheep fell in well."

The ghostly orb giggled and took the shape of a small, silver-haired girl in a long, white dress. She glided over the pond and hovered in front of him. "What's your name?"

The scared boy stammered, "I – my – my name – Siba!"

"What kind of name is this?" the girl chuckled in a soft, silky voice. "Don't be scared. Where are you from?"

Siba gathered his courage and spoke, "I live in the Great Forest. Who are you?"

"I'm the Spirit of Life. I live in this waterfall."

Siba murmured curiously, "The Spirit of Life!"

"You heard me. Yes, the Spirit of Life. My name is Edna. I take care of the life on earth."

Siba asked with raised eyebrows, "The entire life on earth?"

"Yeah! Each and every living being of this planet!"

"You are so small. How can you take care of the entire life on earth? Do you even know how big our earth is?" Siba quizzed.

Edna frowned, "You think it's funny? Don't forget, I'm a spirit."

"Ok! Ok! Don't get angry," Siba chuckled. "How do you do that?"

Edna pointed to the chandelier hanging over her head and said, "With these flames. These colorful flames are emotions. With their help, I control life."

Astonished Siba asked, "You mean those burning flames are emotions? Like my emotions?"

"Yes. Why are you so surprised?"

"I never knew that emotions have colors."

"Life is colorless, just like the water in this pool. It's the emotions that add color to it and make it beautiful. Just like these lights that make this pool look colorful. Joy, happiness, sympathy, sadness, anger are different colors of life." Looking at flames, Edna resumed, "When I want to spread any emotion on earth, I release its flame. The life on earth responds to it and acts accordingly."

Siba's curiosity grew further. "You're a spirit. Do you also feel emotions?"

Edna replied with a smile, "How can I feel them? I don't have a body. I just attain different emotional states."

"What do you mean?" Siba furrowed his brows.

Edna floated to the other side of the pool and told him, "Come here."

Siba tied Celine to the grapevine and told her, "Don't go anywhere." Once he secured the sheep, he swam across the pool of cold water.

On seeing him shivering, Edna chuckled, "Looks like you are feeling cold."

"Of course, the water is freezing cold," Siba scowled.

Edna giggled, "Don't be mad!" She clapped, and a bonfire appeared behind Siba. "Sit next to it. You won't feel cold."

Siba squatted and moved his hands close to the fire. "Thank you! It's nice and warm."

Edna spoke, "Did you notice? Earlier you were feeling cold, and now you are feeling warm. Actually, it's your senses that make you feel different things. I don't have bodily senses, so I don't feel it. Feelings, being sensory in nature, stay for a short duration. Whereas, emotions are states of mind and persist longer. Do you understand now?"

Siba, scratching his head, said, "A little bit."

"Ok, let me put it this way. An emotion is a state of mind that affects the body and those bodily changes are picked by senses, which yoy feel as feelings. Thus, emotions generate feelings. Also, emotions are stronger than feelings. Sometimes you must have experienced that when you are sick, but you are excited to go somewhere, you ignore your pain and go ahead with your plans. On the other hand, when you are very sad, you miss your important appointment, even if your body is perfectly fine."

Siba murmured, "Hmmm! That's why when we recall any memory, its emotional component induces the corresponding feeling in us."

Edna couldn't hear him properly. "What? What component?" Her body turned purple.

"Nothing! I was thinking about my Master. But what happened to your body?"

"Oh, I got confused. That's why!"

"What? I didn't get it?"

"It's the color of the emotion. Earlier I was calm, so my body was white. You confused me, and my color changed to purple."

Siba joked, "Thank God, I didn't make you angry. Otherwise, you would have turned black."

Edna pointed, "Not black! Red! Dark red is the color of anger."

Siba joked again, "We need dresses of different colors for different occasions. You just wear different emotions. That's a smart way to save money."

"You don't want to see me in dark red. Do you?" Edna said, staring at him.

"Hell no! I was just kidding. Jokes apart, can I control my emotions too?"

"Yes, you can, if you know how these emotions work. An emotional state can be recognized by the feelings, thoughts, and desires it generates, but the perfect time to understand emotion is when it's in action. The action being physical in nature can be easily observed, while the other three are mental processes and require special skills. You control your actions; you control your emotions," Edna smiled. "Until you don't control your emotions, they control you. Once you bring them under your control, they become your slaves. Then you can trigger them or hold them on your command."

Suddenly, they heard a big splash. They turned their heads and saw that the chandelier was sinking into the pool, and its flames were dying one after the other. Edna screamed, "Noooo! This can't happen." At once, her body turned blue.

Siba looked on the other side of the pool. Celine was chewing the broken end of the grapevine innocently as if nothing had happened. He yelled at her in anger, "Do you know what you did? Can't you keep your grinders off for some time?" Celine stared at Siba but still kept on chewing.

The chandelier sank completely, and all flames doused. The Spirit of Life fell on the floor. Her brightness began fading rapidly. Siba kneeled and asked worriedly, "Hey, what happened to you?" But Edna didn't respond. He tried to lift her, but his hands passed through her fading ghostly body. Siba panicked. "Please talk to me."

With a great effort, Edna spoke, "My time on earth has come to an end."

Siba said with pain, "No, nothing will happen to you. I won't let you die."

"I'm not dying. I'm a spirit. But," Edna wheezed. Pointing toward the night sky through a narrow opening in the cavern, she said with a painful smile, "That bright Pole Star is Polaris – my home. Finally, my time has come to return home."

Siba asked with teary eyes, "If you leave, what will happen to the life on earth?"

Edna groaned, "The balance of life will be disturbed, and eventually, the life on earth will end."

A sudden gush of panic infused inside Siba upon hearing that. "Is there any way to save the life? I won't hesitate, even if I'll have to fight death to save it."

Edna forced a smile on her fading face. "You don't even know what life is, how will you fight death? First, learn to live. Understand life." She almost disappeared.

Siba asked worriedly, "Is there no way? Is there nothing I can do?"

With a great effort, Edna raised her right hand toward the pool. The chandelier rose from the pool and flew toward them while shrinking in size. It shrank to the size of a bracelet and hovered in front of them. Siba looked at it curiously. It was a black, metallic bracelet with twenty-four grayish-black pearls embedded in it. She grabbed it and handed it to Siba. "This is the only way – the Golden Bracelet. Each pearl of this bracelet represents an emotion. You will have to understand each emotion and bring them under your control. When you do so, then the corresponding pearl will glow. You must bring the Golden Bracelet to Polaris with all its pearls glowing. Only," she sighed painfully, "Only then, the balance can be restored. Follow the star." Pointing to the Pole Star, she vanished.

With a heavy heart, Siba wore the Golden Bracelet and looked at the Pole Star through the narrow opening in the cave. He swam across the pond and stared at Celine who was still chewing the grapevine. "Why do you always get me in trouble?" He yanked the vine angrily, but the innocent look on Celine's face made him forgive her. "It's my fault. I shouldn't have tied you to the vine."

Celine bleated, "Baaa." Siba hugged her, and while thinking about Edna, he fell asleep looking at the Pole Star.

The next morning, distant shouts of Rouble woke Siba up. He went back to the well through the narrow passage. Rouble was fluttering at the top, shouting his name. Siba shouted, "I'm here! At the bottom!"

Rouble flew down but couldn't see anything due to the darkness and crashed into Siba. "There you are! Limpoo told me that you and Celine fell into the well. I was so worried."

"If you were so concerned, then why didn't you come earlier?" Siba taunted.

Rouble gave an excuse, "I came at night but the dark well was very scary. So I waited for the sun to rise."

"I was just kidding. Thanks for coming. I can't climb back. The rope snapped. But I found Celine. She is also here."

"Where is she? I don't see her?"

"Not in the well. There, in that cavern. But there's one problem."

"What happened now?" Rouble asked worriedly. Siba told him about the Spirit of Life. After hearing the tragedy, Rouble said, "Hmmm, this problem is for real! Life on earth is in danger. What are you going to do about it?"

Siba stared at him. "What else? I have to save life of our planet. It's my mistake. It happened because of my carelessness. I shouldn't have left Celine alone in the first place nor should I have tied her to the grapevine. Now I'll have to go to the Pole Star."

"Are you crazy? Do you even know what you just said?"

Siba said worriedly, "I don't know. Edna told me so, and I'm going to follow the star. You should go back now."

"No, I'll go with you. I can't let you go alone," Rouble insisted.

"Alright! But what should we do about Celine? How can we get her out of this well?"

Rouble suggested, "Take her along. There's no way we can send her back through this well."

Siba thought and agreed, "Hmmm! You're right. Let's take her along with us."

"Bow-wow," Limpoo barked from the edge of the well.

Siba shouted from below, "You can't join us. Don't forget your job. You must look after my flock while I'm gone."

Rouble pointed, "Don't you think we should take Limpoo along with us? His sharp senses could be useful. Moreover, you said that life on earth is in danger. So what's the point of leaving him behind?"

Siba yelled at Rouble, "I need him to protect my flock. Don't forget, dogs are loyal servants, and I'm his master." Upon hearing that, Rouble became quiet, and Limpoo ran away from the well.

Siba and Rouble crossed the narrow passage. Inside the cavern, Celine was munching blinking fruits. Siba pushed her through the pool, and the three of them squeezed through the narrow opening in the cavern.

- Chapter 14 -

The Formless Monk

On the other side of the narrow opening, Siba and his companions found themselves in an unknown land of giant coniferous trees soaring hundreds of feet high. They were so high that their tops were touching the clouds. It looked like a lost world completely hidden from humanity. The falling leaves of dry vines were whirling in eddies of autumn winds. The forest floor was covered with cones and dead leaves. Several furry animals were busy stocking cones for the harsh winter to come. The presence of three strangers scared them. They climbed the giant trees and glided away making strange noises.

Amazed Siba watched them gliding from tree to tree. He asked Rouble, perched on his shoulder, "Wow! Are they birds or bats?"

"They are flying squirrels," the scarlet macaw replied. "Where did they go?"

Pumped-up Siba shrugged. "Who cares? I only know that I have to keep going until I reach the Pole Star." The three travelers kept on going toward the north.

After some time, something hit Siba's back. He turned around but nothing was there. He started walking again. A few minutes later, something hit his back again. He stopped and looked behind him, but no one was there. He scanned his surroundings and found a cone on the ground. He picked it up and showed it to Rouble. "Did you throw it at me?"

"How can I throw it? I'm sitting on your shoulder. It must have fallen from some tree," the bird chuckled.

As they resumed, another cone hit Siba's head. He stopped and yelled at Rouble annoyingly, "Stop doing that! It's not funny!"

Rouble shouted, "What happened? I didn't do anything."

Siba shrugged his shoulder. "No more free ride. Get off my shoulder."

Rouble snorted with anger and flew ahead of Siba. Just then, a few cones hit him again. Siba's irritation suddenly changed into fear. He whispered, "Guys! Someone is following us and attacking me with cones."

Rouble suggested, "It must be those flying squirrels."

"No! They went in the same direction as we are going. It's someone else." Siba tied Ultravision around his eyes and carefully inspected the trees. He found a monkey hiding behind a high branch, peeping at him. He removed Ultravision and while tying it back around his waist, shouted at the monkey, "Stop teasing me, or else, I'll teach you a big lesson."

The monkey giggled. He plucked one more cone with his long tail and hurled it at Siba. Siba dodged and picked up the cone. He threw it back at the monkey with his full strength, but it fell way short of his target. The monkey giggled and hurled several cones with his tail, one after the other, like a machine gun. Siba became very angry. The monkey enjoyed seeing him getting frustrated and hurled another round of cones. Siba ran away to escape from the showering cones. The monkey chased him, jumping from branch to branch. The wild chase lasted until they moved out of the conifer grove and arrived at the base of a hill.

Away from the protection of high branches, the monkey came into Siba's firing range. Tossing a stone in his hand, Siba smirked, "Where will you go now?"

The monkey scowled and climbed the hill. Siba became more furious and chased him. After a long chase, when they reached the top of the hill, the monkey got trapped. Siba was standing behind him, while a large waterfall was ahead of him.

The waterfall was so high that from its crest the gigantic conifer trees at its base looked like toothpicks. Left with no option to escape, the monkey snarled and charged toward the boy. Siba panicked and looked around for some stone or stick to defend himself, but he couldn't find anything on the rocky surface. The charging monkey jumped at him. Siba's eyes closed instinctively, and his arm covered his face. To his surprise, he felt his face was being licked. He opened his eyes. It was Limpoo, licking his face.

"Limpoo, you? How come you are here?" Siba looked around. The monkey was not there. "Where did that monkey go?" Limpoo licked his face again. "Oh, Lord! Am I dreaming again?" he said, looking at the sky.

Limpoo said, "No, it's not a dream. I came here to tell you that I am not your servant and nor are you my master. Loyalty is the nature of a dog. It doesn't make you superior to me. And don't take my loyalty for granted. Anyone who'll be attached to me, I'll be loyal to him."

Siba remembered the rude way he shouted at him earlier. "I'm sorry, Limpoo. I was angry at Celine, but you became the scapegoat."

Limpoo resumed, "No, you're fooling yourself. That's not what happened. Because you have this notion in your mind that I'm inferior and you're my master, that's why you vented out that anger at me. If it was Huzo instead of me, you wouldn't have done so."

Siba's eyes widened with wonder. "You're right! I never realized that before. What you just said, that's so true." He got lost in thoughts. After a brief pondering, he asked, "Where did that monkey go? Did you scare him away?"

Limpoo revealed, "It was me. I took the shape of a monkey to teach you a lesson on how it feels to be bullied."

"What?" Siba scoffed, "How's that possible?"

"Like this!" Limpoo turned into a monkey before his eyes.

Siba's jaw dropped, "Who are you? You can't be my Limpoo. Are you a wizard or a genie?"

The monkey turned into a sturdy monk wearing an ochre-colored robe. The monk's head was shaved and shining. His face was glowing, and his eyes were radiating holiness and exuberance. With a serene smile, he spoke, "I'm neither a wizard nor a genie."

Siba fell to his knees. With folded hands, he asked, "O holy saint, who are you?"

The monk replied, "I'm Master of your Master. The strip of Ultravision, which you were wearing earlier, was once part of my robe. I created it by infusing my powers into it." Siba's head lowered with the burden of shame.

The monk held Siba's shoulders and lifted him. "Get up, my child. You don't have to feel bad. You never said anything wrong to me. Whatever you did or said, it was to Limpoo. Those rude actions were not directed toward me."

"I don't understand. You were Limpoo all the time. So it was you, against whom I held those disrespectful thoughts," Siba asked remorsefully.

Instead of answering Siba, the monk asked him a different question, "Now you know that I'm your dog. Will you treat your dog the way you are treating me?"

Siba spoke at once, "Of course, I will."

The monk smiled, "No, you don't have to. You must treat others the way they deserve."

"Aren't you contradicting what you told me earlier in Limpoo's form?"

The monk expounded, "No, they are two different things. Treating others is like a give and take relationship. You must treat others based on what they have offered you. Giving less or more respect than what is offered causes an increase or decrease in your self-esteem. This imbalance generates a superiority or inferiority complex in you, which disturbs your inner peace.

"When you treated your dog badly, it wasn't based on what he did for you, but it was based on your mindset that he's inferior to you. In the same way, if you think someone is superior to you, and you give them more respect than what they actually deserve based on their actions, it is wrong as well. Everyone is unique, having different strengths and weaknesses. If you're stronger than others in some aspect, it doesn't give you the privilege to dominate them."

"I got it!" Siba pressed his lips. "I don't understand why you turned into a dog? You could have stayed like this, as a monk."

The monk revealed, "This was my body form before self-realization. Once I realized who I am, I returned my body to nature and existed as pure consciousness. Now I create any body I want by borrowing elements from nature. And when I don't need it, I return it back. So when I'm a dog, I'm a dog.

When I'm a monk, I'm a monk. Body form doesn't change who I am."

Siba expressed his confusion, "If you can take any shape, then you can appear before me in any form. In that case, how would I know which person is someone else and which one is you?"

The monk smiled politely, "It's the same energy that takes different body forms. So don't go for the form. Instead, focus on what energy is doing in that form."

Siba thought over it and said, "In that case, I should treat everyone with the same mindset."

"Yes, now you are on the right track. That mindset is called – humbleness. Let humbleness guide your behavior all the time."

Siba requested, "O holy saint, please tell me how to attain the mindset of humbleness?"

The monk explained, "Perceive everyone as they are made up of the same energy but manifested in different forms. Never judge or compare, just take everyone the way they are. Always remember, who you are – your strengths, your weaknesses, and your limits. Never attach importance to yourself. When one begins giving importance to oneself; one develops pride, arrogance, and finally, ego. When one perceives everything, including oneself, to be made up of the same energy, only then one can be humble."

Siba silently assimilated the divine knowledge for some time and then expressed a doubt, "When as a monkey you were throwing cones at me, I became very annoyed and tried to defend myself? Is protecting myself the same as giving importance to me?"

"Getting annoyed is different than self-defense. If your focus was on protecting yourself, then you'd have simply moved away. It's because you were annoyed, that's why you retaliated and threw cones back at me. Trust me, you could have protected yourself without getting annoyed," the monk said staring into Siba's eyes. "In your village temple you must have seen a sign saying – 'Cleanliness is next to Godliness.' "

Siba recollected, "Yeah! It's written at the entrance of the temple."

The monk nodded, "Exactly! When you enter that temple you remove your shoes outside so that the dirt sticking to your shoes doesn't spoil its cleanliness. Your mind is also like that temple. In the same manner, don't let the outer filth enter your mind temple and spoil its sanctity. When someone says or does something bad to you, you shouldn't allow it to stir your emotions and disturb your inner calmness. Just take it as a piece of information and decide calmly how to respond, if you need to respond at all. I think Master Sung Tzu must have told you these basics about perception."

Siba recalled, "Yes, Master Sung Tzu explained both these components very well. And I understood perfectly what you just explained. Nothing can disturb your inner peace until you allow it to get disturbed." Siba winked with a smile.

The monk patted him on the shoulder, "Good! Instead of asking why it happened, ask yourself, why you allowed it to happen. Now close your eyes and find humility inside you."

Siba sat down with legs crossed and eyes closed. As he tried to focus on humility, his mind kept on wandering. All kinds of distractions occupied his mind. For one second, he was chasing the monkey; the next second he was riding Gator. From the smiling faces of his school friends to the painful memories of his deceased uncle, everything flashed through his mind. His inner turmoil was visible on his face as well. The monk advised, "Relax! Don't stress your mind. It works better when it's relaxed."

Upon hearing that, Siba took a few deep breaths and calmed his mind. As he focused again, his senses withdrew from outside, and he entered into a meditative trance state. He saw himself walking in the Great Forest. As he was walking, he saw Huzo at a distance. But when he went closer, the elephant changed into monk. Siba bowed before the monk and moved ahead. After covering some distance, he saw Rouble. But when he walked toward him, the same thing happened. Rouble also turned into monk. He bowed again and continued walking. After that, Siba met several other animals, but they also transformed into the monk. He paid obeisance to all of them and felt himself to be very lowly. Finally, he arrived at Emerald Lake. When he looked at his reflection on the water, instead of him, it was the monk again. In the end, he bowed before himself as well.

Siba opened his eyes and fell at the monk's feet. "Master, I found humility inside me. When everything is made up of the same energy, then how I can be superior or inferior to anyone."

The monk smiled and pointed to Siba's Golden Bracelet. Siba looked at it. One pearl was glowing with brown color.

The monk said, "In case, your other emotions overpower your humbleness, imagine me in the other person's place, and you'll become humble again."

In the meantime, Rouble and Celine caught up to where Siba was standing. Rouble asked, "Are you ok? Did that long-tailed monkey hurt you?"

Siba looked at the monk and hiding his smile, said, "I'm ok, and I learned a lot from him."

Rouble exclaimed, "Learned from a monkey? That's something new! Where is he? And who's this half-naked man?"

Siba opened his mouth to tell the reality of the monk. But he realized that he didn't know his name. He asked the monk, "O holy saint, I apologize. I forgot to ask your name."

The monk replied, "I don't have a name. I left everything that confined me, even my name. You can call me whatever you like."

Siba picked a name. "Will it be fine if I call you Master Limpoo?"

The monk nodded smilingly. "Ok."

Upon hearing Siba calling the monk Limpoo, Rouble's curiosity grew further. "Will anyone tell me, what's going on here?" the bird yelled. Siba told him about the monk.

- Chapter 15 -

The Flow Temple

An elegant pure white swan, escorted by flying squirrels, landed near the waterfall and offered greetings to the monk, "Welcome to the Flow Temple."

The monk introduced Siba to the swan, "Thank you, Eva! Meet Siba. He's a disciple of Master Sung Tzu."

Siba greeted her respectfully, "Hello Eva!"

Eva hissed, "So it was you who scared my squirrels." Siba became nervous. Before he could open his mouth to offer an excuse, she chuckled and spoke, "Never mind, I was just teasing you. Welcome to the Flow Temple."

The monk spoke to Siba, "Eva is the priestess of the Flow Temple. She takes care of the temple. You may need her assistance to accomplish your mission. Moreover, you need the blessings of Flow before you begin your journey."

Siba looked around and asked curiously, "Where is the temple?"

Eva looked at Siba in surprise. "This place is a temple. This forest is a temple. Have you never been to any temple before?"

The monk intervened, "Human temples are only symbolic. Not like this one – the real one. They only worship symbols. That's why the human world is full of problems."

Baffled Siba stared at the monk as if he was speaking a foreign language. The monk noticed Siba's perplexed expressions and told Eva smilingly, "Make him a part of Flow. He will understand."

Eva suggested with excitement, "Siba can stay here till Spring Popping Festival. By then, he should become a part of Flow."

Monk nodded with an assenting smile, "Good idea!"

Siba raised his concerns, "But, I must continue my journey."

The monk interjected, "Just follow her. Everything will be fine. I have to go back and take care of your flock." Before the boy could open his mouth, the monk disappeared.

Eva walked toward the edge of the waterfall and called Siba, "Follow me." When Siba walked to her, she flew beyond the edge.

Siba stopped and shouted, "I can't follow you anymore. I can't fly."

"But you can jump," Eva replied.

"Are you crazy? I'll die if I jump." The nervous boy couldn't even look down from the edge.

Eva flew back to Siba and said, "Trust me. You won't die." She pushed him over the crest and Siba fell down the waterfall just like all the other drops of falling water.

Rouble shouted in panic, "Sibaaaaa!" Eva looked at the terrified parrot and chuckled. Rouble gave her a nasty look.

After the great fall, Siba fell with a big splash into the rapids. Eva hurriedly plunged down the waterfall. At the bottom, she saw Siba struggling with the strong currents. She landed next to him and swam calmly through the ferocious rapids and giant whirlpools. Siba got sucked into one of the whirlpools. She shouted, "Don't struggle! Relax! Become a part of Flow, and let it steer you to safety."

Siba stopped moving his exhausted arms and legs. To his surprise, after passing through several rapids and whirlpools, he was safely transported to the river's bank. Eva leisurely swam to him and spoke, "Look! Nothing happened to you."

Siba checked himself. "You were right. I'm shocked. I didn't get a single scratch. How's that possible after falling from such a great height? It's a miracle."

Eva spoke smilingly, "It's the power of Flow. If you surrender to Flow, it takes care of you. If you resist, you struggle. Now that you have been introduced to Flow, should we go up? Your friends must be very worried."

Siba looked up at the majestic, sky-touching waterfall. Even some random clouds were floating around its middle, maybe to get a refill. "My goodness, did I fall from heaven?"

Eva giggled. "No, you fell from One Mile Waterfall."

"Oh, my God! One mile! It will take me days to climb to its top," Siba spoke worriedly.

Eva smiled. "Unless, you fly!" She fluttered her wings, and Siba's arms got covered with wings made from leaves. "Follow me!"

Siba flapped his arms. To his surprise, he got lifted above the ground. The excited boy gasped, "Fantastic! Now I can follow you." Both flew up. Dancing along the incredible murmurations of starlings and passing through the lazily wandering clouds, they arrived at the top. Rouble and Celine were interrupted from their lamenting and grazing. They were shocked to see that Siba was flying and not dead.

Siba bantered with Rouble, "Do you want to go for a race?"

Rouble quipped, "Don't forget, it's autumn! Your leaves will fall even before we start." Everyone laughed.

Eva hissed, "Oaks! I completely forgot. Thanks for reminding me. It's almost winter, and there are so many things left to be done for the Spring Popping Festival. Follow me." She took them deeper inside the Oak Forest. As they marched through the thick woods, Eva tapped the ground in a peculiar way. Tiny holes appeared in the ground and dry leaves on the forest floor got sucked into them.

Astonished Siba asked, "What did you do just now?"

"I'm feeding dry leaves to mushpillers. They live inside the soil and wait for my signal to feed. The more mushpillers we feed the better festival we'll have."

Siba offered, "Can I help with that?"

"Sure! Wherever you see dry leaves, tap the ground in this manner." Eva demonstrated to Siba how to tap the ground. "The mushpillers will do the rest." She picked one red-colored ball-like fruit with white spots and instructed, "These are pomberries. If you find them, please collect them too. We need to stock them as much as we can."

Siba found one of the pomberries and kept it in his pocket. On their way, wherever he saw dry leaves, he tapped the ground to feed the mushpillars and made a makeshift basket from his shirt to collect the pomberries.

At dawn, they arrived at a heart-shaped lake. At the cleft of the lake stood a tall strangler fig tree with a hollow core. Eva flew to the tree top and dropped her pomberries in its hollow cylindrical core. Siba and Rouble also flew to the top and dropped their berries. Looking at the tree's bottom, Eva told them, "We've got to fill this hollow tree with pomberries."

Rouble looked at the depth and remarked, "It'll take at least a year to fill this thing up."

Eva chuckled, "How about some extra help?"

Just then, a group of pelicans arrived there and dropped pomberries from their throat pouches. Siba and Rouble watched the level of fruits rising as the magnificent birds emptied their collections. "That's how you do it, eh?" Siba smiled.

Eva winked. "Always remember – Flow! You become part of it, and it'll take care of you."

Siba nodded with a broad smile. They flew down to the lake and landed on its sandy shore. They all laid back on the white sand, gazing up at the skies.

Gazing at the stars, Siba wished he could fly to the Pole Star with his new wings. He didn't even realize while he was counting stars that he had fallen asleep. In his sleep, he dreamt about his wonderful journey through the stars. He was about to reach his destination in his dream but Celine's bleat woke him up. With half-open eyes, he stretched his arms to yawn. With a sudden jolt, he realized that Celine had eaten his leafy wings. Siba's half-inflated lungs wheezed out. He was about to shout at her with anger, but the monk's words about humbleness rang in his ears – 'In case, your other emotions overpower your humbleness, imagine me in the other person's place, and you'll become humble again.'

At once, Siba imagined Celine turning into Master Limpoo. Suddenly, his state of mind changed, and he swallowed his anger. He thought that she must be very hungry, as she didn't eat anything the previous night. But he was deeply hurt at the loss of his new possession.

Eva was swimming in the lake. She watched the entire incident. She was amazed at Siba's reaction, the way he suddenly controlled his anger. She swam to him. Siba spoke in a gloomy tone, "I'm sorry. I couldn't take care of your gift."

"Never mind, those were temporary anyway. They would have withered at the onset of winter. I can see that you deserve a better and permanent solution." Eva plucked two creamy feathers from her wings and offered them to Siba. "Keep these feathers with you. Whenever you want to fly, just flutter them."

An exuberant smile lit Siba's dull face. Excitingly, he held one feather in each hand and fluttered. To his great surprise, he was flying again. Hovering above Eva, he said loudly, "Thank you, Eva! Thank you so much!"

Eva shouted, "You're welcome! You won't have to protect them from your sheep anymore." Both of them laughed. Siba landed next to Eva. She asked him jokingly, "Where's your bird? Did your sheep eat him too?"

"No, she's strictly vegetarian." Siba guffawed. "But I don't know about Rouble. He should be around somewhere. Don't worry, he'll be back. So, what's the plan for today?"

Eva replied, "Oaks! I forgot completely. I've to go to the Flight School to preside over the flying exam. Thanks for reminding me. I'm already late. Let's go to the Suicide Point. Follow me."

Siba instructed Celine to stay near the lake. Then he excitedly fluttered his new feathers and followed the flying swan closely. He was excited and curious about the planes he was going to see in the flying exam. But he was nervous about the Suicide Point. He asked Eva anxiously, "What is this Suicide Point?"

Eva replied laughingly, "Don't worry. You won't die there."

They landed softly on the top of a cliff, next to a winding river. Rouble was already there, chatting with different birds and their young ones. Siba shouted at him, "What are you doing here? I was looking for you near the lake."

Rouble replied, "Last night, pelicans invited me to the flying exam. They wanted me to share my flying experience with their kids. So I came here to give them a warm-up session." Rouble's reply baffled Siba.

"Do you know how to fly planes? You never told me," Siba asked curiously.

The scarlet macaw became confused as well. "No, when did I say that!"

Eva understood the misunderstanding. She intervened and told Siba, "It's not what you are thinking. The flying exam is for young birds who are going for their first flight."

"Who do you think flies a plane in the forest?" Rouble mocked Siba, "It's a bird thing. Fake birds won't understand it." All the birds laughed.

Eva came forward for Siba's rescue and requested, "Ahem! I think you should share your experience with the nervous kids." Before Siba could open his mouth, she addressed the gathering of the young birds, "Today, we have a special guest among us who learned to fly in just one day even without any prior training or background. Mr. Siba will give you a demo."

Rouble sniggered, "By the way, where are the wings of the recent graduate? Oh, I forgot! Celine ate them."

Siba took Eva's feathers out that he had hidden under his Ultravision belt and smirked, "Don't worry. I got upgraded ones." He fluttered the feathers and showed young kids his flying skills.

As Siba landed, a rooster crowed, "Cock a doodle doo."

Eva said, "Oh! Mr. Rooster has begun the exam. Let's see how many kids will pass today."

Rooster walked to the edge of a big rock protruding beyond the cliff. Young participants formed a line in front of the rock. Most of them were nervous, and a few were panicking, but one little turkey was full of confidence.

Siba asked Eva, "It seems that baby turkey will outperform others. What do you think?"

Eva giggled and whispered in Siba's ear, "Tutu? For sure! That's why humans chose them to represent Thanksgiving."

Rooster announced the eagle's daughter. She anxiously walked to the edge of the Suicide Point. Holding her nerves, she looked down from the cliff and jumped. Everyone fixed their worried gazes at the cliff to see if she would return or not. After a few minutes, she reappeared, fluttering her wings. All the birds cheered. A few nervous youngsters stared in shock, awaiting their turn to perform. Rooster congratulated her for passing the exam.

The tiny son of the hummingbird was next to jump. Without any hesitation, he jumped and returned right away. After him, several other young birds successfully attempted their maiden flights. Toward the end, Rooster announced Tutu, "Your turn, boy."

Eva went closer to the cliff. Siba took a step to follow her, but she stopped him. "Stay here!"

Siba asked, "What's happening?"

Eva replied, "Our confident boy is going to jump. It's because of his family that this place was nicknamed Suicide Point. Don't move!"

Tutu's father yelled, "Go my boy! You can do it this time." Tutu jumped.

Several minutes passed, but Tutu didn't return. Eva murmured, "Not again!" She swooped and dove to the bottom.

The chick was lying face down on a rock, screaming in pain. Siba fluttered his feathers and landed next to them. He noticed that Tutu's leg was broken. The loud screams and agony of the suffering kid traumatized him. He wanted to help, but there was nothing he could do. He felt very sad and helpless.

Eva told Siba, "Move back!"

Siba moved back a few steps. Eva covered Tutu's broken leg with her wings and closed her eyes. After a few minutes, the chick stopped screaming. She opened her eyes and lifted her wings. The broken leg was healed and the chick looked completely normal. Siba's jaw dropped. He couldn't believe what had just happened. Suddenly, the painful feelings inside him turned into amazement. He wondered, "What did you do? How did you fix his broken leg?"

Eva spoke smilingly, "Did you forget? This is the Flow Temple. It's the same energy that flows inside me, you, and him. I transferred some of my energy to heal his leg." She coughed, "Ahem! Ahem! Take him to the top. Others must be worried. I need some time to recover. I'll join you soon."

Siba made a makeshift basket from his shirt and carried the chick in it. Then he whirled the feathers and dropped Tutu at the top.

Tutu asked Siba innocently, "Why were you sad? Did you break your leg too?"

Siba couldn't figure out why he was sad. "No Tutu, I didn't break my leg." It was all he could say with a fake smile covering his turbulent mind.

On seeing his son alive, the turkey wiped his tears. "You made it, son! You made it! It doesn't matter if it was on your own wings or on another's." He hugged his son. "I'm sure, next time you'll make it on your own."

Rooster said to the turkey, "Mr. Turkey, why don't you admit that Tutu can't fly? You already lost your younger brother in his second attempt. You're lucky your son is still alive after three failed attempts."

Turkey said, "I can't fly as I was born with one wing. But my son will fulfill my dream."

"Let him live!" Rooster scoffed. "He better not die while fulfilling your dream."

By that time, Eva reached there. Rooster told her, "Everyone passed but Tutu failed again. Why don't you expel him from the school?"

"He will fail on the day that he stops trying." Eva lifted Tutu's sad face and cheered him up, "Never give up!"

Tutu, with a determined gaze, replied, "I'll try harder next time."

The exam was over and everyone turned to leave. But Tutu's question was still ringing in Siba's head. He couldn't understand that even though he was neither hurt nor in pain, why did he become sad and feel so bad upon seeing the young turkey in distress? Where did his sadness go after Tutu's leg was healed? He tried to run away from these questions by keeping himself busy picking pomberries, but they kept nagging him.

Suddenly, Master Sung Tzu's words rang in his head – "Look within to know beyond." He sat down on a stream bank and closed his eyes. He began analyzing how someone else's suffering could make him feel bad? In his mind's eye, he reviewed the entire episode and analyzed it step by step. He realized that he felt bad as soon as he saw the chick in pain and heard his screams. He figured out that the sympathetic response to another being's distress made him feel that way, as he became happy and was not in distress anymore when Tutu's leg was healed.

After understanding that sympathy made him sad, he went ahead to solve the next piece of the puzzle – how did sympathy work?

After an attentive introspection, he figured out that his subconscious mind was responsible for that. When the images and sounds of the distressed chick entered his mind through his senses, it tried to recognize them by correlating them with his previous stored memories. In that process, the emotional components of the stored memories triggered painful emotions that he felt when those memories were created. So, during the process of understanding the situation, he actually experienced his own emotions attached to similar situations.

Thus, the sad and bad feelings that Siba had felt for the chick were real for the situation, but they were formed from his own previous experiences and not how Tutu was actually feeling at that time. If he had never experienced those feelings before, then he couldn't have correlated to Tutu's situation at all.

The kind of emotional experience one would undergo also depends upon the beliefs one holds for those situations. A particular situation can trigger painful emotions in someone, while in others it may activate hate, anger, motivation, and determination. Siba mused, the emotional response to another being's distress was personal and appeared to vary from person to person. That's why some people can feel sympathy, while some cannot.

He understood that sympathy appraises another person's losses based on the individual's own emotional scale. Evaluation of higher or lower sympathy means one values another person's loss as big or small, respectively. Upon understanding the mystery behind sympathy, Siba opened his eyes and said excitedly to himself, "Now I can answer his question."

"Which question?" Eva asked, appearing on his left side.

Siba shuddered, "You scared the hell out of me. What are you doing here?"

"It should be me who should be asking you this question. What the hell are you doing here?" Eva giggled. "You just vanished after the exam. I was searching for you and found you here, lost in your own world. I didn't feel like disturbing you, so I was waiting by your side."

Siba scratched his head. "I was a little confused. I needed some private time."

"What's the matter? Did you like some chick there?" Eva chuckled, "Just kidding!"

"I was thinking about why I became sad upon seeing Tutu crying in pain?" Siba revealed.

Eva replied, "That's simple, it's because of sympathy. But it's only good for showing affection and concern. It doesn't help in alleviating another person's suffering. You need compassion for that."

Siba asked inquisitively, "You didn't feel sad for him?"

"No," Eva shot a blunt reply. "Instead of feeling sad for him, I felt his pain – the pain he was going through. That's how I found out where to direct the flow of my energy to heal him."

Siba became more curious. "You felt his pain! How?"

"By losing myself and becoming him. Going through his body, his mind, and his feelings, I experienced his pain."

Siba recalled, "My Master told me something similar – to become water."

"Exactly, that's called empathy. You follow others' footsteps and see the journey through their viewpoint." Suddenly, her gaze fell upon Siba's bracelet. She asked, "What happened to your bracelet?"

Siba instantly looked at it and noticed another pearl was glowing with white light. He replied happily, "That must be sympathy."

Eva shrugged with a perplexed look on her face. "Whatever! Let's go back. Your friends are waiting for you." Siba turned back to climb the stream bank. Eva stopped him. "Not that way. Let's take a shortcut." She took him to a huge hanging bridge built from interwoven aerial roots of fig trees. They crossed the valley over the root bridge and arrived at the Heart Lake in no time.

- Chapter 16 -

Pool of Purple Pearls

The dawn sky was still dark. Eva was preening her feathers at the edge of the lake with her head bent downwards. Siba, rubbing his eyes, yawned, "Good morning, Eva."

Eva raised her head, giving him a quick glance. "Good morning, Siba. I was about to wake you up after finishing with my feathers. It's good that you are already up. We need to travel to the far end of the temple."

"So early in the morning? The night is still young. The stars," Siba yawned, "The stars are shining brightly. What's the matter?"

Eva said excitedly, "Purple pearls! Today I'll take you to the Pool of Purple Pearls."

While stretching his arms, Siba looked toward the lake. Steam was rising from its surface and merging into tiny clouds of fog. Suddenly, something caught his attention. He asked curiously, "What's that? A white rainbow?"

Eva looked toward the lake. "Oh, that! It's a moonbow – little brother of a rainbow." She stared at the moon rings and spoke, "Get up and wake your friends. We have a long way to go. Winter is already on its way."

Under the cold, scattered moonlight, the group lazily began their long journey through the dark, leafless oak forest. The clouds of fog floated through the bare woods like aimlessly wandering ghosts. Creaky and spooky sounds made the land of the crooked trees look like a hunting ground of wicked witches. Siba, Celine, and Rouble became scared and huddled together. Eva chuckled, "There's nothing to be afraid of. This is the Flow Temple. Nothing will harm you here." But the three foreigners stuck together until the first ray of the sun hit the horizon.

After a long period of trekking through the wilderness, the tired team arrived at the northern edge of Eva's territory by late afternoon. She led them out of the dry oaks into a small lush green meadow. On one edge, several cascading waterfalls were dropping into a small drop-shaped pool. The pool's shoreline was adorned by a long necklace of purple orchids. Secluded from three sides by towering silver-barked pines, the little natural wonder offered a place of heavenly peace and tranquility.

They were dazzled by the scenic view and rolled down the grassy slopes until they reached the shimmering pool. The relaxing music of the waterfalls and the melodious songs of birds refreshed them, filling them with renewed energy. Siba and Rouble were allured to the sanctuary. Siba removed his shirt and dived into the crystal clear pool. Eva paddled on its serene surface submerging her head under the cold water. Celine joyfully grazed the soft blades of grass around the lake.

After the refreshing break, Eva called, "Siba, come here. We need to collect purple pearls from the bottom of this pool."

Siba refused hesitatingly, "Sorry, I can't breathe underwater."

Rouble teased Siba, "Flutter those feathers and dive."

Eva, controlling her laughter, said, "Feathers won't do. Siba needs snorkel shells."

Siba asked Eva curiously, "What's that?"

Eva replied, "Do you see those pink cone-shaped snail shells next to the orchids? Pick two of them." Siba obeyed and picked two big shells. Eva instructed again, "Not the big ones. Pick smaller shells that can fit perfectly inside your nostrils. Then you can breathe underwater."

Siba picked another two smaller cone-shaped shells and inserted them inside his nostrils. He grunted, "I can't breathe."

Eva chuckled, "Make a hole in them first."

Siba did accordingly. "Ah! I can breathe now."

Eva grinned, "With them, you can breathe anywhere." She plucked two big pitcher-shaped leaves from a nearby pitcher plant and gave one to Siba for collecting pearls.

Siba dived into the Pool of Purple Pearls. To his surprise, he was breathing comfortably underwater. He swam alongside fish and collected purple pearls from the bottom of the pool. He quickly filled his pitcher and went out to get more pitcher-shaped leaves. After filling several pitchers, Eva told him, "That should be enough for the winter. Let's go back."

Siba and Eva emerged to the surface triumphantly. Siba placed his snorkel shells under the folds of the Ultravision belt, alongside his feathers. Suddenly, a snowshoe hare hopped from the silver pines toward Siba. The hare was badly wounded as if someone had been hunting him. His whole body was bleeding and shaking in fear. Siba lifted him to soothe his tremors, but it didn't work.

Siba requested Eva, "Oh, my God! This poor little creature is so badly injured. Can you please heal his wounds?"

Eva refused, "This hare doesn't belong to the Flow Temple. He's from the Silver Forest. Those silver trees don't fall under my dominion. I'm sorry. I can't help him. Moreover, we don't interfere with the creatures of the Silver Forest, and they don't disturb our peace. It'd be better if we leave him there."

Siba persuaded, "But he's innocent."

"Leave him there. Don't feel bad. He's going to die from his wounds anyway."

Hare's heartbeat increased, and he succumbed to his wounds in Siba's hands. Siba became very sad. He laid down the hare's lifeless body in the Silver Forest. With a heavy heart, he picked the pitchers that he had filled earlier with pearls and called, "Rouble! Celine! Come, let's go back." But only Rouble came. Celine wasn't there. He yelled again, "Celine, grazing time is over. We need to return." But again, there was no response. Celine was missing.

Eva also looked around and asked, "Where did she go?"

Siba replied worriedly, "I don't know. Rouble, do you know where Celine is?"

Rouble recollected, "Last time I saw her, she was grazing on the other side of the waterfall."

They swiftly retraced their steps to the other side of the waterfall and found Celine's hoof prints on the wet ground going into the Silver Forest. They followed the hoof prints, and behind a tall silver pine, they found her unconscious and severely wounded body. Celine's gut was cut open as if someone had slashed her belly with a big knife. On seeing the horrific scene, Rouble fainted.

Already grieving from the tragic demise of the hare, Siba broke down completely upon seeing his beloved sheep fatally wounded. Unable to bear the gruesome pain, his soul shattered into a thousand pieces. Streams of painful tears gushed from his eyes. On his knees and with folded hands, he sobbingly begged before Eva, "Please, save my Celine. You said earlier that the creatures of the Silver Forest don't disturb your peace. Then why did they attack my Celine."

Eva replied calmly, "Because Celine doesn't belong to the Flow Temple." After a pause, she said, "Alright, move back."

Siba wiped streams of tears from his face and moved back. Eva covered Celine's entire body with her wings and closed her eyes. In a few minutes, rays of white light emerged from Eva's wings and entered into Celine's body. After a few moments, the sheep open her eyes and bleated, "Baaa."

On hearing Celine's bleat, Rouble returned to his senses and exclaimed, "I can't believe it. She's alive."

Siba, with a budding smile, wiped his tears. "Thank you, Eva. Thank you so much."

Celine stood up with a jerk. She was perfectly healthy, but the wound had left a big crescent-shaped scar on her belly.

Eva got up with difficulty. Her body was very weak. She staggered and said in a feeble voice, "Take me to the pool." Siba picked Eva up gently and walked her to the pool. He laid her in the water. She swallowed several purple pearls and rested in the shallow water with her eyes closed. After some time, she opened her eyes and told Siba, "It'll take a few days for me to recover. I won't be able to fly or do any work. In the meantime, you'll have to perform my duties. Can you do that?"

With folded hands, Siba replied, "I'll do whatever you say."

The next morning, Eva was feeling a little better. But she was still far from being able to fly. She swallowed one more purple pearl to regain more of her lost strength.

Siba inquired, "How are you feeling now? You look better than yesterday."

"Yes, a little better," Eva groaned.

Twisting and hopping, Siba said, "Something is strange about this place. I feel energized as if electricity is running through me."

"I can see that. The water of this pool has magical qualities. Ancient people named this waterfall – the Fountain of Youth." Eva smiled. "Are you ready to perform my duties?"

Siba bowed and replied, "At your service. Tell me what you want me to do?"

Eva instructed, "I want you to collect the resin of slumber trees."

"Alrighty! Where do I find these slumber trees?"

"Do you remember those giant trees near One Mile Waterfall? They are slumber trees. They sleep for hundreds of years. Their flowers release a fluid that hardens as a resin. I want you to collect those solid lumps."

Siba plucked several pitcher leaves of the pitcher plants and flew toward the slumber trees. After arriving at the top of One Mile Waterfall, he hovered above it and watched the majestic waterfall to his heart's content. Still hovering above it, he remembered the last time's miracle. He wondered if he let himself loose, would Flow take good care of him again or not. He hesitatingly felt like repeating the last time's great jump.

Siba landed on the edge of the waterfall and looked down nervously at the gushing water. He inhaled deeply and jumped. But as he was in mid-air, free-falling through the mist clouds, his fear disappeared, and he felt a unique calmness. He felt as if the waterfall was talking to him and saying, "Welcome home, my little drop." All the water which was gushing ahead of him earlier was now falling along his side, like a companion. Soon he felt as if he was not a boy who was falling through the waterfall but was the waterfall itself, smoothly flowing down its course. And in the end, just like all the other drops of water, he merged into the plunge pool.

Again at the bottom of the waterfall, Siba didn't struggle and allowed Flow to take him wherever it wanted. Like a log of wood, he passed through several rapids and whirlpools. And finally, his adventure ride ended on a river bank.

Siba took his feathers out exuberantly and flew toward the giant slumber trees. He playfully hopped from tree to tree and collected amber-colored resin lumps from their top branches. Pretty soon, his pitchers were full. He flew happily alongside the waterfall, saying goodbye, and proudly brought the resin to Eva.

After a few days, Eva fully recovered. With renewed vigor, she spread her wings and flew up into the sky. Siba thanked God upon seeing her flying again. He asked her, "Can I also become a part of Flow, just like you?"

Eva replied, "You are already a part of Flow."

"What do you mean?" Siba asked, furrowing his brow.

"The art of letting go has made you a part of Flow," Eva responded with a smile, "The choice was yours to make, and you made it wisely. When you jumped for the second time in the One Mile Waterfall, you chose to surrender over struggle. You surrendered yourself, and Flow embraced you."

"Eva, I don't understand riddles. Please tell me in simple words."

"Hmm, how should I say this? Okay, listen! Your hands, eyes, legs, and all other body parts work together as one body. Imagine if each one of those body parts starts working for their own good. You'd be in a big chaos. In the same way, we're also a part of Flow. Flow always has its own plans for us. It's we who don't align ourselves with its greater cause. When we become selfish, we become a hindrance to it. Flow is always flowing, irrespective of our choice. Thus, it's up to us to follow its command and become a part of it, or resist it and perish."

"Hmm! Flow works in a very mysterious way. Do you know about its working process?"

Eva explained, "Flow is energy in continuous motion. When energy is stagnant, nothing exists. It's only when energy flows that time, space, and everything else comes into existence."

Siba confirmed, "You mean the same energy that can neither be created nor be destroyed?"

"Yes, the same one. That's why I was able to transfer my energy to your sheep and regained it later from the purple pearls. Normally, one pearl is enough to sustain life for a few months. I lost a lot of energy, so I needed to consume several pearls to regain my strength."

While they were talking, a gust of cold wind blew from the north. They both looked to the skies. Several dark clouds flew toward them and soon, snow flurries swirled through the air. Siba shivered. Eva nudged him. "You must be feeling cold. Your clothes are not good for winter. Let me fetch something warm for you."

Eva flew away and returned with a black leather armor decorated with big pointed scales. Siba opened the suit and adorned it quickly. "Thank you, Eva. It's very beautiful."

"And warm too," Eva added quickly. "Winter is back. It's time for the animals to go into hibernation. We must prepare them for their winter sleep." She gave Siba two pitchers, one filled with purple pearls and the other filled with slumber resins. She also grabbed one each for herself.

"What should I do with them?"

Eva instructed, "First, feed one pearl to every animal. It will provide them energy during hibernation. Then rub this resin on their noses to put them to sleep for the entire winter." They both flew with their pitchers and started nannying the animals. While feeding the pearls and applying the resin, Eva sang the song of sleep.

"Winds from north, snow from seas.
Birds and leaves have left the trees.
Close your eyes, dream so deep.
O my friends, it's time to sleep."

With the strong pine scent of resin and the song of sleep, the animals went into hibernation.

Ω

Siba woke up inside a crevice. His body was buried under the furry arm of a sleeping grizzly bear. He carefully lifted the grizzly's arm and crawled quietly out of the bear's den. Outside, the snow was melting into the soggy soil. Siba scratched his head and tried to recall how he ended up there. But he couldn't remember anything. Unable to figure out the mystery, he took his feathers out and flew above the bare oak trees to look for Eva. After hovering above the bare forest for some time, he spotted Eva. She was sitting next to a dead raccoon. "Aha! There you are," he shouted from the sky and dived straight down to her.

Eva asked him, "How are you feeling, refreshed or dizzy?"

"A little absent-minded," Siba replied. "I can't remember what happened yesterday. The last thing I remember, we were singing the song of sleep. But how I fell asleep in a bear's den, I can't recall that."

Eva chortled, "At the end of the song, you smelled the resin and went into hibernation. Don't you remember that?"

"I went into hibernation! What do you mean?"

"Winter is over, my boy! It's springtime!" Eva giggled. She touched the dead raccoon with her wings, and it turned into bright-blue butterflies. They fluttered their gleaming wings and spread throughout the forest as harbingers of spring.

"Wow! What a miracle!" Siba exclaimed, staring at the dazzling butterflies wondrously.

"No, that's Flow. Remember, the energy can be transferred from one form to another."

"Can I do that too?" Siba asked eagerly.

"Yes, you can, with compassion and the blessings of Flow. But the first step to compassion is to be empathetic. You should feel the way others feel and think the way others think."

Siba avowed cheerfully, "Ok, I will."

"Alright, that's enough talking. I'm very busy. It's springtime, and I have so many things to do." Eva hurriedly moved closer to a fallen tree trunk and touched it gently. The dead tree turned into a bunch of beautiful tulips.

Eva told Siba, "It's time for the spring song." She started humming the spring song and flew through the forest.

"O spring! O spring!
It's time to sing.
Return back to where you belong.
Let's all sing the beautiful spring song."

Wherever Eva saw any dead tree or animal, she turned them into flowers and butterflies. Upon hearing her song, the animals woke up from hibernation. New leaves began appearing on dry branches. Fresh green blades of grasses emerged from the ground. Creepers and climbers sprawled over the forest floor and tree trunks. The entire forest blossomed with beautiful flowers and their exotic fragrances filled the air. Birds returned to their nests and began singing along with Eva. Butterflies, ladybugs, and hummingbirds danced to the spring song. Siba flew next to Eva, rejoicing and enjoying the warm sun rays and the beauty of spring.

- Chapter 17 -

Spring Popping Festival

Gazing at the star-studded midnight sky, Siba took his feathers and snorkel shells out of the Ultravision's folds. He inserted the shells in his nostrils and flew toward the sky. He passed the wandering clouds and moved out of the earth's atmosphere. After entering space, he paused and looked at the Pole Star. Then he flew toward it and quickly crossed Mars, Jupiter, and eventually, the entire solar system. After going deep into space, Siba looked back. The Milky Way was spinning like a vortex around its bright, foggy core. He got mesmerized by the grand view.

Suddenly, a voice came from the core of the spinning galaxy, "What are you doing in space?"

"I'm going to the Pole Star," Siba replied. "Who are you?"

The voice came again, "I am Flow. These stars, their planets, and all creatures living on them are part of me."

Siba became confused. "I thought only the creatures of the Flow Temple were part of you, and lately, I also became your part when I jumped from the waterfall."

"You and everyone else are already part of me. It's only when you try to go against me and struggle that you feel you are not part of me."

"If I am part of you, why can't I perform magic like Eva?"

"It's not magic, it's a sacrifice. If you are willing to sacrifice your share for others, then make an earnest request to me. I'll transfer myself from you to others."

Elated Siba bid adieu, "Thank you. I'll pray to you when I need your help."

As Siba turned around to continue his journey, instead of the Pole Star, Tina was standing there, spinning her glowing tail with her hand. She said, "Wake up, Siba. I want to show you something."

Siba said, "No, I don't want to get up."

"Get up, Siba," Tina said again.

Siba opened his eyes. Eva was in front of him, saying, "Get up, I want to show you something."

With half-opened eyes, Siba looked around. It was the middle of the night. The stars were twinkling, and the full moon was illuminating the night sky. Eva said excitedly, "This is the moment we all have been waiting for. Today is the Spring Popping Festival. Under the full moon, the mushpillers will emerge from the ground. Follow me to see the magic."

Siba yawned and rubbed his eyes. He lazily took Eva's feathers out and followed her to the top of the hollow strangler fig tree. Eva picked up one of the stored pomberries and checked it. The white spots of fruit had turned black. She threw it into the Heart Lake and said excitedly, "Just watch now!"

Within a few minutes, white glowing mushrooms started popping up around the lake. Soon, the entire shoreline was glowing with candle-like mushrooms. Siba was spellbound by the magnificent view. He exclaimed, "Wow! These glowing mushrooms look like a sparkling necklace around the Heart Lake."

Eva spoke cheerfully, "Yes, we call it Heartbeat!"

In the next few minutes, the entire forest floor lit up with glowing mushrooms. Soon after that, they began rocking and crawling toward the lake like caterpillars and finally, submerging under its water. Eva cheered excitedly, "Look! Mushpillars are migrating."

Siba wondered, "I understand now, why you call them mushpillars." Eva smiled. Siba said jubilantly, "No wonder, you've been waiting for this grand magical moment for so long. It appears the entire forest floor is draining into the lake."

Animals, birds, and all other creatures of the Flow Temple followed the migrating mushpillars and assembled around the Heart Lake. As more and more of those glowing creatures entered the lake, the lake began to glow. By the time all mushpillars entered the lake, it was glowing fully. Then, from the top of the strangler fig, Eva addressed the gathering, "Hello friends! This is the moment, we've been waiting for. Finally after one year, our wait is over. I welcome you to our amazing Spring Popping Festival."

The crowd cheered. Flying squirrels made holes at the base of the strangler fig and round pomberries rolled down into the lake. Slowly, the glowing lights in the lake faded away.

Siba asked Eva worriedly, "What's happening to the mushpillars? Are they dying?"

"No, they are eating the fermented pomberries and transforming into mushpops. With the first rays of the sun, they'll emerge above the surface of the lake to dry their wings and then, live their lives until the sun sets."

Just then, the sun emerged from the east, and its warm welcoming rays fell upon the lake. Several minutes later, tiny winged creatures emerged onto the surface of the lake. Their curved, cylindrical bodies were covered with stripes of different colors, unique to each mushpop. They had four long transparent wings which were displaying holographic patterns under the sunlight. They each had one big, round eye in place of their face, which was shining like a mirror. With six thin, long, black legs, they were comfortably walking on the surface of the water as if it was just a fluffy mattress. Soon, the entire lake surface got covered with the buzzing mushpops, and it seemed like millions of tiny winged rainbows were dancing on the surface of the lake.

Siba said, "They must be very sad. I feel sorry for these colorful bugs that they are going to live only for a day."

Eva stared at Siba. "No, you should not. Who told you they're feeling bad about their life? Go and live their life for a day. Then you'll understand the beauty and happiness that life offers in one day, which we don't recognize. If lived well, one day is enough. I wish I had a life like them – to live for a day, which feels like you have lived forever."

Siba apologized, "I'm sorry. I shouldn't have judged. You are right. I don't know how they feel. I was looking from my viewpoint. I should have looked at life from their viewpoint."

"That's right! Everything changes when you change your viewpoint. Make sure to choose the right viewpoint when you analyze anything. When we don't consider others' viewpoints and think that only our viewpoint is correct, it leads to misunderstandings, which are the root cause of disputes. So try to see the world through others' eyes as well," Eva pointed. She took him to the shoreline to watch them more closely.

One mushpop spoke to Siba, "Why are you standing there? Join our Swarm Carnival." Siba looked at Eva, seeking her permission. She nodded smilingly.

Siba entered the chest-deep water with his arms spread out. The mushpops playfully climbed on his arms and head. The excited bugs were busy interacting with each other. Siba tried to catch multiple conversations from their buzzing hustle and bustle.

"What's your name?"

"My name is Joy."

"I'm Happy."

"I told you, it's Hope."

"Carol, nice to meet you."

Amidst all sorts of buzzing voices, one mushpop flew and sat on Siba's nose. He curiously stared into Siba's eyes, one after the other.

Siba asked him, "What's your name?"

Still staring into Siba's eyes, the mushpop replied, "Only One."

"What kind of name is that?" Siba twitched.

The mushpop buzzed, "You have two eyes. I have only one. So, I'm Only One. But you can call me O O."

Siba giggled, "Ok! Mr. O O! How do you feel after coming into this world?"

O O replied, "Actually, I feel very blessed that I got this life. A chance to see this beautiful world, blue sky, white clouds, green plants, amazing animals, colorful birds, and more than anything else, lots of mushpops. I'm so lucky, luckier than those mushpillers who didn't get a chance to become mushpops. I'm so happy. Wait, should I change my name to Happy?"

Another mushpop shouted, "Already taken."

"Never mind, Only One is good too," O O said loudly to the other mushpop. "Moreover, to be happy, all you need is an open mind and a big heart. And I have both."

Siba chuckled, "I'm luckier than you. I got a chance to meet you – the most amazing creature in the entire world. Can we be friends?"

"Of course, there's no time to say no. Everyone is welcome to join our life, our celebration, our joy, and most importantly, our family. There's no place for judgment or prejudice in a mushpop's life."

Suddenly, the swarm clouds of mushpops rose and spread over the surrounding trees. O O fluttered his wings and hovered in front of Siba. "Let's go and explore the beauty of this wonderful place." O O made a short flight before crashing into the velvety petals of a tulip garden. Siba was closely following him. The curious mushpop asked Siba, "What's this soft thing? It smells so good."

Siba replied casually, "Oh! That one? That's just a tulip. Let's go, I'll show you amazing things."

O O gave a stern look and said, "It's not just a tulip. It's The Tulip. You might know what it is, but I don't know. Everything is new for me."

Suddenly, Eva's words echoed in Siba's mind – "try to see the world through others' eyes." Instantly, time froze for him, and he forgot that he was Siba. He imagined himself to be a mushpop who was born just a little while ago. He realized that he knew nothing. A fresh energy of curiosity gushed inside him, and he looked at everything from a completely different perspective.

With a brand new outlook, Siba felt the same way about the world as the mushpops were feeling – excited and curious about everything and marveling at the wonders of nature. He wanted to explore and learn everything the way it was, without the filters of prejudices and beliefs. He could feel the same emotional currents that were running inside the mushpops. After attaining the same mindset, he was able to read O O's thoughts and predict his behavior. As Siba understood empathy, another pearl of his Golden Bracelet lit up, radiating peach-colored light.

Poking his head out of the tulip, Only One asked, "My friend, you didn't tell me your name."

"My name is Siba, and you can call me Siba," Siba chuckled.

"What? Making fun of me?" O O buzzed.

"No," Siba chuckled. "Let's go! I want to introduce you to my friends." He took the mushpop to Rouble and Celine who were enjoying the Voodoo Dance of peacocks. A group of peacocks was dancing in a wide circle with their iridescent blue-green tail feathers spread as big fans. At the center of the circle, some mushpops were trying to imitate their twirling dance moves. Siba and Only One also stood there to watch their enchanting dance performance.

Standing on Siba's shoulder, O O asked him, "Who are these birds with beautiful feathers?"

The peacock's leader, dancing next to them, spoke, "We are peacocks – king of the birds! What do your wings tell you?" Only One and Siba looked at each other, confused. The peacock spoke again while spreading his tail feathers to make a fan, "Spread your wings like this and shake them."

Only One did accordingly. To their surprise, under the sunlight, O O's holographic wings displayed an erupting volcano. The peacock rolled his eyeballs up and prophesized to Siba, "Your life on earth will end in a volcano."

"What? What do you mean?" Siba asked, giving a perplexed look.

The peacock told Siba, "The mushpops make only one friend and their holograms show the last moments of their friends on earth. In a way, mushpops give a warning to their friends as a token of their friendship. Your friend's wings showed a volcano, so you'll die in a volcano. Stay as far away from volcanoes as possible." The peacock joined his dancing group and began prophesying about other mushpops' holograms.

Siba took it lightly and joked with Rouble, "Did your mushpop tell you where you'll die?"

Rouble replied, "No one made me a friend yet."

Just then, a group of wicked ravens interrupted their celebration. One big, fat raven yelled, "Party time, folks! Happy feast to all!" Savage ravens attacked the mushpops. All mushpops flew here and there for their lives.

One old peacock shouted, "Don't kill them! The feast is after sunset."

The fat raven bullied the old peacock, "We feast when we are hungry. And we are hungry, now." The ravens continued pecking the helpless mushpops more voraciously.

Siba looked for Only One but couldn't find him. The worried boy searched all around, but his little friend was nowhere. Grief-stricken, he sat on a rock with his head down on his knees.

"Did they leave?" Only One's voice came from above.

Siba looked up at once and checked his surroundings but couldn't see him. He whispered, "O O, where are you?"

The tiny mushpop emerged from Siba's long messy hair and walked down from his head to his nose. Staring into Siba's eyes, he said, "Here I am." Siba's face lit up with happiness on seeing his new friend safe and sound.

Several mushpops, riding various birds and animals, stopped in front of Only One. One mushpop, riding a hoopoe, asked O O, "Did you make anyone your buddy?"

Pointing toward Siba, O O replied, "He's my buddy."

"Cool! You're eligible to join the race – Ride Your Buddy. Do you want to participate?"

Only One cheered, "Oh yeah! I'd love to."

"Come on then. The race is going to begin soon."

Siba placed O O on his head and followed them. They arrived at the Suicide Point. There, Eva was already addressing the gathering. She shouted, "Are you having a good time?"

The crowd cheered loudly, "Yeah!"

Eva shouted again, "I didn't hear."

The crowd cheered more loudly, "Yeaaahhhh!"

Eva spoke loudly, "Now it sounds like fun. Alright! All participants will follow the winding Snake River, and the race will finish behind those twin mountains in the Valley of Flowers. Those who don't have a buddy can go there directly. They don't have to follow the river. Are you ready to ride your buddy?" The crowd roared.

The rooster crowed loudly to signal the beginning of the race, "Cock a doodle doo."

With mushpops on their backs, the participating birds flew above the river, whereas animals raced along its banks. Siba also ran along the meandering river. After passing through the dense grooves, crossing gorges, hiking hills, and climbing waterfalls, finally through a narrow pass, they arrived at the Valley of Flowers.

It was a big lush green meadow carpeted with exotic alpine flowers. The cool refreshing breeze was loaded with exotic fragrances of jasmine, daisy, buttercup, primrose, marigold, orchids, and poppies. Honeybees and butterflies were humming and collecting nectar from the wildflowers. The enclosed valley was guarded by mighty peaks from all sides and several white clouds were resting leisurely near its edges. A small pool in its middle was the cherry on the cake and elegant white swans were swimming in its shimmering water.

Eva was the first one to reach there. She landed in the pool next to the other swans. Shortly after her, others began to arrive there as well. Pretty soon, the splendid valley was teeming with birds, animals, and mushpops. Siba, confident about Eva's victory, congratulated her, "Congrats! You made it."

Eva asked, "For what?"

"For winning the race."

Eva said calmly, "Everyone, who completes the race, is a winner. That's how it works here; otherwise, the birds will obviously win all the time."

Only One poked his head out of Siba's hair. His gaze fell upon another stunning mushpop riding on Eva's back. He asked her, "Hello beautiful, what's your name?"

The other mushpop replied shyly, "Achoo."

O O asked, "Achoo? Why did you pick that name?"

"Achoo!" She sneezed. "I'm allergic to everything. That's why. What's your name?" She sneezed again.

"My name is Only One, as I've only one eye."

"What's special about it? Achoo!" She sneezed. "I too have one eye."

"Yeah, but my buddy has two eyes. That's why. Would you like to be my dance partner?"

Achoo asked nervously, "Me?"

"Yes, I like the way you sneeze."

Siba muttered, "Seriously? Is that your pick-up line?"

O O whispered, "Shut up! I'm not a pro. It's my first date. I'm already very nervous." He flew from Siba's head and hovered above her, offering his hand. Achoo nervously held his hand. He pulled her closer to him and joined other dancing mushpop couples. Siba and Eva waved at them cheerfully.

Eva shrieked, "Oh, I forgot to introduce you to my family." She introduced Siba to the swans in the pool. In the meantime, Celine and Rouble also arrived there.

Eva welcomed them, "Are you enjoying our festival?"

Celine bleated joyfully, "Baaa."

"Thank you, Eva, for inviting us to join this wonderful festival," said Rouble.

Eva smiled and revealed, "The best is yet to come. Where's your buddy?"

Rouble frowned, "No one wants to be my buddy."

Siba laughed and consoled, "Don't be sad. You've got me."

"But you can't show me my last moments on earth. I wanted to see how I'll die."

"Why are you worried? You won't die before me," Siba joked.

"What if I do?" Rouble uttered seriously. At once, Siba's face turned silent and grim.

Eva coughed to break the silence. "Siba, why don't you go and ask O O to find a buddy for Rouble?"

"Good idea!" Siba looked around. "O O and Achoo were right there. Where did they go?"

Eva guessed, "They must be somewhere inside the forest, looking for a safe place to lay their eggs. Don't worry. They'll come back for their final dance – the Dance of Romance. I have to meet others. You enjoy the festival." She flew to welcome other arriving teams.

Siba heard some familiar screams. He followed them, and to his surprise, he found Tutu getting his leg stung by a bunch of wasps. Siba giggled at the chick's funny facial expressions.

"Don't laugh at my son. Can't you see how bravely he's enduring the pain?" Tutu's father shouted.

Siba hid his giggle behind his hand. "Yes, sir. I can see. But what is he doing?"

"Are you blind? Can't you see my son has a buddy? He's getting a friendship tattoo."

"Tattoo from wasps?" Siba wondered.

Tutu's father scowled, "From who else? Butterflies?"

Siba blushed, "I meant, why is he getting a friendship tattoo from wasps?"

"When you make your first buddy, you get a tattoo as a souvenir. Don't you have any buddy yet?" the turkey asked.

Siba replied, "I do."

"Then why are you staring at my face. Stand in the queue, and wait for your turn."

Siba looked around. "Which queue?"

The turkey pointed behind him. "This queue! I am the queue. Idiot!"

Siba stood behind the turkey and murmured, "Wait for Thanksgiving."

The turkey glared, "What did you say?"

"I said I want to thank you for giving me this piece of information." Siba refrained from any further conversation with him. After the turkeys left, Siba got a nice tattoo of O O on his hand. He went looking for Rouble to show him his tattoo. Rouble was learning to paddle on the water from the swans. Siba, with his arm in the air, yelled from the edge of the pool, "Rouble, look what I've got."

"What is it?" Rouble tried to look with a raised head.

Siba shouted, "Come here." The scarlet macaw paddled to him. Siba showed him his hand excitedly. "I got a tattoo. My first tattoo."

"It's beautiful! Is it O O?"

"Yes," Siba replied smilingly. "Where are O O and Achoo? Most of the mushpops have returned. Don't you think they should have returned by now?"

"Maybe they want to enjoy more private moments," Rouble suggested.

Siba hinted, "Or maybe they're in trouble. Let's go and find them."

"Hmmm, maybe. But where shall we look for your tiny friend in this vast forest?"

"Let me think." Siba closed his eyes and employed his recently learned skill – empathy. He imagined himself to be Only One and began to think and feel like him. Based on the places that O O had been since he emerged from the lake, Siba pondered over the best place where he could have taken Achoo. After a little contemplation, Siba opened his eyes. "Follow me," he said to Rouble. Both of them flew to the tulips garden but their tiny friends were not there.

Rouble inquired, "Where are they?"

"Shh!" Siba hushed, "Be quiet! Listen!"

They heard boisterous caws at a distance. "Ravens!" both shouted.

Siba raced toward them at once, grabbing some stones on his way. He pelted stones at the commotion of ravens around a hole in the ground. Few of them were digging the hole with their sharp claws and pointed beaks. Two ravens flew toward Siba to attack him. But Rouble saved him just in time by crashing into them. Siba broke a dry branch and wielded it like a sword. All the ravens fled away cawing.

When Siba went near the hole, he spotted one broken wing of a mushpop. He yelled anxiously, "O O! Achoo! Are you here?" He heard Achoo's sneeze from inside the hole. She came out of the hole, dragging injured Only One.

Siba picked up O O and his broken wing. Filled with anger and pain, he uttered, "I won't leave those filthy bastards. They will meet a gruesome death."

Only One groaned, "Leave them, my friend! Don't fill your heart with anger and revenge. Mushpops never hold grudges and resentments. Ravens had no personal enmity with me. I'm mere food for them. Forgive them, my friend! Life is too short to be hateful. Instead, spend your time with me – with love, joy, and happiness."

Siba controlled his anger but was still very distressed. Only One told Achoo, "My love, find another dance partner for you. I'm sorry. I won't be able to dance with a broken wing." Upon hearing that, tears came to everyone's eyes.

Achoo sniffled, "I don't care about the dance. We have only a few hours left. I want to spend them in your arms." All became very sad and emotional.

Siba paused for a moment and thought about why he was feeling sad. He didn't have to be sympathetic. Eva had already told him that sympathy doesn't help. If he really wanted to help O O, he would need to develop compassion for that. His mind calmed down at once, and he closed his eyes. Devoid of his own sympathetic feelings, he empathetically focused on how O O was actually feeling inside. To his surprise, he not only felt his tiny friend's physical pain but also realized that the emotional pain of not being able to perform his final dance with his beloved was far more painful than the tremendous pain of the injury. This realization jolted Siba to his core.

Siba took that pain and suffering to be his own. He understood the difference between sympathy and compassion.

Earlier, under sympathy, he was feeling sad at his friend's suffering and was thinking how the tiny little creature would come out of that great tragedy. But once he accepted Only One's suffering to be his own, he himself was feeling that great emotional suffering and physical pain. Now his mind was focused on what he could do to alleviate his friend's sufferings, and that was true compassion.

Siba realized compassion is not just the ability to feel and take others' sufferings to be his own but sticking to that pain and feeling it until it is released. Therefore, once a person owns another's suffering, it keeps on hurting him and that motivates him to get rid of it by taking necessary actions. And as the source of the pain and suffering is not his own loss but the loss of the actual sufferer, he can get rid of it only by helping the real sufferer.

After this great realization, suddenly, a spring of energy oozed from his heart and clouded his mind's eye. The cloud of energy in his mind churned and turned into a galaxy that he had seen in his dream. Suddenly, Flow's voice echoed in his mind, "You impressed me with your compassion. Tell me, what do you want?"

Siba requested, "I want to help my friend. Can you please heal his injuries so that he can relish the last moments of his life?"

"I can do that, but are you willing to pay the price? Are you prepared for the sacrifice?"

"Yes, I am," Siba replied confidently.

The rotating galaxy turned back into a cloud of fog and vanished. Siba opened his eyes. To his wonder, the broken wing of O O was attached to his body, and he was perfectly hale and hearty.

Rouble pointed, "Siba, your bracelet!"

Siba looked at the glowing pink pearl. "That's compassion," he smiled gently.

Only One flew from Siba's hand. Achoo joined him as well. Siba tried to get up but couldn't. He felt very tired and weak. Only One, hovering above him, asked, "What happened to you?"

Siba lied, "Nothing, my friend. I ran everywhere looking for you. So I got a little tired. I'll be fine after some rest."

After a brief rest, Siba and all his friends flew back to the Valley of Flowers. There, mushpops were swarming and getting ready for their final dance – the Dance of Romance. The sun was heading toward the horizon. Mushpop couples were holding each other's hands, which they were supposed to hold till the end of the dance. O O merrily held Achoo's hand and flew toward the swarm.

Every eye was on the sun. As it touched the horizon, the long-awaited dance began. The swarm rose and covered the sky like a giant floating blanket. Suddenly, the blanket melted and the mushpops dropped from the sky like shooting stars. Just before hitting the ground, they flew up again to form a giant revolving donut. It marked the beginning of their dance.

Millions of tiny mushpops twisted and turned, and changed directions and patterns almost instantaneously. One moment, they formed twinkling stars, the next, they swirled like tornadoes. From flowing waves to slithering snakes, they formed several beautiful formations while dancing in the sky. Awestruck spectators watched the amazing dance without blinking their eyes.

When half of the sun slipped below the horizon, they formed a giant circle. Slowly, the circle started revolving, and its speed kept on increasing. Mushpops who couldn't maintain the increasing speed got tossed out, and the size of the circle began to shrink until only one couple remained. Above that victorious couple, other mushpops formed a circular disc by holding each other's hands, and their flapping wings formed a giant hologram.

Eva flew to that couple to congratulate them. She announced loudly, "This year's prince and princess are Only One and Achoo." The giant hologram displayed the winning couple, hugging and rubbing their eyes. Everyone cheered. Siba whistled. Eva landed back on the ground next to the whistling boy.

O O and Achoo rose to join the other mushpops. The hologram disc broke into individual couples. As the sun dipped below the horizon, all the mushpops soared up to stay in the vanishing sunlight. Just as they missed the last rays of the sun, their tiny bodies exploded with popping sounds and colorful lights, displaying one of the most spectacular fireworks Siba had ever seen. Their popped heads fell from the sky like rain, and shortly after that, their transparent wings glided down like snowflakes.

While everyone else was cheering and shouting with joy, appalled Siba froze with shock. In an instant, the world turned upside down for him, and the frenzied festivity changed into doom. He couldn't believe what he just witnessed – a holocaust. But that's what it was – the Spring Popping Festival.

The cheering crowd feasted happily upon the popped heads that looked like popcorn. Siba found himself completely alienated from everyone else who were busy gorging themselves. Frozen in time, he just kept on watching others like a statue. Suddenly, the familiar voice of Eva brought him back to his senses. "Hey, Siba! Why are you not eating? Enjoy the delicious feast of the Spring Popping Festival."

Siba was momentarily startled by Eva's behavior. He responded, "So many mushpops died in front of your eyes, don't you feel anything? O O died, Achoo died, all of them died right here! How can you celebrate their deaths? How can you even think of eating them? Don't you have a heart?"

Eva confronted him, "Siba! This is the true nature of existence. Life and death are two sides of the same coin. Every beginning has an end, and every end leads to a new beginning. Embrace it, the way it is. Always remember, nothing takes birth, nothing dies. It's the same energy that transforms from one form to another."

Siba wasn't impressed with her answer. With narrowed brows and a wrinkled nose, he still kept staring at her with dissatisfaction.

Eva continued, "Different forms take shape from the perpetual flow of energy, and in the end, they dissolve back into it. The dead leaves turned into mushpillars, mushpillars into mushpops, mushpops into animals, plants, you, and me. And when we die, we will turn into mushpillars. Then, there will be new mushpops, another Spring Popping Festival, and another Dance of Romance. This is how the cycle keeps on going. If the cycle stops, the flow of life will stop."

Siba cooled down a bit. His little mind was busy assimilating this deepest secret of the Flow Temple. He understood that his life was just a tiny fraction of this perpetual cycle, and there was nothing to grieve about.

Eva spoke with a smile, "Cherish this amazing marvel of nature. Make this wonderful moment a sweet part of your memory. Appreciate these amazing creatures that remind us how short our lives are, and how we should live it with love, joy, and happiness. Thank them for teaching us how we should live each day of our life as if it was our last."

Siba's eyes gleamed and his face blossomed. He sighed, "Yes, we should."

With a charming smile, Eva said, "I'd say, you should eat a few popped heads and make them part of you. Moreover, they're delicious as well."

Siba picked one popped head and placed it in his mouth. "Mmm! Yummy! It just melted on my tongue." He savored another one. "Thank you, Eva, for enlightening me with your wisdom. Now I have a complete understanding of the real meaning of Flow."

Eva spoke softly, "You are welcome." They picked more popped heads and ate them graciously until their bellies were full and slept soundly on the forest floor.

When the sun rose, Siba thanked Eva, "I don't have any words to express my gratitude for your generosity, and what you did for me and my friends. Thank you for sharing your world with me. I want to spend more time with you, but my journey is waiting for me. I must take my leave now."

Eva replied, "I must admit, you have learned a lot in such a short time. There's nothing more for me to teach you. You have become a part of Flow. Now, Flow will take care of you." She gave him one pitcher full of purple pearls and several lumps of slumber resins. "Keep it. You may need them for your journey."

Siba's eyes became wet. He kept the gifts inside the pockets of his black leather armor and hugged her. "Thank you, Eva. Thank you so much."

Turning her head toward the north, Eva said, "You better move fast. Try to cross the Snow Mountains before winter falls. The dangers lurking there are nothing compared to the ruthless cold of its winter. And when you cross the Pool of

Purple Pearls, grab some extra snorkel shells for you and your friends. Up there, everything freezes, even the air."

Siba looked toward the north and said, "I will."

Rouble landed on Siba's shoulder and asked, "Are you ready?"

Siba cleared his throat and replied, "I am." He bid adieu to Eva and marched ahead with Celine and Rouble.

Eva yelled, "Good luck! Have a safe journey."

Siba turned his head and waved his hand. "Thank you, Eva. I'll see you again."

- Chapter 18 -

Ghosts of the Snow Mountains

After crossing the oak forest, Siba and his companions arrived at the Pool of Purple Pearls. He picked up snorkel shells for all three of them and kept them safely under the folds of the Ultravision belt tied around his waist. As he was packing his stuff and was ready to move, they heard a loud howl from the silver trees.

Rouble became scared and moved closer to Siba. He swallowed, "What's that sound? Are you sure we have to go that way?"

Siba looked in his eyes and said, "We need to go north, and that is north."

"I know that is north. But do we have to go through these scary trees?"

"Rouble, you can still fly. Look at Celine. Does she look scared to you?"

Celine bleated meekly, "Baaa"

Siba patted her, "Don't be scared. I'm with you. Let's go." But she was so frightened to enter that she didn't even move. Siba rubbed her shivering fur. "You got attacked because you didn't listen to me. When I told you to graze near the pool, why did you go into the woods? Now move. I don't want any excuses."

They entered the Silver Forest slowly and cautiously. The needle-shaped leaves of the silver-barked trees were sharp and strong like the quills of a porcupine. Siba and Celine marched ahead close to each other, while Rouble was flying just above them. After going a little deeper inside the shady forest, several needle leaves became lodged in Rouble's wings.

"Ouch, Ouch," Rouble squeaked.

Siba yelled at him, "I told you to stay close to me. Come here now." The bird, fluttering in pain, perched on the boy's shoulder. Siba carefully removed the sharp spikes.

Rouble flapped his wings. "That's better."

Just then, the frightened sheep moved closer to Siba. He asked her, "Now what happened to you?" Suddenly, he heard rustling sounds of dry leaves behind him. As he turned his head, the sound stopped. He whispered, "Someone is following us. Let's get out of here fast." They moved fast, but the sound came again. While walking, Siba twisted his head to look back but couldn't see anyone. The rustling sound became more intense, scaring the hell out of them.

Celine bleated in panic and ran. Siba also ran behind her.

Suddenly, Rouble screamed, "Siba, wolves!"

While running, Siba turned his head and saw a black wolf chasing him closely. The wolf jumped on him to attack, but Siba escaped narrowly. Ahead of him, two gray wolves were chasing Celine. He picked up a log and hurled it at them. The log hit the hind legs of one wolf, knocking him down. The second wolf stopped and sniffed his fallen mate. Siba and Celine raced from there like never before. But the three wolves chased them down in no time.

The black wolf flanked by the other two gray wolves cornered Siba. With his canines fully exposed, the black wolf snarled and growled. Siba took a step back and tumbled.

The black wolf attacked. Instinctively, Siba's eyes closed and his arms moved in front of his face. The wolf's claw struck against the boy's armor and broke. The black wolf screamed in pain. Siba opened his eyes and was surprised to find that nothing had happened to him.

The furious black wolf yelled, licking his paw, "You little trickster! You stole my hare the other day. But today, who'll save your sheep from me? Watch carefully how I devour her. Because after her, you are next on our menu."

The wolves snarled and surrounded Celine. Upon seeing death drooling from their bared fangs, Celine's trembling eyes closed in fear. Suddenly, a big snow leopard leaped between the wolves and sheep. He twitched his thick long tail and growled, "Grrr, I think you three are on my menu."

The stunned wolves shouted in fear, "Ghost of the Snow Mountains!" They fled hastily with their tails between their legs. Beholding the snow-colored, thickly furred beast with dark-gray rosettes, Rouble, Siba, and Celine became even more frightened.

The snow leopard spoke, "I meant the three wolves, not you three." He bowed before Siba and said, "I'm here to protect you – Dragonslayer."

Feeling frightened and bewildered, Siba gulped, "Dragonslayer?"

The snow leopard held Tiger's claw hanging around Siba's neck. While staring at it, he said with a budding smile, "Welcome, Dragonslayer!"

Siba pulled his necklace back and asked, "Who are you?"

The snow leopard replied, "I am Ajax – the King of the Snow Mountains. My uncle and I were hunting when we saw you entering the Silver Forest. He recognized you by this

Tiger's claw. We were coming to greet you. Unfortunately, those mongrels attacked you first."

Siba inquired, "Where's your uncle?"

"I am here!" a panting shout came from a distance. They all turned to watch as an old, gray-furred snow leopard with black rosettes walked toward them. While catching his breath, the old snow leopard said, "These old bones don't catch up with the young blood." He puffed, "I'm glad you are safe, Dragonslayer."

Ajax told Siba, "Meet my uncle – Musa."

Siba said, "You appeared like angels and saved our lives. I don't know how to thank you."

Both snow leopards said, "It's our duty to serve you, Dragonslayer."

Siba spoke, "My name is Siba. Not Dragonslayer."

Musa smiled. "Siba – the Dragonslayer. It sounds even better. We must cross the Silver Forest before those mongrels return with their entire gang. We two can't fight all of them." The three outsiders followed the two snow leopards.

Rouble asked Musa, "Are you taking us to the Snow Mountains?"

Musa replied, "Yes, those mountains are our home."

"The Snow Mountains! They appear to be very romantic. Aren't they?" Rouble fantasized.

Musa coughed to hide his chuckle. He cleared his throat and spoke, "The Snow Mountains are cruel and unforgiving – mighty peaks, sliding rocks, and distances so vast that you will get lost covering them. Food so scarce and far-flung that you die searching. A loose rock, rolling down the slope, can make you vanish in an instant, leaving behind no trace of your existence. A single carelessly placed step can slide you into abysmal depths as if you never existed. And I haven't even mentioned the real danger – the snow."

"Ahem!" Siba interrupted Musa, "Why are you scaring my parrot?"

Ajax giggled, "Who's getting scared, your parrot or you?" Siba didn't speak.

Musa resumed, "I'm not trying to scare you. I'm warning you about what you are about to experience. The Snow Mountains are not a fantasyland. It's a real and dangerous place to be, especially for furless and clawless beings like you," Musa spoke, staring at Siba from head to toe. "Only the strongest of the strongest can survive in this treacherous and rugged terrain, where every day, one has to outrun his death to survive."

Siba asked, "If it's so dangerous, then why don't you leave the Snow Mountains?"

"We are born to live there – fully adapted and well designed to face all its challenges. It's dangerous for outsiders. If you are not familiar with the perils, then they can prove to be your death traps, as they became the death trap for Tiger," Musa spoke, looking at Siba's necklace, and got lost in his thoughts.

Surprised Siba asked, "Tiger?"

"Yes, Tiger," Musa replied. "A long time ago, my elder brother, Sultan, the previous king of the Snow Mountains, found Tiger lost and nearly unconscious in the great expanses of those mountains. Tiger was fatally injured and very weak. Sultan fed him wild goats and blue sheep for several days before he could walk. Tiger stayed with us and regained his full health and power. He learned our ways and became a part of us. That year, the winter came early. Tiger wanted to leave, but Sultan requested him to stay until the winter was over.

It's too dangerous to travel during the coldest months of the year. He stayed with us and survived one of the harshest winters. Later, when the snow began to melt, we started hunting together. Sultan, Tiger, and I were chasing a wild goat on higher slopes. Suddenly, a dragon dived from the sky, grabbed that goat, and flew away."

Awestruck, Siba and Rouble blurted, "A dragon!"

"Yes, you heard me right. Dragons live in the Frost Mountains. They don't hunt goats. And before that day, they never hunted on our lands. Sultan told us to let it go and hunt another wild goat. But I doubted his pride and courage. I wanted to take revenge on that dragon and argued with my brother. He stated that the winter was long and harsh, so the dragon must have been very hungry. Else, it wouldn't have attacked our prey. He insisted on not taking it seriously and suggested going back and hunting the next day," Musa narrated.

Siba, immersed in his story, inquired curiously, "Did you listen to him?"

In a dejected voice, Musa replied, "No. I told him that if he couldn't muster his courage to fight the dragon, he could leave. Sultan was a wise king, but before that, he was my elder brother. He didn't utter a single word and left quietly for his den. I was young and naive. I took his silence for cowardice and went ahead with Tiger, who like me, knew nothing about the dragons. We both were prowling when we spotted the same dragon devouring that goat. I expressed my ire to Tiger to teach that creepy reptile a lesson for hunting in our territory.

"Filled with rage, I advanced stealthily and leapt on that flying serpent from behind. But the dragon sensed my presence and whipped me with his tail. I got smashed against a big rock. Tiger roared with anger. His thundering roar stunned me and the dragon. Before we could return to our senses, Tiger attacked the dragon. His strong claws pierced through the dragon's black scaly neck. The dragon pushed him away but the damage was already done. The dragon suffocated and died. Unfortunately, during this lethal assault, Tiger lost his claw."

Siba clasped the claw hanging around his neck.

Musa continued, "Afterward we both sighed with relief. Tiger made a coat from the dragon's black wings to withstand the cold." Staring at Siba's armor, Musa said, "But I think after leaving the Snow Mountains, he never needed it again."

After crossing a tiny creek on a fallen tree trunk, Siba asked, "What happened after the dragon's death?"

"I thanked Tiger for saving my life. I picked up his broken claw and told him to give it to someone who was as strong and courageous as he himself was. He smiled in assurance and left. That was the last time I saw him."

Ajax spoke, "Look, listening to Uncle's story, we didn't realize how fast we crossed the Silver Forest. Behold the mighty Snow Mountains before us!"

A huge glacier rested at the base of the mighty mountains. The peaks were completely covered with shimmering white snow that aptly justified the title – the Snow Mountains. Dazzled by the majestic view, Siba exclaimed in awe, "Wow! This must be the way to heaven."

A stream of chilled water, gushing through big boulders, marked the end of the Silver Forest. The fresh blades of grass next to the stream were indicating that the spring had just arrived. The terrain was completely devoid of bushes and trees, although patches of mosses and lichens were thriving well on the moist rocks.

Musa told Siba to remove his coat and give it to Ajax.

"Why?" Siba asked, throwing a suspicious look.

Musa answered, "To distract the wolves. Ajax will go through the Marmot Pass. That is the shortest way to reach our kingdom. If the wolves are following you, they will follow your scent left behind by your coat. Instead, we will go through this stream. It'll be a little longer but safer. And we won't have to worry about them."

Rouble jittered. "But the water is icy cold."

Siba mocked, "Are you going to walk with us through the water?"

"No," Rouble replied, lowering his head. Everyone laughed.

"Then, why are you worried? Just fly! Musa is right. We can't leave our scent marks behind and put our lives in danger," Siba replied, giving his black armor to Ajax. The young snow leopard crossed the stream and headed straight toward the Marmot Pass, while the others entered the stream. They waded through the shallow water for some distance and then followed it along its other bank.

After a day-long journey throughout the valley, Musa looked at their cold, tired faces and said, "You all look exhausted. We will take shelter in a crevice for tonight."

Rouble, shivering from cold, joked, "No, I'm not exhausted. Don't you know I'm used to this treacherous landscape?"

Musa chuckled, "Maybe you are not, young bird, but I'm very tired." They cramped inside a confined crack in the mountainside.

Siba asked, "How far are we from your kingdom?"

Musa replied casually, "Just four more days away."

"Four more days!" Rouble gasped, shivering with cold. "Siba promise me, if I die en route to his kingdom, you'll bury me in the Great Forest. I don't want my body to freeze for eternity in this land of rocks and snow."

Siba chuckled, "How come you are shivering? Celine doesn't have any problem."

Rouble stuttered, "I don't have thick fur like her, Dragonslayer."

Siba giggled and offered a purple pearl to the scarlet macaw. "Nothing will happen to you. It will give you warmth and energy." Rouble swallowed the pearl and stopped shivering. Without his armor, Siba was also feeling cold. He took a pearl too.

Musa spoke, "The Winter Capital is our closest settlement to the Silver Forest. Through the Marmot Pass, we could have reached there in three days. Anyway, Ajax will be waiting there for us. Then, along with everyone else, we will proceed together to our Summer Capital."

Rouble suspected, "And how far is that from the Winter Capital?"

Musa, hiding his laughter, replied, "One week away." The bird fainted.

Ω

The next morning, Siba woke up yawning and stretched his arms. "Shh!" Musa hushed.

Siba whispered, "What happened?"

Musa pointed toward the other side of the valley. A large pack of wolves was crossing the Marmot Pass.

Siba expressed his concerns about Ajax, "Will Ajax be fine?"

Musa replied, "Don't worry about him. He's very fast, just like an avalanche. He must have crossed the pass by yesterday evening. But we couldn't have done so."

Siba said, "Thank you for saving our lives."

"I know the secrets of these mountains. Don't worry, you are safe," Musa spoke with a caring smile. "Although no one is following us, still we shouldn't move from here until they cross the pass. Once they can't see us, we are good to go."

Upon hearing this, a gentle smile gleamed on Siba's face, and the teachings of the Great Forest echoed in his mind – "Sound is just one form of communication. You still have to work on touch, smell, taste, vision, and most importantly body language. You should master these skills too." Lost in his thoughts, Siba said, "Yes, I will."

Musa asked in surprise, "What?"

"Nothing. Just an old memory," Siba replied while coming back to his senses.

After some time, Musa said, "Ok, we can start now. I can't see them anymore."

Walking on a narrow icy trail alongside the high mountains, Celine slipped. But Musa grabbed her and saved her from falling into a steep gorge. He warned, "Be careful! The melting ice is very slippery, and your feet are not fit for this terrain. Follow my footsteps. Always secure the first foot, before moving another."

After a long day of rough and risky trekking, Musa halted and gazed at the sun sliding behind the mountain peaks. He predicted, "Ajax should have reached our Winter Capital by now."

Rouble asked, "You said it takes three days, didn't you?"

"Three days for us, not for Avalanche," Musa smiled.

The next day, they arrived at a mountainous meadow. Musa's eyes twinkled upon seeing a herd of ibexes grazing tender blades of wild grass. "Siba, let's hunt that wild goat with long curved horns," he whispered, pointing to one ibex.

Siba asked to confirm, "The one grazing next to the stream?"

"Yes. I'm going to hide behind that rock. You'll be the driver. Let's tear some flesh," Musa instructed. Siba stared at him with a blank look on his face.

"Don't say you never ambushed before," Musa gasped. Siba nodded his head, acknowledging that statement. "Really!" Musa exclaimed. "I'm hungry. I need to eat something," he said while looking at Celine. She got scared. Musa giggled. "I'm not going to eat you. The way you were longingly staring at the grass, I thought you must be starving too."

Siba agreed, rubbing Celine's thick fur, "Yes, she is." He looked into Musa's eyes and said, "I can learn how to hunt. All I need is your guidance."

Musa smiled and taught Siba some basic hunting lessons. "You stealthily go close to the prey and drive it toward me. When it will come close enough to me, I'll attack and hunt it down."

Musa stalked the prey with Siba's help and not long afterward they had an ibex for dinner. Siba collected some dry twigs and made a fire to cook the prized catch. Celine grazed on the fresh blades of grass, and they slept satisfyingly with full bellies in the open meadow for the night.

- Chapter 19 -

Fire & Fury

The following day, the group lazily followed Musa alongside a gushing gorge. "Pick up some speed guys. We have to travel a lot today," Musa said. "We must cross the Valley of Yaks before nightfall." The group increased their pace upon hearing that. After crossing a narrow ridge, they followed a tiny stream rushing down the steep slope. Several hours later, they reached an open valley. Musa told them, "This is the Valley of the Yaks. Do you see those tiny dark specks on the green grassy carpet?"

Siba replied, "Yes."

"They are wild yaks. Move fast. We have to cross the valley before evening. This valley is more famously known as the Valley of Death or the Hunting Ground of Dragons," Musa said, furrowing his eyebrows.

Rouble became scared. He stuttered, "Dragons!"

Musa spoke, "Don't worry. They don't hunt every day. And if they do, they do it after sunset. But we must be very careful, in case today is that day."

The group walked swiftly through the valley. When they arrived near the yaks, Siba noticed crescent-shaped scars on some yaks, similar to the one left on Celine's body after she was healed by Eva. He asked Musa about those scars.

Musa told him, "These scars tell the grim tale of their life. The yaks with scars are the lucky ones who managed to escape from the dragons. Many others were not that fortunate." Siba stared at Celine's scar. Musa said, "Only a dragon's fang could leave a scar like that."

At once, Siba's face turned red with anger. He blasted, "Dragons attacked my Celine! I will not leave those monsters alive."

Musa told him, "Calm down, Dragonslayer! Wait for the right moment to take revenge." Siba listened to him and controlled himself. They continued their journey and crossed the valley before evening. Around sunset, Musa suggested, "We should hide under these loose rocks. Be extremely careful. They are unstable and dangerous. Place each step cautiously, and don't put extra pressure, or else they'll collapse."

Rouble asked, "Why don't we cross these rocks and take refuge in some safer place?"

Musa replied, "The sun is about to set. Dragons can come anytime. We won't be able to cross these rocks before that. If we continue, they'll notice our movement, and we won't find any place to hide. We are out of the danger zone. I insist we should stay here for tonight."

Siba agreed, "Rouble, he's right. My teacher told me once – 'Mind only notices the change.' We shouldn't make any movement."

Just when the sun was about to hide behind the mountains, several black-skinned dragons dived from the sky to attack the yaks. The scaly, serpentine monsters hovered above the hoofed animals and spewed streams of fires to isolate their prey. The yaks stampeded for their lives but couldn't escape from the ferocious attack of the fire-breathing reptiles. Smoke and fire engulfed the entire area. Dragons swooped up several yaks and flew back. Hiding safely behind the loose rocks, Siba watched the entire horrifying episode.

Musa exhaled, "We are safe now. They won't return for a few days."

Siba, filled with anger and horror, asked Musa, "There must be a way to obliterate these ghastly demons."

Musa looked at Siba with hope and said, "You are the way, Dragonslayer!"

Siba got irritated and yelled, "Why do you keep calling me Dragonslayer? I haven't killed any dragons. In fact, I saw them today for the first time in my life. I'm just a boy. You don't know anything about me."

"It's true, I don't know about you. But the spirits know."

The baffled boy asked, "Which spirit? The Spirit of Life?"

"No, the spirits of the Smoky Mountain."

Bewildered Siba stared at Musa. "Now what's that? Stop throwing puzzles at me."

Musa narrated, "When Tiger left me, I returned back to our kingdom. I told council members about the cowardly act of my brother. Also, how bravely Tiger and I fought and killed the dragon. I even brought back dragon's fang as proof. Sultan rebuked me for killing the dragon and making them our enemies. He believed it was an invitation to destruction. I didn't agree with that notion. In front of our council, I demanded that he must step down as king and go into exile for diminishing our honor. The council supported my claim. He accepted his punishment.

"Just then, the dragons attacked our kingdom. Fire rained down from the sky. Death and destruction ravaged our kingdom. We attacked them, but our claws and canines couldn't penetrate the thick scaly skin of dragons. On that dark night, hundreds of snow leopards were butchered or burned to ashes. The young and old paid the price for my anger and arrogance. Apparently, my brother might have been familiar with the fact that our claws weren't strong enough for dragons. Before I could ask him about that, one dragon flew toward me, spitting fire. Sultan jumped between us and pushed me away. I rolled down from the cliff and fell unconscious.

"When I gained consciousness at dawn, I climbed up. The half-burnt body of Sultan was lying there along with uncountable others beyond recognition. The few, those who survived this holocaust, were severely wounded. Their screams were piercing through the smog of burnt flesh. I regretted not following my king and, even more so, not listening to my elder brother. I felt guilty for questioning his courage. He was right.

"At that time, Ajax was just a cub. He was weeping and pushing Sultan's dead body to wake him up. I limped to him and lifted him. I announced – 'Sultan was a great leader. A wise and strong king. For the first time in history, he united the solitary snow leopards of the Snow Mountains under one kingdom. He sacrificed his life to save mine. We will avenge his sacrifice and the death of our brothers and sisters. I will find Tiger and seek his help in destroying dragons.' The surviving snow leopards requested me to become their next king. But I announced Ajax to be our king and vowed to spend my life serving him."

Siba spoke, "So it's Tiger that you need. Not me."

"No." Musa resumed, "After accepting Ajax as our king, we went to the Smoky Mountain to seek blessings from the spirits of our ancestors. We requested them to help us in finding Tiger. The spirits told us that it was not Tiger's but someone else's destiny to bring peace back to the Snow Mountains. Someone with the courage of Tiger and a heart as pure as snow. They also told us that we don't have to look for him, destiny will bring Dragonslayer to us.

"Since then, we've been waiting for you, living a very concealed and secretive life. Hiding and avoiding confrontations with dragons, waiting for the right moment to strike. But when I saw Tiger's claw around your neck, I realized at once that it was you whom the spirits were referring to. You are our emancipator. You are the Dragonslayer."

Confounded Rouble stared at Siba with wonder and awe.

Gazing at the star-studded sky, Musa spoke again, "While telling you our story, I didn't realize how fast the time passed. We should sleep. We've had a long day, and tomorrow, a day-long climb is awaiting us. We should get some rest before we reach our den."

After a long night of rest, the sun's rays scattered across Siba's eyes, awakening him. He opened his eyes and noticed that Musa was staring at his hand. He pulled his hand back.

Musa asked, "What's that mark on your hand?"

Siba gently touched the tattoo of Only One with his other hand and replied, "He was my friend."

Musa asked, "Was?"

"He's no more. He passed away," Siba exhaled.

"Oh! I am sorry."

Rouble and Celine moved closer to them. Rouble interrupted, "It seems you all had a good sleep. I was up all night. The crackling sounds of these rocks didn't allow me to sleep."

Musa chuckled, "Once we reach the Winter Capital, you can sleep as much as you want. But now, we must hurry."

They ventured carefully across the loose rocks. "We have safely crossed the danger zone. Now we only need to climb that mountain to reach our den," Musa said, looking at a giant mountain.

Rouble looked at it and scoffed, "Huh! Just climb! I need a break before ascending that thing." He flew and perched on a huge overhanging rock. But as he placed his feet on its top, the rock began to wobble and some pebbles rolled down the slope. He flew at once.

Musa said, "After snowmelt, you never know how delicately some rocks are balanced. Didn't I warn you earlier that this place is not a fantasyland?"

Siba giggled. "Perhaps you should have listened to Musa," Siba shouted at Rouble.

As the group marched ahead on a narrow slippery trail on the mountainside, they spotted a dragon sleeping at the bottom of the mountain. A half-eaten yak's body was lying next to him. The rolling pebbles dislodged by Rouble hit the dragon, waking him up. Disturbed from his sleep, the dragon hissed with rage and flew toward them. Siba told Musa to roar and scare the dragon.

Musa told him, "The vocal cords of snow leopards are different than tigers. We can purr, but we can't roar like them. So we better run and hide."

Musa and Celine slid into a small crack, while Rouble took refuge behind a rock. Siba couldn't find any spot to hide. He ran on the narrow slippery trail. The dragon hovered next to Siba and spewed fire at him. Siba crouched down to dodge the fire, but his foot slipped, and he rolled down the steep slope. The dragon dived down chasing the rolling boy and landed in front of him. As he inflated his lungs to blow fire at Siba, from the top Rouble and Musa pelted stones and pebbles at him. The dragon cowered and covered his head with his wing. He turned and looked up at them with anger and hissed loudly. After scowling and hissing, the dragon turned toward the boy, but Siba was not there.

With the help of Eva's feathers, Siba had flown to the loose rocks. The dragon was looking around for Siba when suddenly, he heard a whistle. He looked up. Siba was hovering above the big overhanging rock, upon which Rouble had tried to sit earlier. Before the dragon could understand what was going on, Siba touched the rock with his feet. The big rock rolled down and dislodged several other rocks on its way. The resulting rock slide crushed the dragon to his death.

Musa and Rouble cheered, "Dragonslayer! Dragonslayer!"

Musa pulled out the fangs of the dragon and gave them to Siba as a token of victory. They resumed their journey and later that evening, arrived at the Winter Capital. Ajax and the other snow leopards welcomed them. Musa told everyone how bravely Siba had killed the dragon, just by himself. All snow leopards became excited upon hearing Siba's heroic story. But the council was suspicious of him being the Dragonslayer, as he had neither claws nor fangs like Tiger.

Ajax rose and announced, "I understand Siba doesn't have claws or canines like Tiger, yet he's the only other person who has killed a dragon. He proved the prophecy. Our days of suffering and hiding have come to an end. He will restore our lost glory and bring peace back to the Snow Mountains. Siba is the Dragonslayer." All hailed and cheered.

Rouble joked to Siba, "I never knew you'd become so popular here. They think you are strong like Tiger." The scarlet macaw chuckled.

"So, what's wrong with that? I killed the dragon with my sharp brain. I don't need any claws like Tiger. Even Tiger lost his claw, and look at me, I didn't even lose a single hair," Siba replied in a serious tone.

Rouble became silent for a moment and then spoke, "Musa and I saved you first by distracting the dragon. It was only then that you were able to kill him."

Siba spoke arrogantly, "So you think I couldn't have saved myself? Don't forget, I saved all the animals of the Great Forest from the alligators. It was because of me, my school team won the Annual Huntzman Games for two years in a row, almost. I helped Only One to fly again. I know who I am and what I am capable of."

Dumbfounded Rouble stared at Siba as if he was not his friend but some stranger. Just then, Ajax approached them. "You must be very tired and hungry. Let's go eat and then you can have a good sleep."

After eating, Siba said, "Rouble and Celine can take rest. But I must find the dragon that attacked Celine. I can't rest until I have killed him."

Ajax asked curiously, "How will you find that dragon?"

Siba told him, "Musa was talking about the spirits of the Smoky Mountain. I'll ask those spirits. Can you take me there?"

Ajax pondered, "Hmmm! Alright! The Smoky Mountain is close to our Summer Capital. We'll proceed to the Summer Capital tomorrow. From there, I can take you to the Smoky Mountain."

The following day, as they started their journey, Ajax handed the black armor back to Siba. "You'll need it. We'll be walking alongside a glacier for a week." Siba adorned it with a gentle smile.

Ajax and Siba walked in front, while the others followed closely behind. During their journey alongside the glacier, Siba inquired, "Before Tiger visited your kingdom, how did the snow leopards defend themselves against the dragons?"

Ajax replied, "Dragons hunt only yaks and only in the summer. During winter, they hibernate in the Ice Castle in the Frost Mountains. We don't hunt yaks. We hunt wild goats and other small animals. So there was never any conflict between us and them. We used to live peacefully in our small kingdom. But when Tiger killed the dragon, they attacked our kingdom and began hunting down other solitary snow leopards of the nearby mountains. Then, all the snow leopards of all the mountain ranges joined together to fight the common enemy. We went to the Smoky Mountain to seek the blessings of the spirits before declaring war, but the spirits told us to wait for the Dragonslayer to lead us."

Siba questioned again, "What about the wolves? Are they your enemy too?"

Ajax scoffed, "Wolves! They are just scavengers, opportunistic wild dogs, living in a pack. A wolf is no match to a snow leopard. They can't even hunt alone. They just live in those woods. Sometimes they steal our leftovers from the Snow Mountains, but that's ok, as we also hunt in the Silver Forest during winters. So it's a mutual understanding, and we don't engage with each other."

Rouble flew toward them and perched on Siba's shoulder. Siba shouted at him, "Can't you see? We are discussing something important. Go and sit somewhere else."

Rouble fluttered and hovered in front of them. "I just saw dragons coming this way. I thought of warning you, but I think you don't need my help, Dragonslayer," he said angrily.

Suddenly, panic engulfed the snow leopards. Ajax yelled, "Everyone, to the glacier! Take cover in the crevasses."

Siba looked back to find Celine but couldn't find her in the commotion. "Celine, where are you?" He shouted, but to no avail. He took Eva's feathers out and hovered above the glacier to find his sheep. He saw her grazing on a tiny patch of moss, way behind everyone. He flew swiftly toward her and hustled her inside a small crack in the glacier.

After hiding Celine, as Siba moved out of the crack, he saw the dragons were attacking his friends. They swooped and snatched the snow leopards with their steel-like claws. Streams of fire turned the ice into clouds of steam. Watching the snow leopards slaughtered and torn into pieces, Siba ran toward them to help. As he reached there, one dragon blocked his way and spewed fire at him. Siba ducked. The stream of fire hit the black armor but didn't burn it. Siba was surprised to find himself unscathed. He remembered the armor was made from the dragon's skin.

He got up at once and climbed the glacier. But his leather slippers slipped on the molten ice, and he fell inside a shallow crevasse. He felt a sharp pain in his right arm. He looked at it. His arm was injured and bleeding. He took his feathers out but couldn't flutter with his right arm. He struggled with one hand but couldn't balance to fly out of the hole.

After a long struggle and several attempts, Siba emerged out of the crevasse. But by that time, the dragons had already left, and their dance of death was over. Many snow leopards died. Many more were injured. Ajax emerged from one crevasse with one leg badly injured.

Musa shouted, "They are gone." Several other snow leopards emerged out of the glacier from all directions. Holding his bleeding arm, Siba arrived there in tears.

Ajax limped toward Siba and forcing a smile on his face, spoke, "It was bound to happen. You killed one of them. They came to kill us all. I should have foreseen that."

Siba spoke with teary eyes, "No, it's my fault. I brought this destruction upon you and your clan."

Musa said, "Don't blame yourself. It's not your fault. This is what they are – savages."

Rouble crawled out of a fissure. He saw Siba holding his right arm. He taunted, "What happened to you, Dragonslayer? Oh! You must have hurt your arm while killing the dragons."

Siba became very shameful and spoke apologetically, "No, Rouble. Don't call me that, please. I'm just a small boy who became arrogant after killing one dragon by luck. I'm extremely sorry for my behavior."

Rouble spoke with a cheerful smile, "No, you are not just a small boy. You are Siba, my Siba."

Siba wondered, "I don't know what happened to me? I'm not sure why I behaved like that?"

"I don't care. I'm glad you are back." Rouble fluttered and perched on Siba's shoulder.

Musa announced, "We will stay here under the refuge of the glacier and resume our journey, once the injured are healed."

- Chapter 20 -

Words of Wisdom

At dawn, Musa took the healthy snow leopards with him to hunt and bring food for the others. Siba took Celine to an isolated patch of moss near the glacier to feed her. He sat there on a rock with his head down on his knees, thinking about why he had changed and behaved in that rude way.

A caravan of two-humped Bactrian camels passed along the glacier. An old camel with flabby humps trotted toward Siba. His brownish shaggy winter coat was molting off, exposing thick patches of his bare grayish skin. He lowered his long neck and stared curiously at the boy. Siba was still lost in his thoughts and didn't notice the approaching camel.

The old camel flapped his floppy split upper lip and asked, "You don't belong here. Did you get lost?" The camel's rough voice and zombie-like appearance startled the daydreaming boy. The camel asked again, "You look confused. Are you searching for something?"

Siba looked curiously at him and his other marching companions who looked like walking corpses. "Are you the living dead?" the boy stuttered.

"No, I'm alive," the Bactrian camel sputtered. "My name is Wize. I'm the leader of my nomadic caravan. We are traveling through the Snow Mountains. You didn't answer my question. Are you traveling too?"

Siba replied, "You are right! I don't belong here. I'm traveling north. But for the time being, I'm helping the snow leopards."

Wize shot a suspicious look. "Hmm! In my entire life, I've never seen them seeking help from anyone. They are too proud of themselves. Won't their honor get hurt by taking help from a stranger? By the way, may I know what sort of help you are providing them?" Siba stayed silent and looked at him with suspicion. Wize sniffed, "Don't tell me if you don't want to. But be careful, lad. Pride is contagious. It appears to me that their pride has rubbed onto you."

Siba denied, "No, nothing like that. I'm helping them to kill the dragons so that peace can return to the Snow Mountains."

Wize chortled, "That was a good joke."

Siba yelled angrily, "That's not a joke. I killed one dragon already."

The old camel stared at Siba with suspicion. He lowered his long neck, sniffed the right side of the boy, and then, his left side.

Siba yelled annoyingly, "Move back! What are you doing?"

Wize concluded, sniffing the boy, "Hmm! You were telling the truth. You really did kill a dragon. I smell arrogance in you. Killing a dragon has given you too much arrogance. Otherwise, a lad like you can't have that much arrogance."

"Arrogance!" Siba panicked. He remembered the Great Forest's words – "the seeds of arrogance" and became sad and upset.

Wize asked him, "What happened to you, lad?"

Siba told the old camel worriedly, "I knew the seeds of arrogance were in me. But I don't know how and when they sprouted."

Wize told him, "Arrogance doesn't appear in a day. It takes time to build."

Siba stood up and asked, "How?"

Wize cleared his throat and spoke, "It begins when a person performs some task better than others. For performing any task, three things are required – pertinent knowledge, resources, and skills. If he possesses better knowledge, resources, or skills than others, then he can outperform them. When that person as well as others acknowledge that particular ability in which he is better than others, it generates a feeling of happiness and superiority in him. Happiness arises because outperforming others is his achievement, while superiority arises because he is better than others.

"Now, the more he performs that activity for experiencing a feeling of happiness of outperforming others, the more skillful and confident he becomes at it. That confidence in one's skill and the feeling of happiness of outperforming others join together and become pride. If that particular skill or ability has less value in the his society, then the associated pride will be less. If that skill holds a significant value in his society, then the pride will be huge.

"Taking pride in one's strengths is fine. The problem occurs when an individual begins to think of himself as a person to be better than others instead of realizing that he is better just at a skill or ability. In that case, the his focus is always on the quality at which he is better, and he doesn't appreciate the other qualities and skills of other people. He starts considering himself to be superior to others. He begins to think whatever he does is right, and his way of doing things is the correct way. Instead of understanding that there are many different ways to perform a task, he starts viewing those ways as right or wrong. When someone doesn't perform the way he wants, he gets irritated and angry.

"The next mistake that person makes is, instead of recognizing the conditions under which he can perform better, he thinks he can perform better under any conditions. It's known as over-confidence. When something doesn't work, he thinks that the fault doesn't lie in his lack of understanding of the situation or his way of working, but it lies in others. And he starts blaming others for his failures. The superiority component doesn't allow him to see anyone performing better than him. So when he fails while others succeed, he becomes angry instead of focusing on where he fell short. This over-confidence and the feeling of superiority jointly become arrogance."

"Got it. But how did you smell arrogance inside me?" Siba asked.

Wize answered hesitatingly, "Actually, I smelt nothing. I just pretended so that you'd listen to me carefully."

Siba frowned, "Then how do you know it was arrogance? It could be pride too?"

Wize moved his head closer to Siba and stared into his eyes. "You serve what you have, and you react the way you are." Wize moved his head back. "First, when I doubted your abilities, instead of verifying or double-checking how you would kill the dragons, you became angry at me. Secondly, you told me that you killed one dragon. Without recognizing the conditions under which you killed him, you were confident that you could kill others too. You tell me, lad, is it pride or arrogance?"

Siba became ashamed of his behavior and apologized, "The Great Forest had warned me about keeping my attention on my behavior to prevent the seeds of arrogance from growing inside me. But I didn't realize how it happened."

Wize replied with a gentle smile, "If you don't know, then you must find out. The answer lies within you." His gaze fell upon his fleeting caravan. "Oh! I've got to catch them. You carry on with your northward journey and your inward journey." The camel trotted to catch up to his caravan.

Siba waved and shouted, "Thank you, Wize."

Wize turned his long neck and shouted, "All the best!"

Siba sat down on the rock again and began to ponder his conversation with Wize as well as what the Great Forest had told him earlier. He closed his eyes to analyze how it began. In his mind's eye, he saw himself as a small baby, running away and climbing a tree to escape from getting spanked by his uncle. He understood how he honed the skills of running faster and climbing trees at such an early age. Later in school, during the games, his friends and teachers praised him for these skills. Even Mr. Drock acknowledged them.

Unlike other kids whose parents would help them in hard times, Siba had no one to rely upon or look for support. So, instead of whining and complaining, he learned to face problems head-on and find practical solutions. It made him self-dependent and mature for his age. That's how he earned extra respect from his elders.

He realized that even after gaining advanced knowledge and superhuman abilities from the Great Forest and Master Sung Tzu, he wasn't arrogant but proud. This was because the Great Forest, Huzo, Edna, and Eva had experience and knowledge superior to him. But when he arrived at the Snow Mountains, the snow leopards placed him at the same level as Tiger and even far more superior than themselves. They also praised him all the time for their own interests and motives.

He felt like he was at the top of the world, better than everyone else. That's when arrogance overtook him.

Arrogance deluded his thinking, he realized. The killing of the dragon made him falsely believe that he could fight all other dragons head-on. It didn't allow him to reason that it was not his intelligence alone but also the prevailing conditions, which helped him to kill that dragon. After the whole analysis he realized that he was already proud of his abilities before arriving at the Snow Mountains and with external praise from the snow leopards, this pride fostered arrogance deep within him.

Siba opened his eyes and looked at the Golden Bracelet. Two more pearls were glowing – violet for pride and dark purple for arrogance.

He said to himself, "Hmm, that's what the Great Forest meant by a higher level of awareness. I should be aware of my strengths and weaknesses, instead of feeling proud or worried about them. And most importantly, I should always keep in mind – every creature is unique. No one is superior or inferior. Never judge or value yourself based on what others say about you. You must always know who you are and should act accordingly."

In the meantime, Musa returned with his hunting team. He saw Siba sitting alone on a rock. He went closer to him and asked, "Are you still upset? Don't blame yourself for that. We hunted some snow rabbits. Come, fill your tummy. You'll feel better." Musa shared food among the survivors.

Soon a heavy white fog covered the valley, hiding everything under its blanket. Siba left his food and started looking around at the mysterious fog.

Musa chomped, "They are snow clouds. In these mountains, you never know when the weather will change its mood.

A snow blizzard can take a bright sunny day by surprise, and the very next minute, the sky turns blue as if nothing had happened."

After finishing his food, Siba brought Rouble and Celine under the cover of his armor to protect them from the snowfall and blasts of cold winds. They huddled together for warmth.

Ω

Siba took his feathers out and flew toward the Great Forest. As he landed there, he vomited out a few shining seeds. He was gazing at them when suddenly, the Great Forest's voice echoed, "Welcome home, Bumblebee! We thought you forgot about us."

Siba blushed, "Nothing like that. In fact, today I was thinking about you and came to see you."

"You look tense. Is everything alright?" the Great Forest asked.

Looking at the seeds, Siba wondered, "I didn't eat any fruit or vegetable for the past few days. I am not sure how these seeds entered my stomach?"

"Ask the seeds. They should know," the resounding voice echoed.

Siba furrowed his brow in confusion but still asked the seeds. They replied one after the other, "I'm your tree climbing skill."

"I'm your running ability."

"I am reasoning."

"I'm your sharp intelligence."

Siba spoke loudly, "Hold on! You mean you are my skills?"

The seeds replied together, "Aye!"

The Great Forest spoke, "Your strengths are your seeds of arrogance. If you don't watch them properly, they grow inside you to become arrogance."

Siba said, "If my strengths are my seeds of arrogance, then I don't need them."

"No, Bumblebee. You need them. All you should do is to be aware of them," the Great Forest advised.

Just then, a dragon swooped down and took Siba away. Flailing his arms and looking down at the seeds, Siba yelled, "I need my seeds. I need my seeds."

Rouble slapped Siba and said, "Let us sleep. Get your seeds in the morning."

Siba opened his eyes and realized that it was the middle of the cold night. He looked at the stars and thanked God, "Thank you, Lord, for curbing my arrogance before it could reach the next level when I would have dictated and blamed others." He hugged Celine and slept again.

- Chapter 21 -

Boy with the Dragon Fangs

Musa asked Siba, "How's your arm now?"

Siba tried to lift it but couldn't raise it much. "A little better. It'll be fine in a few days."

Musa pointed, "On the other side of this mountain, there are hot springs. They've got healing powers. Even if we walk slowly, we should be able to reach there before night. You and the injured snow leopards will recover quicker in the miraculous waters."

"Ok," Siba agreed, picking up his armor. They marched toward the hot springs. When they arrived on the other side of the mountain, clouds of steam rising from the warm pools welcomed them. Everyone merrily jumped into the warm waters to unburden their fatigue from the day-long trekking. After relaxing for some time, Siba lifted his right arm. To his surprise, the pain was gone. He said to Musa, "You were right. These waters do have magical healing powers."

"I know these Snow Mountains like the back of my paw," Musa said smilingly. "How did you get hurt? I don't see any sign of a dragon's attack. No burns or crescent scars."

Siba blushed, "Actually, my slippers slipped on the molten ice, and I fell into a crevasse."

Musa looked at his slippers lying outside the pool. "How can you walk with those things on ice? No wonder you slipped.

Let me get you something better." He went and brought two rabbit hides. "From now on, you walk with them. They are warm and have a solid grip."

Siba cheerfully formed the hides into snow shoes using the leather strips of his old slippers and wrapped them around his feet. "They are much better and warmer. Thank you, Musa," Siba said with an appreciative smile.

"Pleasure is all mine," Musa responded cheerfully.

They stayed at the pools for a few days until everyone was healed. Then they resumed their journey to the Summer Capital. They kept on going even after the sunset to make up for the lost time. Siba was leisurely following the snow leopards, looking at the clear star-studded sky. He pointed toward the last star of the Little Bear's tail and told Rouble, perched on his shoulder, "Rouble, look! That's the Pole Star. We have to go there."

Rouble responded, "Thanks for the offer, but I'm good here on earth."

Suddenly, Celine bleated, "Baaa."

Siba and Rouble twisted and looked behind them. A small ball of fire was following them. Siba became scared and stopped. The burning ball also stopped. Siba took one step ahead. The ball moved a little ahead too. Siba became extremely scared and ran toward the snow leopards, screaming. He sprinted so fast that Rouble fell from his shoulder. Celine and Rouble turned back. The flame ball was still chasing them. Both screamed and raced toward Siba.

Siba dashed into Ajax. He pointed toward the flame ball, panting fiercely. "Ajax! There is something following us!"

Ajax looked behind and shouted, "Glowl!" The burning ball stopped. All the snow leopards stopped as well.

Siba asked him, "What's that?"

Ajax whispered, "Shh! Look around you."

Siba twisted his head. More burning balls were approaching them from all sides.

Ajax spoke softly, "We call them – Glowls. They are mature spirits who are ready to take birth. If they have arrived, it means the females are ready to deliver cubs in a few days. We better hurry up and reach our Summer Capital."

They continued their journey toward the north. As they marched ahead, more and more burning balls followed them and adhered to the bodies of the female snow leopards. Siba, a little bit scared and unaware of what was going on, kept sticking close to Ajax. After a few days, they reached the Summer Capital. It was a big cave, overlooking an extended mountainous meadow. Herds of ibexes and wild sheep with long curved horns were grazing in abundance. Several migratory birds nestled around a small lake at the center of the meadow. Celine raced to the meadow to graze. Rouble flew there as well and joined the birds.

On one side of the meadow stood a mountain fully shrouded by dense clouds with only its tip visible. Ajax noticed Siba looking at that mountain. He went closer, placed his paw around Siba's shoulder, and said, "That is the Smoky Mountain."

Siba expressed his heart's desire, gazing at the mysterious mountain, "When are you taking me there?"

Ajax replied, "When the spirits call you."

Siba twisted his head and stared at him. "What do you mean?"

"When its tip is not visible, that's when the spirits call. We must wait for the signal."

Siba twitched his eyebrows and nodded, "Alright!"

Ajax smiled and spoke, "Come, let me show you our den."

They walked inside the cave. The bodies of the female snow leopards were almost fully covered with the balls of fire. Musa and several other snow leopards were taking care of them. One glowl floated close to Siba. He hesitatingly touched it with his index finger. "It's not that hot," Siba uttered. The glowl kept on floating and attached to the body of one female.

Musa said, "It just looks hot, but it's not. They are warm, the same as body heat. They provide warmth to pregnant females and merge into their bodies. The brightest glowls sticking to their bodies will take birth as cubs, while the others will become spots on the cubs' fur."

Ajax showed Siba the rest of the cave. Snow leopard skulls were lined along its inner walls. Ajax told him, "They are the skulls of those who died in the Great Battle against the dragons." While crossing them, Ajax stopped in front of one skull and became silent.

Siba said, "Sultan was a great king. You must be proud that you have his blood in your veins."

"I am," Ajax asserted, nodding his head, and moved ahead.

At the end of the cave was a skeleton of the dragon that Tiger had killed. Siba went closer to it and touched its skull. A cavity just below the base of the dragon's long neck intrigued him. "Do you know what this hollow space is?" Siba asked curiously.

Ajax guessed, "Might be the heart cavity."

Siba thought for a moment and spoke, "Yes, you are right. It must be here, where this monster's heart throbbed. Do you remember where Tiger attacked him?"

"Musa told us that Tiger attacked his neck," Ajax recalled.

Siba smiled. "Yes, that's what he told me too. Now look here." He pointed to a bone at the back of the cavity. There was a cut in it. Siba removed his necklace and placed Tiger's claw in that cut. It fitted perfectly in it. Siba looked into Ajax's eyes and smiled. "Do you see?"

Ajax pulled his brows together in confusion. "See what?"

"Musa was whipped against the rock. He must have not recalled the fight properly. Tiger didn't attack the dragon's neck. It was the chest, right here, on the monster's heart. When his claw struck against this bone, it broke," Siba explained enthusiastically.

Ajax asked, furrowing his brow, "Then what?"

"This is the soft spot of the dragons. This is where their armor is weak. If you attack here, even you can kill them."

Ajax, trying to comprehend what Siba had just told him, blurted, "Really?"

Siba with a broad smile nodded his head. "Yes!"

One snow leopard came running and informed, "My king, Musa called for you." Ajax and Siba dashed to the outer chamber.

Musa was holding two cubs in his paw. He said to Ajax, "They look just like you when you were born."

On becoming a father, jubilant Ajax licked his cubs. He addressed the gathering, "I promise you. Soon we will end these dark clouds looming over us. Our cubs will grow in a kingdom free from fear and hiding, just like our fathers and our forefathers." Everyone cheered.

Ajax looked at Siba and said, "Our families are safe in this cave. We can go and teach those demons a lesson – what it means to attack our families."

After listening to Ajax's encouraging speech, Siba asked him, "What's your plan?"

Ajax revealed, "We will ambush them in the Valley of Yaks. When they come there to hunt yaks, we will attack them."

"How will that help? Your claws can't penetrate their thick skin. Isn't there any better way to commit suicide?" Siba refuted his plan.

Ajax questioned, "Didn't you propose earlier that we attack their hearts?"

"Yes, I said that, and I stand by it. But how will you attack exactly at the heart of a dragon when he's flying in an open area and spewing fire at you?"

Ajax realized the blunder he was about to commit. "Then what should we do?"

"Give me some time. Let me think. Surely, there must be some better way of committing suicide." Siba smiled.

The next morning, Siba called Musa and Ajax to discuss his strategy. He revealed, "You told me that the dragons hibernate in some Ice Castle. We should go there and kill them all."

Musa blurted, shaking his head, "No, no, no! That's not possible. Their guards will see us coming, even before we make it to the Frost Mountains."

Siba spoke, "I think you didn't hear me properly. I said 'hibernate'. We'll go there in the winter when they are hibernating. Then no one will see us coming."

Musa and Ajax blurted at once, "Are you crazy?"

Musa spoke, "Do you even know what you are saying? Going to the Frost Mountains, and in the winter! Do you know why they are called Frost Mountains? Because they stay frozen even in summers, and during winters, even the air freezes over there. They are so high that clouds touch their feet and their peaks are in heaven. Moreover, we need to take care of our cubs during winter. We can't leave them alone."

Ajax added, "And what if the dragons wake up? We don't have the numbers to beat them."

Siba spoke again, "The plan is not over yet. That was just the first half."

Ajax asked, "And what's the other half of this crazy plan?"

Siba revealed, "Asking for the wolves' help." Both snow leopards scoffed.

Ajax said, "Are you really crazy or just playing around with us? If your pranks are over should we discuss something serious?"

"Even the golden eagles hunt down those mongrels, and you think they can fight against dragons," Musa scoffed. "Moreover, why would they ally with us? They are opportunistic liars who can never be trusted."

Siba smirked, "That's the reason they'll join you."

The perplexed snow leopards stared at Siba's face and asked together, "What do you mean?"

Siba explained, "Look, they won't do anything unless they see something in it for them. We'll give them an offer that they can't refuse. Once the dragons are gone, what's left for you are yaks. You allow them to hunt yaks. You don't hunt yaks anyway."

Ajax asked, "What if they don't agree?"

Siba proposed, "Then you can offer them to hunt in the Snow Mountains as well."

Musa refuted right away, "No way! Those dogs can't enter our territory."

Siba questioned Musa, "During winters, you hunt in the Silver Forest, which is their territory. How fair is that?"

Musa replied proudly, "We are rulers. We are more powerful than them. We can hunt wherever we want and whatever we want."

Siba stated, "The same rule should apply to the dragons too. They are more powerful than you. What's wrong if they hunt your prey or even you?"

Musa furrowed his brows. Staring at Siba with furious eyes, he asked arrogantly, "You tell me, why you became angry when someone attacked your sheep? Obviously, someone more powerful than her must have attacked her."

Siba couldn't answer. He became silent for a moment and couldn't utter a single word. After a brief period of silence, he asked, "So, what do you suggest?"

Musa smirked, "I like your suggestion, but partially. If the wolves agree, we can make them our allies. But after killing the dragons in their deep sleep, we'll return back from the Frost Mountains, alone. If the wolves are lucky, they'll find their way back home, or else, they'll freeze to death after their supplies exhaust."

Musa looked into Siba's eyes and said, "As you said, our deal will be to attack the dragons together. After the dragons are killed, they'll be on their way, and we'll be on our way. I mean, literally. And I think we don't have to tell them that. It's obvious. Isn't it? So, the question of sharing our territory only arises if they survive the winter of the Frost Mountains. And for your knowledge, it's only me who knows the way to the Ice Castle."

Ajax commented, "I like this plan. Let's kill two birds with one stone." But Siba didn't appear to be comfortable with the plan.

Musa said to Siba, "Don't forget, those wild dogs attacked you and your sheep in the Silver Forest. Had Ajax not reached there on time, you both would have been dead."

Siba frowned, "Let's do it."

Musa asked, "But who'll negotiate with those dogs?"

Siba took the initiative. "I will. I don't belong to you, neither do I belong to them." He smirked and proposed, "They'll listen to the Dragonslayer."

Musa suggested, "Alright Dragonslayer, take five of our best warriors with you for your protection. Those wolves are savages. You never know, they may devour you, even before you open your mouth."

Siba spoke with a smile, "Don't worry. I'll be fine. I have a plan. You keep your strongest warriors ready. I'll bring theirs."

"Don't bring them here," Musa blurted. "Meet us near the glacier at the first snowfall of the winter. The path to the Frost Mountains starts there."

Siba nodded and bid adieu to them. He took his feathers out and flew southwards toward the Silver Forest. When he arrived near the silver trees, he saw a musk deer carcass. He speculated that wolves would come for it. He landed there and climbed a nearby silver tree. Then, sitting on a high branch, he waited for the scavengers.

In the middle of the night, two wolves arrived there and dragged the carcass. One of them sniffed an unfamiliar scent and followed it to the tree where Siba was hiding. He howled, and soon, several other wolves gathered around that tree. The black wolf, which had attacked Siba earlier, also arrived there. He sniffed and recognized Siba's scent.

The black wolf howled, "I know you are hiding up there. I must thank you for coming back. You don't know how desperately I was waiting to tear your soft flesh into tiny pieces."

"I must say sorry because that day is not today," Siba shouted from the top, "Who is head of your pack? I brought a message for him."

The black wolf asked suspiciously, "What message?"

Siba replied, "It's a secret message from Ajax - the King of the Snow Mountains, only for your leader. Tell me, which one of you is your pack's leader?"

The black wolf sniggered, "O poor messenger, come down and give me that message. I'll be pleased to deliver your message to our leader along with your sweet little head."

Siba shouted, "If you won't take me to your leader. All I need to do is to give a signal. The snow leopards hiding on the other side will kill you all. Will you take me to your leader now or not? You decide."

The wolves agreed, "Ok, we'll take you to him."

The wolves led Siba deep inside the Silver Forest. A large gray wolf walked out of the dark woods. Under the moonlight, Siba peered at his face. A deep hideous scar ran across his face, starting a little above the missing left eye, curling to right, and slicing through his long muzzle. He howled and spoke in a very rough voice, "I am Taziki – the King of the Silver Forest. What is this message for which you risked your life?"

Siba looked carefully at Taziki's scar. It was similar to the one on Celine's body.

Taziki moved closer to Siba and stared into his eyes. "Do you have something to say or should I tell my boys to serve you on my plate?"

Siba rolled his finger down the wolf's scar. "I came here so that this should not happen again."

Taziki backed off and frowned, "What do you mean?"

Siba revealed, "I am Siba – the Dragonslayer. I've come here to protect you from the dragons."

Taziki guffawed and so did every other wolf. While others were still laughing out loud, Taziki pulled his eyebrows together and snorted, "That was a good joke. But now Dragonslayer, who will protect you from me?" Taziki lifted his paw to slice him.

Just then, Siba raised his hands, revealing the dragon fangs.

The King of the Silver Forest fell back, frightened. He blurted, "The boy with the dragon fangs!" He murmured, "The prophecy is true." He got up and announced, "He's Dragonslayer. All hail the Dragonslayer." Other wolves became confused and motionless. Their frozen eyes kept on staring at the boy with the dragon fangs.

Siba spoke loudly, "I know the pathetic life you are living – hiding under these trees, feeding on the dead and rotten, living at the mercy of the snow leopards and the dragons. Don't you want to live free and roam free? Don't you want to hunt in those Snow Mountains? I've come to offer you a choice that can change your life."

All wolves blurted, "What is it?"

"Freedom! Join me in the war against the dragons. The snow leopards have already joined me."

Taziki expressed his concern, "We are not snow leopards. They can afford to fight with the dragons. In case they lose, they've got caves to hide in. But we can't. If dragons set ablaze our forest, we'll burn to death, alive."

Siba remarked, "Well, your concerns are valid. But the rewards are promising as well."

Taziki asked, "And what are those?"

Looking into his eye, Siba said, "Exclusive rights to hunt yaks and freedom to hunt in the Snow Mountains as well. Not to mention, no more danger from the dragons."

Taziki licked the excitement of the offered prospect as it drooled from his fangs. He asked anxiously, "What do you want us to do?"

Siba sighed, "Along with the strongest warriors of the snow leopards, during winter, we will attack the dragons hibernating in their Ice Castle."

Taziki scratched the scar on his face with his claw and mused for a moment. "Alright, we'll fight for you."

The black wolf interrupted, "But my king!"

Taziki growled at him, "I know what I am doing."

Siba said loudly, "Get your supplies ready. We'll march at the first snowfall of the winter."

The wolves made wooden sleds from hollow trees and filled them with meat. Taziki filled several sleds with giant cones of the silver trees.

Siba asked Taziki, "What are you going to do with those cones?"

Taziki told him, "When these cones come in contact with fire, they burst with loud explosions. The dragons are scared of loud sounds. When you hold them in front, they rarely breathe fire." He winked. "That's why the dragons never come to the Silver Forest."

Siba furrowed his brows with thoughtfulness.

- CHAPTER 22 -

THE GREAT BETRAYAL

The time passed quickly. The days grew shorter and colder. The wolves stocked enough supplies to last an entire season. And finally, that moment arrived, which they had all been waiting for. The first snowflake of winter glided down the sky and melted on Siba's face. He announced in excitement, "Winter is here!"

Taziki howled to assemble everyone, and the band of assassins began their epic journey. The King of the Silver Forest led the cavalcade from the Silver Forest through the Marmot Pass. The wolves comfortably dragged their sleds loaded with supplies on the fresh snow. On their way, Siba came across the caravan of nomadic Bactrian camels again. But this time, he couldn't recognize Wize. With long wooly summer coats, those zombie-like creatures had transformed into beautiful plush giants. One camel with a long beige mane approached Siba and asked, "Don't you recognize your old friend?"

Siba recognized that voice immediately. "Wize, you look so different! I mean, you look fabulous. I couldn't even recognize you," Siba spoke in awe.

Wize spluttered, "Don't get deceived by the looks. My appearance doesn't change me. I'm still the same. But you look completely different now. I mean from the inside."

"Yeah! What you told me helped me a lot. Thanks again."

Wize smiled and looked at his fleeting caravan. "Oh! No one stops for an old camel. See you later. Keep up your good work."

Siba smiled and waved at his trotting old friend. Siba also ran and joined his group of warriors. By the time they arrived at the glacier, dense clouds crept into the valley. Unable to see anything, the group halted and settled down next to each other. The fog grew denser and darker. While they were waiting for the fog to disperse, a giant shadow appeared in the fog and moved toward them.

The black wolf stuttered, "Dragons! We are doomed!" Suddenly, panic prevailed. The wolves closed together as a pack to protect themselves.

Taziki growled, "It can't be a dragon. They should be slumbering in their Ice Castle by now."

Just then, the billowing fog parted and revealed the entity behind it. Ajax growled loudly as he appeared through the thick fog, flanked by his accompanying snow leopards.

Siba rose with relief and excitement. He ran and embraced Ajax, complementing, "Now I know why they call you the Ghosts of the Snow Mountains."

Musa and Ajax chortled and greeted Siba gleefully. Then they looked at the wolves and scowled at them. The pack growled back at the snow leopards.

Siba jumped in the middle. "Guys, guys, guys! Do away with the enmity and make peace with each other. Please remember, we have a bigger enemy to fight. Let's make a pact to watch each other's backs, or else we won't be a strong army against the dragons." The Ghosts of the Snow Mountains and the Warriors of the Silver Forest exchanged uncertain paw shakes as the fog dispersed and the sun emerged.

Taziki asked Siba, "What's next?"

Siba looked at Musa and announced, "Musa knows the route to the Ice Castle. He will lead us there. Any questions?" Everybody remained silent. Looking at Musa, Siba requested with a smile, "Alright then, lead us to the Frost Mountains."

They moved day in and day out on the thick sheets of ice covered in deep snow. Several unfortunate souls perished in the abysmal crevasses and cracks of the glacier concealed under the blanket of snow. A few others simply froze to death. Some succumbed to extreme altitude sickness from the lack of oxygen and severely low air pressure.

Siba was no different. He was breathing heavily and hallucinating. He was about to faint when suddenly, he had a vision of Eva, offering him snorkel shells. He took several deep breaths and forced his eyes to open wide. He took the snorkel shells out from the folds of Ultravision and inserted them inside his nostrils. To his great relief, he was able to breathe normally again. The others also gradually acclimatized to the extreme conditions.

Their expedition was getting worse and worse with each passing day. Snow blizzards marred them continuously, impeding their already slow advance. The icy trails along the exposed sky-high steep slopes punished them with powerful gusts. The winds were so strong that several adventurers were knocked off the edges into the abysmal depths. Avalanches buried many unlucky travelers alive in grim snow graves.

After one grueling month of suffering and torture, marching on a narrow, frozen trail near the mountain top, they came face to face with their biggest nightmare – a serac. The huge overhanging wall of unstable ice that could topple without warning was awaiting them.

Musa instructed everyone to halt. Then he carefully moved closer to the narrow passage under the hanging wall of ice to inspect its stability. Just when he was about to step under the serac, a huge chunk of ice shattered above him and fell inches away from him. He barely escaped getting crushed under the ice chunk and falling into the fathomless depths.

Musa took a sigh of relief, "Phew!" He turned back and addressed his startled followers, "This is the only path to our destination. We must cross it. But as you have witnessed, it's extremely dangerous and risky. We'll cross it one at a time. When the first individual makes it safely to the other side, then the next shall proceed. I'll go first and give a signal when I cross it." He closed his eyes and prayed to the spirits. Then he moved ahead, placing each step with extreme precaution. After making it across safely, he shouted, "It's clear. Next!"

Taziki crossed after Musa followed by Ajax. But when Siba was crossing, a block of ice cracked. It knocked him off the frozen trail and washed him down in a current of snow and ice down to the bottom of the frozen mountain. Siba finally crashed on a big ball of soft snow.

"Ouch!" a scream came from the snowball.

Siba stood up quickly rubbing his head and took a few strides away from it. The big snowball rose into a giant ape-like creature, covered from head to toe in thick white hair. Only his red eyes and black nose were visible.

Siba screamed in panic, "Snow monster!"

The ape-like creature also screamed, "Snow monster! Help!"

Suddenly, a large number of similar creatures rose from the snow around them and began yelling, "Snow monster! Run for your life! Help!"

Siba was puzzled. He shouted, "Silence!" All the ape-like creatures quieted down at once.

The creature whom Siba fell on, asked him, "Where's the snow monster?"

Siba asked with a perplexed look on his face, "Aren't you a snow monster?"

He replied, "I am no snow monster. I am Neti."

Siba asked, "Neti? Neti, what?"

The ape-like creature replied, "We are yeti, and my name is Neti. This is our village. Who are you, and why do you come here to scare us?"

Siba giggled. "Did I scare you? I'm sorry if I scared you. Actually, it should be the other way around. Anyway, I am Siba. I and my friends were crossing the frozen trail at the top of the mountain. My foot slipped, and I fell upon you. I need to climb back to the top. They must be worried about me."

Neti asked innocently, "What is climb?"

Siba twitched his eyebrows in surprise and then scrambled several meters up the steep face of the frozen mountain. From there, he shouted, "This is climbing."

Neti asked curiously, "Is this how you want to get to the top?"

Siba replied, "Yes, of course. This is how climbing is done."

All the yetis burst into laughter. One yeti said, "It will take you months to reach there by climbing."

Siba scoffed, "Do you know a better way?"

Neti moved next to the frozen mountain and squatted, bringing his hips as low as he could. Then he jumped and clung to the mountain above Siba with his sharp claws, piercing through the ice. He looked down at the astonished boy and said, "This is how you hip-hop to the top. Come on, we'll take you there. We are also going to the other side of this ridge."

Neti lowered his palm. Siba climbed onto it and dropped onto the yeti's back. Siba clung to Neti's back, clasping his long white hair. Other yetis hip-hopped and clung way above Neti. One of them looked down at Siba and asked, "Are you ready, climber? Let's hip-hop this rock." Siba gently nodded his head with a smile.

The yetis hip-hopped the steep face of the mountain. Soon they arrived at the frozen trail. Siba got down from Neti's back and walked toward his companions. Upon seeing him alive, smiles returned on the grieving faces of snow leopards and wolves.

Ajax said, "We thought you died and our hopes died with you. I'm glad you are ok."

Musa spoke with a smile, "Let's resume our journey and climb to that mountain."

Siba said, "Not climb! Hip-hop!"

Musa blurted, "Hip-hop?"

Siba pointed down the slope. The yetis were clinging to the steep face of the mountain just below the narrow frozen trail. Siba smirked, "We got a ride."

The snow leopards and wolves rode the yetis, crossing the mountain range in no time. The yetis brought them to the other side, upon a large frozen lake. Several groups of yetis were already present there, skating on its frozen surface. Neti told Siba, "This is our rink. We have an ice hockey tournament with the yetis of the other villages."

Siba and his companions thanked the yetis for their help and marched ahead on the frozen lake. Taziki said to Siba, "Hop on my sled. Now watch, how we roll!"

Siba nervously boarded the sled pulled by the wolves. They dragged the sled very fast, just like huskies. Siba enjoyed the high-speed ride. After crossing the frozen lake, they arrived at the base of a giant dormant volcano. The ice sheets on the sides of the volcano were so thick that it appeared to be a colossal cone of ice.

Looking up at the volcano, Musa announced, "The Ice Castle of the dragons is up there, at the top of this volcano. We'll begin our final ascent tomorrow morning. It'll take us a few days to reach there. Be strong and be ready by tomorrow."

Ω

The next morning, they began ascending the giant ice cone with their sharp claws. Siba used the dragon fangs as ice axes to make pigeon holes and hike. During the night, they rested inside the cracks of ice sheets. After a few days of extreme ice climbing, they finally reached the summit. The crater of the volcano was covered by a thick ice cap.

Musa addressed everyone in a muffled voice, "Dragons hibernate in this Ice Castle. Be exceptionally careful. Don't make any sound. If they wake up, you know what will happen to us. And remember, aim only for their hearts. That's the only place where they are vulnerable. Target that and pierce your fangs through their bloody hearts."

The group stealthily climbed down into the crater. After crossing a huge pile of yak bones and skulls, they came across a hollow tube carved inside the glacier. Large icicles hung at the entrance of the icy cave. Siba sneaked inside the cave and found one dragon sleeping near the entrance. He moved closer quietly, held Tiger's claw firmly with both hands, and stabbed the dragon's heart. The dragon hissed and died right away.

Siba signaled others to enter the Ice Castle. Wolves dragged their sleds filled with giant cones of silver trees inside the ice cave. As Siba moved deeper into the cave, it grew bigger and darker. When the outside light got completely cut off, to his surprise, the color of ice turned blue. Under the pale blue light of ice, he saw three dragons sleeping close to each other. He took out a lump of slumber resin from his armor's pocket and very gently rubbed it on their nostrils. After that, he pierced their hearts with Tiger's claw. The dragons died in their sleep without making a sound.

Through a tunnel, they entered inside a big splendid chamber. The chamber was brighter than the tunnel. Its roof was loaded with long pointed icicles. In the middle of the chamber, a huge sapphire-blue-hued column of ice was supporting the ceiling. Numerous burrows were present all along its circumference. But only two of them were occupied by dragons, and both of them were sleeping and snoring. Siba got suspicious. He whispered to Musa, "Why are only two of these burrows occupied?"

Musa replied in a muffled voice, "I don't know. Maybe they are sleeping somewhere else inside this castle."

Siba peered under the dim blue light and found one more tunnel at the other end of the chamber. He moved cautiously through the other tunnel to investigate what lay beyond it. That passage led him outside the Ice Castle. "Oh! This must be the other entrance," he thought.

While returning through the same passage, he found another hidden chamber. He peeped into it. A dragon was sleeping there on a heap of dry leaves and twigs. He quietly entered into that chamber and held Tiger's claw firmly in his right hand. As he took a few silent strides toward the sleeping monster, he heard the sound of an explosion. Unable to comprehend, Siba paused at the very spot. The dragon woke up from the blast and yawned, "Is winter finally over?" His gaze fell upon Siba.

The dragon frowned and hissed, "Who are you? What are you doing here?"

Siba clasped Tiger's claw with both hands and spoke with angry eyes, "I came here to seek revenge for the havoc one of you unleashed upon my sheep in the Silver Forest. Get ready to die, you filthy monster!"

The dragon guffawed. "You are a funny little creature. I don't know if I'm laughing at your innocence or stupidity." The winged reptile controlled his laughter and continued, "I don't know what sheep you are talking about. Don't you know? Dragons kill only yaks, and we never go to the Silver Forest. The sharp needle leaves of the silver trees puncture our wings and their cones explode with our breath. If I take that as your ignorance and pardon you for sneaking into our castle, I still can't forgive your stupidity for entering the royal chamber without permission, calling me a filthy monster, and daydreaming about killing me." The dragon inflated his lungs and sprayed fire at Siba.

Siba crouched and covered himself with his armor. The stream of fire struck against the black armor leaving the boy unscathed. But the flames set the heap of leaves and twigs on fire. The dragon hissed with rage. Just then, Taziki arrived there with a sled. He jumped and slashed one big icicle hanging above the dragon with his sharp claws. The icicle broke and pierced through the dragon.

The dragon screamed in pain, "You will have to pay for this. Ra will find you and burn you to ashes." The dragon croaked and died.

Taziki grasped one burning stick between his jaws and raced out of that burning room. Siba chased him to the main chamber. The splendid chamber had turned into a hellish battlefield. The snow leopards and wolves were fighting the two dragons. Several wolves were huddled around the central column, hurling cones from their sleds to prevent dragons from spewing fire. Many half-burnt bodies of ghosts and warriors were scattered all over the floor. Smoke and the smell of burning flesh sullied the air.

Siba charged toward the dragons with Tiger's claw in his hand. Suddenly, standing at the mouth of the back tunnel, Taziki howled. Upon hearing their king howl, the fighting wolves sprang and assembled behind him. Caught by surprise, Siba, the snow leopards, and the dragons paused, turning their eyes toward the King of the Silver Forest. Taziki threw the burning stick at the sleds of cones huddled around the central column.

Siba screamed, "Everyone! Run!"

Before the others could hear Siba's scream, the cones exploded and the ice column shattered. The pointed icicles fell from the roof like spears, killing dragons and many snow leopards. A big crack ran across the roof. Taziki looked at the crack and ran into the back tunnel. Other wolves followed him. Siba and the surviving snow leopards dodged the falling icicles and ran into the front tunnel of the chamber.

Taziki hurriedly entered the chamber where the heap of dry leaves was burning. He pushed aside the burning leaves and unveiled a golden egg hidden underneath. He carefully lifted the egg, placed it in his sled, and covered it with unburnt leaves. Suddenly, a thundering cracking sound rocked the castle. Taziki swiftly fled from the back entrance with his pack following him and dragging the sled.

At the front of the main tunnel, Siba and the snow leopards narrowly escaped from the Ice Castle, just as it collapsed.

Loud thunder and a cloud of shattered ice particles engulfed the crater. Unable to see, the snow leopards yowled to locate each other and gathered near the heap of yak bones. They waited there until the cloud of ice particles settled down. As things started becoming clearer, Siba saw that Musa was badly injured and breathing heavily.

Siba swiftly took a purple pearl out and offered it to Musa. But he refused and groaned, "My time has come to an end. I'm not scared of death. I avenged the death of my brother. I'm leaving with honor and dignity."

Taziki and his pack panted at the back entrance, surviving the devastating collapse. The black wolf asked Taziki, "My king, why did you choose the back exit? We don't even know the route. How will we return to our Silver Forest? This egg won't even serve us as a single meal. We all will freeze to death."

Taziki slapped him. "Idiot! Don't even look at this egg. This egg is the key to our emancipation, the path to our glory. The snow leopards humiliated us, despised us, and treated us like outcasts. The time has come for them to pay for their every crime and sin." He raised the egg and spoke loudly, "Behold the egg of Ra – the Queen of Dragons. This egg is under our control. It means the dragons are under our control. From now on, they will do what we tell them to do."

One wolf asked, "But my king, the dragons are dead. We just killed them and their bodies are buried under the ice."

Taziki guffawed and spoke, "Do you think the population of dragons was only seven? Fool, they were just the guardians of the Ice Castle. Ra – the Goddess of Fire and the other dragons were at the Fire Temple taking their fire baths."

Another wolf asked, "My king, how do you know all this?"

Taziki smirked, "How do you think I got this scar? Follow me. We have a long way to go." He placed the egg back in the sled and covered it with leaves again. Pointing to the black wolf, he said, "You! Pull this sled very carefully."

Ω

Siba was very disturbed. Dragon's words were ringing in his head. He mused out softly, "The dragon was telling the truth. It's not possible for such a large dragon to roam in the thick and dense Silver Forest; there isn't enough space for them. Moreover, the needle-like leaves of silver trees can definitely puncture their wings. They did so to Rouble. The dragon was right about the cones as well. When the wolves were hurling cones in the main chamber, the dragons didn't breathe fire. As far as I have roamed into the Silver Forest, I have never seen any sign of dragons there. And if I remember correctly, there were no broken branches or burnt woods at the spot where Celine was found badly injured." He sighed, "If it was not a dragon, then who else attacked her? Definitely, it was not a wolf or a snow leopard as her scar is crescent-shaped. Who else would have done that?"

Musa, suffering from pain, noticed wrinkles of distress flowing across Siba's face. He inquired, "Why are you upset? You should be happy and proud of yourself. You fulfilled the prophecy. You proved that you are the Dragonslayer."

Siba, with his eyebrows pulled together, expressed his muddled mind, "I don't know should I be happy or should I be sad?" He sighed and spoke, "I don't know why I did what I did? Was it right or was it wrong? I don't know. I feel lost." He pressed his lips, closed his eyes, and took a deep breath.

Musa groaned in pain and dragged himself closer to Siba. He asked, "Tell me, what's troubling you?" Siba told him everything that the dragon had told him about Celine. Musa moaned, "Yes, that's true. Dragons didn't hurt your sheep."

Siba became completely baffled. He asked angrily, "Then who attacked Celine? Tell me, I will kill that swine."

Musa lowered his gaze and said, "It was me. I am that swine." Musa's words shocked and shattered Siba.

Siba's anger and aggression vanished into thin air, and he pleaded, "No, no, no! You are lying. That's not true. Please say you're lying."

Musa looked into Siba's eyes and said, "It's true. I injured your sheep."

Tears rolled down Siba's cheeks like rivers. "Why? Why did you do it?" That's all he could say before he lost control over his voice and words.

Musa groaned, "I was in the Silver Forest on that day, keeping an eye on the wolves' activities. They were hunting a hare. That's when I saw you for the first time. You were with your friends near a pool. You removed your shirt to dive into the water, and the Tiger's claw around your neck became visible. I recognized it at once and knew that you were the Dragonslayer.

"I conceived a plan to bring you on our side. I lured your sheep by placing magic mushrooms on the trail leading to the Silver Forest. She ate them quickly and entered the woods. Soon she began hallucinating and fell to the ground. I stealthily went closer to her and inflicted a wound on her belly with a dragon's fang, exactly the way they do. I was watching you when you went there with your other friends. I was going to tell you that dragons attacked your sheep, but your priest-ess friend healed her and you left. I visited that place every day to see you again. And finally, I saw you again when those wolves were chasing you. The rest, you know."

Siba, burning with anger and pain, asked, "You didn't tell me, why did you do that?"

Musa gasped and groaned, "Tell me honestly, would you have helped us to defeat the dragons, if I had just requested it of you? Would you have risked your life to come to this frozen desert to fight and kill those monsters on your own accord?" He moaned in pain, "I didn't want to kill her. I just gave her a wound to convince you. Now the dragons are dead. Our future is safe. I'm your culprit, and I'm willing to pay the price. Kill me and finish my life. This is my punishment for not listening to my brother, for his death, and for the havoc unleashed upon my kingdom. I won't live much longer anyway. I beg you, kill me."

Siba wept and cried. He placed Musa's head in his lap and sniffled, "No. How can I kill you? I'm a culprit too. I killed the dragons who did nothing wrong to me."

"That was your destiny. Don't feel bad about what you did. It was not you; it was your anger. Anger is the most violent force that doesn't know anything other than destruction and devastation. Untamed anger makes you its slave. You only do what it tells you to do. I also fell prey to it when I lost Sultan. But the spirits told me to control this power and wait for the right moment," Musa gasped deeply and moaned loudly, "Sultan is calling me. He's calling me to go with him to the Snow Mountains." Musa looked at the sky and lifted his paw. "I'm coming brother." The old snow leopard limped forward and died.

Siba hugged him and cried. The other snow leopards encircled their greatest martyr, grieving heavily. Siba wept and spoke with teary eyes, "Musa was a great leader and a good friend. He cared for his kingdom and gave his life protecting it. May his soul rest in peace."

- Chapter 23 -

The Reign of Horror

Siba and the snow leopards passed the night there, huddled together under the frozen sky. But no one slept that night. Siba's conscience kept haunting him over and over again. He was not able to justify the dragon massacre to himself. Because of his decision, not only did dragons die but many wolves and snow leopards also died, including Musa. He tried to convince his conscience that he was innocent by blaming it on Musa, the prophecy, the destiny but not on himself. But nothing worked. He realized he would have to accept it and live with it. He said to himself, "No matter how hard you try, you can never lie to yourself. Your heart always knows what the truth is."

Siba remembered Tiger's words – "With higher position and power, comes higher responsibility." After correlating it to the current situation, he understood when a person is making a decision that involves and impacts others, then he must verify all facts and foresee its consequences.

After analyzing Tiger's teachings, Siba's mind switched to Musa's last words on anger. He closed his eyes and looked for anger inside him. In his mind's eye, he replayed the incident where it all began. He visualized the moment when he found Celine behind the silver tree, wounded and unconscious. He was panicked and worried at that moment, but there was no anger. When Eva healed her, the panic and worry disappeared, and happiness overtook him instantly. He figured out that still at that point, anger was nowhere around because he didn't think about the cause or perpetrator of that gruesome act. His only concern was the well-being of his sheep.

Later when he saw similar scars on yaks in the Valley of Yaks, and Musa told him that only a dragon's fang could leave a crescent-shaped scar, it was then that a volcano of anger erupted inside him. A sudden gush of brute force rushed through his nerves, tensing his muscles and jaws. This force overpowered his brain, shut down all its activities, and concentrated its focus only on lashing out at the culprit. Even now, just by recalling that memory, he could feel the heat and intensity associated with its emotional component. That's how powerful anger is.

Siba realized anger is like a volcano that erupts when a person focuses on the cause of affliction or loss, and it destroys everything that comes in its way. If the person focuses only on the affliction or loss and not on the cause, then he experiences pain, worry, and sadness.

To understand the mechanism behind this mysterious force, Siba delved deeper into the labyrinth of anger and found that from the moment a person is born, he gradually builds a replica of himself and the world around him inside his mind based on the information he gains through his senses. The foundation of this imaginary world is an individual's perception, beliefs, and logics. This replica of the outer world is known as the inner world, and it may or may not be a true representation of reality. While the replica of himself contains all the attributes that he considers to be his own, and this is what the Great Forest called self image.

When an individual feels that some harm or damage is inflicted upon him or his self-image, then an instinctive protection mechanism overtakes his body and mind. It bursts out an impulse of energy to protect him. If the individual knows the perpetrator and perceives it to be less powerful than him, then that energy takes the shape of anger. It forces him to strike at the perpetrator to balance out the injustice. On the other hand, if he cannot find the cause of damage or perceives it to be more powerful than him, then that energy becomes fear and provides him the strength to run away from the danger and save himself.

After understanding the secrets of anger, several old memories related to anger cropped up in Siba's mind. Especially the incident of the Evil Bud when he shouted at the Great Forest for calling him an animal. He figured out that if something keeps on irritating a person over a period of time, then those small bursts of feelings of injustice keep on accumulating as negative energy. When it crosses the person's threshold to contain it, it explodes as anger.

He also remembered the way he shouted at Rouble with anger when he was intoxicated with arrogance. It didn't take Siba much time to recognize the connection between anger and arrogance. He found that under the influence of arrogance, a person has an inflated self-image, and he thinks himself to be superior to others. His superiority makes him set high standards for himself, and he expects the same from others. Even the slightest deviations from his higher expectations annoy him. Arrogance fuels these annoyances and they explode as anger.

To make things worse, arrogance doesn't allow an individual to take the blame for his own miscalculations and mistakes. If something goes wrong because of the individual himself, arrogance provokes him to blame it on others. When an arrogant person tries to blame others for his own mistakes, it involves not only anger but aggression as well, and in extreme cases, violence. This is so because, to make an innocent accept a mistake that he has not committed, the arrogant must inciting fear in him by using aggression and violence.

He also figured out when an individual is not able to find a solution, he becomes frustrated. This frustration keeps on accumulating and takes the shape of anger. Then, either he suffers from this negative energy or someone else becomes its victim.

In the end, Siba realized that anger is a form of energy, that can't be destroyed but only be released. All that matters is how an individual releases it.

After understanding what anger is and how it works, Siba stumbled upon another question. If anger is a sudden burst of energy, then what kept it alive in him for so long that it lasted until he killed the dragons in the Ice Castle?

Siba connected all the incidents to get a broader holistic view. The first piece of the jigsaw puzzle was his belief that if someone else kills another animal for food, that's an act of cruelty. He was shocked at this revelation because if he or his friends hunted for food, he didn't consider that being cruel. For example, when the snow leopards killed ibexes, blue sheep, or other animals, he didn't become angry. The second clue was when he saw scars on yaks. It reminded him of the tragedy of Celine. Moreover, when he watched dragons attacking yaks, he considered that attack to be similar to the one on Celine. So, while watching dragons attacking yaks, he imagined them attacking Celine in the same manner and felt the atrocity inflicted upon her. To add fuel to this pre-existing fire, a dragon attacked him as well near the loose rocks. These instances constantly provoked his anger against the dragons.

The next parts of this jigsaw puzzle involved external factors. Snow leopards treated Siba like a messiah and called him the Dragonslayer, and that inflated his arrogance. As Ajax had saved their lives from the wolves, so he had become an obvious friend. Siba considered Ajax's enemies to be his own. Tiger also killed a dragon for saving Musa, giving Siba another solid reason to declare dragons as his enemies. All these factors fanned his unresolved anger, to simmer as revenge deep within his heart.

Upon deep contemplation, Siba further realized that self-image is not limited to the image of one's body only, but it also includes all those entities that a person considers to be his own. That may include his family, his friends, his belongings, his possessions, his language, his land, and so on. This self-image keeps on changing. It grows when a person considers outside things to be his own and shrinks when he excludes things that he considers don't belong to him any longer. Siba figured out that he included snow leopards in his self-image as his friends, so any harm to them would be considered harm to himself.

In the end, arrogance comes to play its nefarious role. It can't bear when a person or his self-image is harmed. It holds the anger that originates when the damage is done until it inflicts damage to the perpetrator and becomes superior again. Anger is like a wildfire. Until it is held inside, it can cause damage to the person as well. But arrogance doesn't care about the damage it causes to the person. Its only concern is to make the other being lower than itself.

After taking revenge, when an individual gets rid of the simmering anger, he realizes the damage anger did to him and his self-image. But now, the damage can't be undone and the arrogance repents on the loss it did unto itself.

Siba finally understood that revenge is a blend of arrogance and anger. He found answers to all those burning questions that were troubling him. He opened his eyes. Another pearl of his golden bracelet was emitting dark red light, representing anger. He looked at the Pole Star and said, "I'm making progress."

Ajax heard Siba's murmur and spoke, "You didn't sleep yet. The night is almost over, and we have a long way to go. Take some rest." Siba closed his eyes and slept.

After a few hours, Ajax woke him up. Several severely injured snow leopards couldn't survive the bone-chilling frozen night of the Ice Castle. Survivors dug up a mass grave in ice and buried their dead. A long perilous journey still lay ahead of the war-torn survivors. Ajax led their way back home through the same path that Musa had shown them earlier. But their spirits began to wear out due to injuries, lack of food, and extreme weather. Few gave up their hopes of ever returning back to their families. Siba gave a purple pearl to each one of them. After swallowing that, the snow leopards gained the energy and strength to continue their journey back home.

The condition of the wolves was not much different. They were also struggling and suffering on their way back. They were facing even more troubles than the snow leopards because of the longer and tougher route, and they were forced to drag their sleds on the icy and bumpy trails. But they didn't care much about the sleds, as there were many other major life-threatening concerns to worry about.

By the time the snow leopards returned, harbingers of spring were already knocking at the door of the Snow Mountains. After spending a long, dark winter in the frozen icy world, the sight of early bloomers and the chirps of robins infused new life in them. When they arrived at the Summer Capital, their families and young cubs welcomed them like returning heroes. Rouble and Celine also welcomed Siba as if they had been missing him for ages.

The entire kingdom turned into a big festive party to celebrate their victory over evil. Songs were sung about the bravery of Siba and other war heroes. Special events were hosted where public homages were paid to their martyrs. Traditional rituals were performed for the smooth journey of their souls to the afterlife. Everyone was celebrating their full unchallenged claim over the Snow Mountains. There was no more hiding, no more living in fear. They were the apex rulers now.

Amidst their celebrations, an old griffon vulture crashed from the sky. Her tail feathers were burnt and her skull was bleeding. The horrified vulture's heart was beating so fast as if it was about to explode. Ajax and other snow leopards gathered around her. Siba also ran toward the crowd. Unable to catch her breath, she wheezed, "What have you done? Why did you enrage Ra? No one will survive her wrath. No one." The vulture died from a panic attack. The lavish and exuberant festival suddenly turned into a stampeding nightmare.

Ajax and Siba looked bewilderedly at each other. Suddenly, they heard a shrill cry from far away. They looked in the direction of the Frost Mountains. The sky above the mountains was black with smoke. They saw the distant Snow Mountains and valleys burning. Ajax froze with fear upon seeing the horrifying view. A huge cloud of fire and death was moving toward them. Terror and horror engulfed every living soul. Everyone was crying and yelling, "Death! Death! Death!"

Siba, terrified to his core, asked Ajax, "What's that?"

Ajax, frozen in fear, uttered, "End of the world!" He turned toward Siba and looking into his eyes, pleaded with hope, "Mountains are burning! The sky is dark! Day has turned into the night! You are our last hope. Only you can save us, Dragonslayer."

Before Siba could say something, another shrill cry sent shivers down their spines. They turned their heads and watched the unspeakable horror unfold before them. Through the clouds of smoke and fire, emerged a giant bird of flames, flanked by dragons. Flying in a row, their spewed wall of fire scorched the entire surface of the mountains and valleys.

Upon seeing the angels of death coming toward them, Rouble fluttered to Siba, yelling, "Maybe the Spirit of Life was referring to this moment that the balance of life will be disturbed and finally, the life will end. This is how we are going to die."

Siba's fear grew further. He moved his arm forward for the hovering bird to perch on. His gaze fell upon the tattoo on his hand. He remembered the peacock's prediction that his last moments on the earth would be at a volcano. He recalled the actual hologram on Only One's wings, which clearly showed a volcano. He said to the scarlet macaw with determination, "This is not the end of the world."

Perplexed Ajax asked, "What do you mean?"

Siba replied to Ajax, "I don't know. I only know that I can't die here. You always told me that the spirits prophesized I would be bringing peace to the Snow Mountains. I'm going to the Smoky Mountain to find out how." Both looked at Smoky Mountain. Its tip was covered with clouds.

"The spirits are ready, but it doesn't matter now. Even before you get down to the meadow, those monsters will reach there and burn you alive," Ajax warned Siba.

Siba replied with a smile, "Unless, I fly there." He took Eva's feathers out and told Ajax, "Distract them until I return. And trust me, I'll be back soon." He flew at a very high speed and reached the next mountain in no time. Unable to see in the dense fog, he shouted, "Spirits of the Smoky Mountain, I am Siba, friend of Ajax – the King of the Snow Mountains. I seek your help to fight those demons. You prophesized, I will kill the dragons and restore peace in the Snow Mountains. But I don't know how. I need your guidance. Please show me the way."

The spirits of the snow leopards emerged from the fog, floated around him, and merged back again into the fog. The spirits spoke to him one after the other, as they appeared and disappeared.

"You know the way."

"You've found the way."

"We don't have it."

"So you have to do it."

Siba watched them with great wonder as they glided around him. "What is it that you don't have? Which way have I found?" the puzzled boy asked.

The spirits replied, "Sometimes, what you don't have is what is required."

"You better not have what creates problems."

Siba thought for a while about what he didn't have that could be the cause of the problem. He uttered at once, "Arrogance! I don't have arrogance. Arrogance is the root cause of this problem. The arrogance of snow leopards! The arrogance of Musa! The arrogance of me!"

Siba paused and then spoke in a low voice, "Actually, I had it earlier. But you're right, I don't have it now."

The spirits spoke, "You know the way."

"You've found the way."

Siba asked again, "But I don't know the way. I don't know how to kill that giant bird of flames."

The spirits replied, "Killing the enemy is not the way."

"Killing the cause is."

"Don't fight the enemy."

"Fight the evil inside the enemy."

"War is won not on a battlefield."

"War is won in the mind."

"First, conquer your mind."

"Then, conquer the war inside your mind."

"And you've already won."

Siba became confused with the riddles of the spirits. But he got some clues at least. He closed his eyes and tried to focus his mind on finding a way to defeat those demons. But he couldn't focus. His mind was full of fears, and fears didn't allow him to concentrate. He understood what spirits meant by "First, conquer your mind." Instead of focusing on how to fight, he switched his mind's focus on his fears.

After deep contemplation, he figured out that when the mind receives outer information from the senses, it first tries to recognize that information by matching it with the information stored in the memory. If the stored information with which the outer information is matched is dangerous, then the mind raises an alarm as fear.

If the mind correctly matches the outer information with the stored one, then the alarm is real. But if the mind wrongly matches the outer information to a stored dangerous memory, then it's a false alarm. The mind can do this mismatching due to many reasons. The most prominent one is the lack of information about the outer object. Based on the circumstances, if the limited available information is matched to something dangerous, then the mind tries to fill in the missing information with all the possible dangers to warn and protect an individual.

Siba also understood that in reality, the mind doesn't fear the object but the damage it could possibly cause to the person. But the potential damage is only in the mind as it has not occurred yet. This prediction of damage generates a sudden gush of energy called fear to help him escape from the danger.

In case the anticipated damage is not imminent but in the distant future, then the energy produced as fear can't direct the person anywhere to escape from the danger. He can't avoid the situation until that time arrives, so this energy stays in his body and mind as anxiety. Anxiety hijacks all internal resources and doesn't allow them to be used for any purpose other than worrying about the anticipated danger.

If the mind keeps on producing an excess of this negative energy, it can have serious negative impacts on a person's health. For imminent danger, this negative energy in the form of intense fear can lead to a panic attack. Whereas, in case of anticipated danger in the future, this negative energy keeps on building up until that moment arrives and can cause an anxiety attack.

Siba understood that fear is a good tool for survival, as it senses danger and protects an individual. But it lacks rationality. It makes a person a pessimist and doesn't help him either in understanding the real problem or finding its solution.

He opened his eyes and found one pearl of his Golden Bracelet had turned black for fear. He said to himself, "Now

I know what fear is. Let's focus on the next part – conquering the war in my mind."

Siba closed his eyes once more and imagined himself fighting against the Goddess of Fire and her army of dragons. But he couldn't do much, except helplessly watch them burn the snow leopards and other animals to ashes. He tried to fight with Tiger's claw, but there was no way he could attack the flying dragons that were spewing fire at him. At most, he just covered himself with his armor to protect himself from the streams of fire. The fire-spewing monsters burned all the snow leopards and his friend, Ajax. Finally, Ra cornered Celine and Rouble and burned them to ashes as well. Siba couldn't bear that happening in his imagination. He opened his eyes and said to himself, "Until I'm alive, I can't let this happen to Celine and Rouble."

He took a few deep breaths and mused, "When the snow leopards were killed, I felt bad. When I imagined Ajax's death, I felt anger but was still scared to fight. It was only when I saw Celine and Rouble burning to death that I couldn't bear it, and without caring for my life, I was charged up to fight and die. Why so? What gave me that courage to fight to the death?" He closed his eyes and pondered over it.

He realized it was his love for Celine and Rouble that gave him the courage to fight against all odds. This love could be for anyone or anything. It could be for a person's own life, his family, his friends, his land, his honor, or many things. When a person sees his loved ones in danger, love gives him the courage to overcome fears and fight with full strength.

Siba opened his eyes and noticed one red-colored pearl glowing for courage. His determined face was radiating courage and fearlessness. He was fully equipped to take on the Goddess of Fire and her fire-breathing monsters.

Sultan's spirit appeared from the fog and warned him, "Siba, Ra is the fire of the volcano. Fire can't be killed."

Siba replied with a smile, "Sometimes, killing the enemy is not the way." Sultan's spirit smiled back and disappeared into the fog. Siba fluttered his feathers and flew toward the Summer Capital.

Ajax was anxiously waiting for Siba's return, but there was no sign of him. Ra and her army of dragons were coming closer with each passing moment. Soon the flood of fire arrived at the valley and flowed over the mountainous meadow, scorching everything in its path. Overlooking from the cave, Ajax heard the shrieks and screams of ibexes and other unfortunate animals of the meadow, making desperate attempts to survive.

Ajax turned his head and looked at the Smoky Mountain for one last time. But his desperate eyes still couldn't find any sign of the Dragonslayer. After losing his last hope, he inhaled and mustered his scattered courage by thinking about his friends, family, and responsibility as a king. In the meantime, Ra, flanked by her army of fire-breathing demons, arrived at the snow leopards' cave.

Ajax jumped between the Goddess of Fire and his snow leopards. He spoke loudly, "I am Ajax – the King of the Snow Mountains. I take full responsibility for the attack on the Ice Castle. I am your culprit. Kill me, but spare the animals of my kingdom."

Ra thundered with burning rage, "How dare you and your spotted cats enter my palace, kill my babies, and destroy my home. You buried my heir under the ice grave before even she could come into this world. How can you beg before me to spare the lives of your loved ones?" With her flaming wing, she smashed Ajax against a big rock. Ajax flew into the air, landing with a sickening crack against the sharp edges of rock. He opened his eyes weakly as Ra looked down upon his bloody and burnt body. She roared, releasing her burning rage. The flames of her body cooled down and revealed her golden plumage. She ordered her dragons to burn everyone.

- Chapter 24 -

The Final Assault

Siba flew back swiftly and landed near Ajax. He lifted his friend's head, but Ajax was dead. A gush of anger ran through Siba's body. He took a few deep breaths and controlled himself from doing anything reckless. Siba slowly laid his dead friend back on the ground and removed his armor to cover the dead body of Ajax. He inhaled another deep breath and stood up facing Ra and the dragons. Pulling his eyebrows together, he stared straight into Ra's eyes.

Ra thundered, "Aren't you scared of me, you little worm? Even these mighty mountains tremble upon seeing me."

Siba walked toward her and in a very composed voice, replied, "No."

Upon hearing that, Ra's face became furious like wildfire. Her body once again turned into flames. She yelled in a burning rage, "Burn this insolent pest."

The dragons flew toward Siba, spewing fire at him. Siba kept on walking toward Ra. He closed his eyes, held his head high, and spread his arms out to welcome and embrace the streams of fire. Ra smirked. But to their surprise, the fire didn't hurt the boy. Instead, grass, flowers, and butterflies appeared around Siba. As he moved toward Ra under the showering fire, he left behind a trail of grass adorned with beautiful flowers and fluttering butterflies. When he reached close to Ra, he opened his eyes and raised his right palm to touch the giant flaming dragon.

Ra shivered in fear, flames on her body vanished, and she stumbled back in panic. The dragons panicked and stopped spewing fire.

Ra quivered, "Who are you? Wizard? Ghost? Prophet?"

Siba replied calmly, "I am Siba – the Dragonslayer."

Ra wondered worriedly, "Why did the fire not burn you?"

Siba replied, "Fire is a form of energy. I transformed your dragons' destructive energy into life energy. But don't worry, I won't hurt you or your dragons. I've nothing against you."

Ra asked suspiciously, "I just killed your friend. Aren't you angry?"

Siba replied, "I'm not angry about that. Do you see anger on my face? An eye for an eye will make everyone blind. Moreover, why should I be angry at a slave?"

Ra cautiously moved a little closer to Siba and asked, "What do you mean? I am the Queen of the Frost Mountains, the Goddess of Fire. I am the most powerful being in this world. I am a slave to no one."

Siba smirked, "Yes, you are. You did what your anger made you do. You think you are a queen or goddess, but instead, you are a slave of your own arrogance. Your every thought, action, desire, and even revenge is guided by arrogance. You took so many innocent lives without even investigating who the real culprit was."

"We did find the dead bodies of snow leopards buried under the ice in front of our destroyed castle. They are always behind my babies. It was them, who attacked and destroyed my home," Ra spoke with pain in her eyes.

"Yes, you are right. They went there and attacked your castle. But it was my plan. I took them there," Siba revealed.

Perplexed, Ra blurted, "You? We never did anything wrong to you. You don't even belong here. Why did you destroy my home, my family?"

Siba replied, "I was also mistaken just like you. Someone attacked my sheep, and I thought dragons did that. So I led them there to take revenge. But I was wrong. I'm responsible for your loss, not these innocent lives."

Ra realized her mistake, but her arrogance didn't allow her to admit it. She looked for an excuse and tried to hide under the blanket of blame. She tried to justify herself, "These wild cats are not innocent. They never gave us the respect that we deserved."

Siba said, "Respect is not given but earned. What have you done to earn it? A long time ago, when your dragon was killed, your other dragons slaughtered the innocent snow leopards. At that time as well, you didn't care to find who the real culprit was."

Ra scoffed with attitude and defended herself, "We are stronger than them. They are like pests to us. What happened if we killed a few of them to make it clear who the boss is?"

Siba replied, "You don't become great because you are strong. You become great if you are wise. And a wise person never kills less powerful ones for fun or to satisfy his arrogance. You should kill only those that you need for your survival. And if you consider yourself to be strong and powerful, then use your strength to help the needy."

Ra asked another question, "Why should we care about the weak?"

Siba replied, "Actually, no one is weak or strong. It's just a relative term based on the comparison of one or more aspects. You should appreciate the qualities of others in which they are strong. It will earn you their respect and trust. That's how you grow together, as a family." Siba paused and stared into Ra's contemplating eyes. "If any anger is left inside you, your culprit is before your eyes, burn me alive. But don't let arrogance ever dictate you again."

Ra spoke with a remorseful face, "How can I kill you? You opened my eyes. I was living in a world of illusion, deluded by my power."

Just then, Taziki arrived and spoke loudly, "Did anyone miss me? Let me guess, no!" He walked toward them and clapped. "Well done, Ra! Congratulations! It seems you have extended your brood to include these wild cats that killed your children. Trust me, I'm happy for you from the bottom of my heart. I think you should retire and spend time babysitting their cubs. And it's time for a true king to rule these vast expanses." He sniffed. "Oops! Ajax is dead. That makes me the only surviving king. I promise I'll take good care of it." He winked.

Enraged Ra thundered, "I have only abandoned my arrogance, not my honor. You picked the wrong time to show up. Did you forget? Last time you escaped into the Silver Forest. But this time, you won't find any place to hide."

Taziki smirked, "I think I don't need to hide anymore. In fact, you should follow the command of your new king and kill this boy and the snow leopards."

Ra chuckled, "And what makes you think so?"

Taziki said, "If you love your Golden Egg, the only Golden Egg that you could have in your life, which gives birth to a queen instead of dragons, then you must follow my command and kill them."

On hearing about her egg, Ra became sad and spoke in a painful voice, "I understand my egg got crushed under the Ice Castle, but it doesn't mean I should kill them."

Taziki revealed, "No, your egg is safe." He shouted, "Boys, bring her egg." The wolves dragged the sled filled with dry leaves to Taziki. He announced, "Your egg is here. If you want it back, then you must follow my command."

Helpless Ra looked at Siba. Her eyes, brimming with tears of pain, were holding the surging anger. She said, "Sorry, Siba! I can't lose my Golden Egg again. I must save it, or else my clan will become extinct."

Siba moved right in front of her and said smilingly, "You got to do what you got to do." He closed his eyes and stood there bravely, offering his life.

Ra's shining golden plumage turned into flames. She filled her lungs with air to blow fire at Siba. Just then, the black wolf shouted, "My king, the egg is not here."

Everything came to a standstill at once. All eyes turned toward the sled. The black wolf was searching for the Golden Egg inside the sled full of dry leaves. Taziki pushed him away and began searching for the egg, spilling out the leaves. Unable to find the egg, Taziki giggled nervously and in a low voice, scolded the black wolf, "Couldn't you've kept your mouth shut for a few more minutes?"

Ra's flames grew bigger and brighter. She roared, "Where is my egg?" The pack became petrified with fear and began trembling upon seeing her coming toward them.

Suddenly, a panting voice came from below the cliff, "Siba, are you there?"

Everyone looked at the edge. Neti jumped from below the cliff and landed near the edge. He looked at the Siba and said, "I think you dropped something while crossing our village." He opened his hand to reveal the Golden Egg.

Upon seeing her egg perfectly safe, Ra's flames doused and two tears rolled down from her eyes. Siba breathed a sigh of relief. The snow leopards and dragons encircled Taziki. Siba kissed Yeti's hand and said, "Thank you so much for bringing it back." He picked up the egg and offered it to Ra.

Ra commanded the enraged dragons, "Spare the wolves. We should give them a chance to live and become a part of our family. Let us all forget our past and start a new life as a new family."

The dragons and snow leopards moved back. Ra looked at Siba. He gave her a smile, appreciating her choices. She smiled back, nodding her head.

Taziki moved closer to her and picked both of Ra's tears that had turned into small beads of glass. He gave them to Siba with a shameful face and spoke, "I apologize for what I did. You deserve to keep the tears of the Goddess of Fire – the rarest thing in the world, rarer than even the Golden Egg. They hold the power to bring the dead back to life."

Siba, filled with wonder and suspicion, walked over to Ajax's dead body. He uncovered Ajax's face and placed one glass bead in his mouth.

Ajax's wounds healed instantly. He groaned and woke up as if he was waking up from a deep sleep. Opening his eyes, he shouted, "Kill me, but don't hurt my family and friends." All laughed.

Ra went closer to Ajax and said smilingly, "No one will ever hurt your family. We are all family, a big family." She announced loudly, "We can't change our past, but we can build our future together with peace and harmony." She flew back to the Frost Mountains with her dragons.

After waving at Ra, Siba told Ajax, "My job is over. I fulfilled the prophecy. Peace has been restored in the Snow Mountains. It's time for me to leave for my journey."

Ajax said, "Thank you, Dragonslayer. Thanks for everything." Siba smiled.

Neti asked Siba, "Are you going back to the Frost Mountains?"

Siba replied, "No, I have to go to the north."

Neti offered his help, "I'm going that way to Yeti Summer Camp. If you want, I can take you there."

Siba said, "Alright, but my other two friends are also with me. Can you take us all?"

Neti replied, "Sure, hop on. Let's hip-hop!"

Siba said goodbye to Ajax and Taziki, and the three travelers rode Neti. After crossing the Snow Mountains, Neti stopped at a rocky shore of an ocean. He dropped them there and said, "I can't take you any further. You'll have to cross the ocean by yourself."

Rouble asked, "How can we cross this vast ocean? We are not fish."

Neti told them, "I heard that a pirate ship anchors here every full moon night. And tonight is a full moon night. Maybe you can request the captain of the ship to take you across the ocean."

"We'll figure out some way. Thanks for your help." Siba showed his appreciation with an affectionate smile and gave the yeti a warm, goodbye hug. Neti hip-hopped and disappeared into the Snow Mountains.

Siba turned and gazed across the rocky shore and wondered where the next journey would take him.

The End

BOOK TWO COMING SOON

CONTINUE THE JOURNEY WITH SIBA

Thank you for reading!

Reviews are always appreciated!

B. Singh grew up in a small city, Chandigarh, located near the foothills of the mighty Himalayas in northwest India. Since his childhood, he has always had an inquisitive mindset. He doesn't settle for the pre-existing answers if they don't make sense to him. Instead, he explores, experiments, and finds the answer himself. He has traveled across India from north to south not only for his education but also to explore different cultures and values. To continue his journey of exploration, he moved from India to Canada. After graduating from the University of Windsor, Canada, he conceived the idea of compiling his learnings in the form of a spiritual fantasy book. This well-crafted and awe-inspiring adventurous journey into a fantasy world is full of chiseled gems of wisdom that will enrich the lives of every human being on earth.

You can learn more on Instagram:

@returntonature_